LITTLE,
BROWN
LB
LARGE
PRINT

ALSO BY JAMES PATTERSON FEATURING ALEX CROSS

Target Alex Cross
The People vs. Alex Cross
Cross the Line
Cross Justice
Hope to Die
Cross My Heart
Alex Cross, Run
Merry Christmas, Alex Cross
Kill Alex Cross
Cross Fire
I, Alex Cross
Alex Cross's Trial (with Richard DiLallo)
Cross Country
Double Cross
Cross (also published as *Alex Cross*)
Mary, Mary
London Bridges
The Big Bad Wolf
Four Blind Mice
Violets Are Blue
Roses Are Red
Pop Goes the Weasel
Cat & Mouse
Jack & Jill
Kiss the Girls
Along Came a Spider

For a complete list of books by James Patterson, as well as previews of upcoming books and more information about the author, visit JamesPatterson.com or find him on Facebook.

CRISS CROSS

JAMES PATTERSON

LITTLE, BROWN AND COMPANY

LARGE PRINT EDITION

Little, Brown and Company
Hachette Book Group
1290 Avenue of the Americas, New York, NY 10104
First edition: November 2019

Little, Brown and Company is a division of Hachette Book Group, Inc. The Little, Brown name and logo are trademarks of Hachette Book Group, Inc.

ISBN 978-0-316-52688-3 (hardcover) / 978-0-316-53564-9 (large print)
LCCN 2018958420

10 9 8 7 6 5 4 3 2 1

LSC-C

Printed in the United States of America

CRISS CROSS

CHAPTER 1

IT WAS A MISERABLE MID-MARCH afternoon, chill and sleeting, as John Sampson and I ran to the main gate of the Greensville Correctional Center, a hexagon-shaped high-security prison in the rural, southern part of the Commonwealth of Virginia.

We ducked inside the security shack, showed our badges and identifications, and surrendered our service weapons. A gate rolled back, and we walked through.

As a homicide detective with the DC Metropolitan Police and as a behavioral specialist with the FBI, I have been to many jails, prisons, and penitentiaries over the years, but I am still unnerved by the sound of steel-barred gates slamming shut behind me. We passed through seven such gates, following Warden Adrian Yates and several reporters who'd arrived before us.

One of them, a journalist named Juanita Flake, said, "Is it true, he chose?"

The warden kept walking.

"Can you—"

Warden Yates spun in his tracks and glared at her, looking barely in control. "I don't wish to talk any further, Ms. Flake. I'm not in favor of this, but it is my job to see it done. You want it different? Call the governor."

Yates, who had been criticized by the media, went to the next gate, which slid back. Three gates later, we entered a small amphitheater with perhaps thirty seats.

Twenty of the seats were already taken. Despite the years that had gone by since I'd seen them, I recognized many of the people gathered there. They recognized us as well. Most nodded and smiled weakly.

A fivesome sitting together sneered and, I'm sure, spoke bitterly about us under their breath. Those three men and two women were by far the best-dressed people in the room.

The men—two brothers, both middle-aged,

and their father—wore well-tailored, dark three-piece suits. The women—one in her sixties and the other in her twenties—were dressed in charcoal-gray Chanel outfits; their hair was perfect, their jewelry flashy.

Sampson found us seats facing a long rectangular window. Drapes had been drawn closed on the other side.

I started to question my decision to come here almost immediately. I had good reasons, of course, but they didn't stop the doubts from creeping in.

"You framed him," a woman said.

I looked up to see the older of the two fashion plates beside me. She was a petite woman with dyed ash-blond hair and the kind of tight facial skin that suggested she had a high-dollar plastic surgeon on retainer.

"Mrs. Edgerton," I said wearily. "That was your son's defense in his trial and during his appeals."

"His *appeal*, not his *appeals*," Margaret Edgerton hissed. "You get only one appeal in this primitive, eager-to-kill state."

"And the Supreme Court of Virginia upheld his conviction and sentence, ma'am."

She trembled with rage. "I don't know how you did it, but you did, sure as I'm standing here. And I hope to God you carry to your grave the knowledge that you put an innocent boy on the other side of that curtain, Dr. Cross."

"No, ma'am, your son put himself there, a long time ago," I said.

"He's innocent."

Warden Yates said, "We need to begin."

"My son is innocent!" Mrs. Edgerton shouted. "You can't do this!"

"The law demands this," Yates said. "If you'd rather not be here, I understand."

He left the room.

She glared at me. "Remember this moment. It's when you doomed your soul. You will burn in hell."

Then she stormed away to her husband's side, where she broke down sobbing.

A few states in the country allow the doomed man to choose his method of execution; in Virginia, the choice is lethal injection or electrocution. The drapes rolled back and revealed not a gurney but a heavy oak chair with arm, leg, and chest straps.

Two corrections officers entered the death chamber. Warden Yates followed them and watched his officers open the only other door in the execution facility.

A shaved-headed man in his early forties stepped

out. He was tall and lanky and appeared slightly drugged. He looked not at the electric chair but through the window at us.

Michael "Mikey" Edgerton drew himself up to his full height and then walked to the chair of his own volition, as if he welcomed what was about to happen.

"Mom, Dad, Delilah, Pete, and Joe, you know why I chose old Sparky?" Edgerton said over the intercom. He took a seat, laughed, then looked straight at me. "I'm not going out like some kid going night-night. I want Cross and Sampson and everyone else who helped frame me to see me crackle, to see the smoke coming out my head and the skin on my arms and legs splitting from the lightning they're gonna send through me—me, an innocent man."

His mother, older brother, and sister began to sob. Only his father and his younger brother remained stoic.

"You did it!" a middle-aged woman in jeans and a Georgia Tech sweatshirt shouted at him from a seat near us. She jumped to her feet. "You did it, and you deserve this! I hope when they throw the switch, you disintegrate, you sick bastard!"

CHAPTER

2

MIKEY EDGERTON GOT HIS MACABRE last wish.

I had never seen a man die in the electric chair, and the sight of two thousand volts ripping through him shook both Sampson and me so badly, we were barely able to stand after Edgerton was pronounced dead, and the curtain closed on his life.

We left the witness chamber, trying to ignore Edgerton's mother, who alternated between emotional collapse and spitting rage.

"I will see you both destroyed for this!" she screamed at one point. "With every last cent I've got, I will see you both sitting in that chair for what you did to my son!"

We had to listen to that and the angry responses

from the relatives of Edgerton's victims until the final steel gate slammed shut behind us and we walked out of the penitentiary into drizzling rain and fog.

The Edgerton family came out moments later and walked to a waiting limousine. We went in the opposite direction, toward the squad car we'd driven down.

"Dr. Cross? Detective Sampson?"

I turned, expecting a journalist to shove a microphone in my face. Instead, Crystal Raider, the woman in the Georgia Tech sweatshirt, was standing there looking at us with an expression that was a rough sea of emotions and thoughts.

"He did that to torture us," she said. "To stick the knife in us after all that he did to my sister and the others."

"He did," I said. "And he succeeded."

Crystal raised her head defiantly. "Maybe. But I think somewhere my Kissy is thinking it was a good thing, how he went. I bet the other girls think so too."

"Go home now," I said softly. "Find Kissy in her son and let this all be a bad memory that you rarely visit."

She cried at that and gave us both a hug. "Thank you for standing up for her, Dr. Cross, Detective

Sampson. Neither of you ever judged her, and I'm grateful for that."

"Pole dancers are people too," Sampson said. "Good people. Like your sister."

She cried through a weak smile, then she gave us a weaker wave and walked toward a waiting pickup truck with Florida plates.

The three-hour drive north was quiet and uneasy, both of us lost in our thoughts.

It wasn't until we were almost to Washington, DC, that the rain stopped. Sampson cleared his throat. "I wasn't expecting that, Alex," he said in a hoarse voice.

"None of us were expecting it. Except Edgerton," I said, suppressing a shudder.

My lifelong friend glanced at me. "Alex, right now I don't know whether I should be satisfied at justice served or praying for my sins."

My stomach soured, but I shook it off, said, "Mikey Edgerton did the dirty work on the eight and maybe more. There's no doubt about it in my mind."

There was a long pause as Sampson took the exit off 95 onto the Beltway, heading toward my home on Fifth Street in Southeast DC.

"No doubt in mine either," Sampson said at last. "But still, you know?"

I swallowed hard. Before I could respond, my phone buzzed in my pocket. I pulled it out, saw a familiar number, and answered. "This is Cross," I said. "How are you, Chief?"

"I should be asking you that," said Metro Police chief of detectives Bree Stone, my wife. "But I don't have time, and neither do you."

I sat up straighter, said, "What's going on?"

She gave me an address in Friendship Heights and said to go there immediately. Then she told me why, and the sourness that lingered in my stomach became the worst kind of nausea, that terrible taste you get at the back of your throat just before you say goodbye to everything you've eaten all day.

"We're on our way," I said, then hung up.

"What's the matter?" Sampson said.

"John," I said in a hoarse whisper. "What in God's name have we done?"

CHAPTER 3

WE DROVE TO FRIENDSHIP HEIGHTS, in the far northwest corner of DC, parked on Forty-First Street, and ran up the sidewalk to Harrison Avenue, where a patrol car with lights flashing was in front of a barrier.

"Which one is it?" Sampson asked the patrol officer.

"Third on the right, sir. There's a few plainclothes there already."

"And I imagine there will be more," I said, moving around the barrier toward a gray Craftsman house with a tidy front yard and a medical examiner's van parked out front.

On the scene, there were three uniformed

officers and two in plainclothes whom I recognized as junior homicide detectives Owen Shank and Deana Laurel.

They were talking to two very upset women in their late thirties. Laurel spotted us, excused herself, and came over.

She told us that the two women—Patsy Phelps and Anita Kline—were neighbors of the Nixons, who owned the Craftsman. Gary Nixon, the father, was a successful attorney on K Street. Mr. Nixon had taken his two young children on a four-day trip to see his ailing mother in San Diego. Katrina, his wife of fifteen years, had a successful speech-pathology practice and couldn't make the trip.

"They said the Nixons made it a point to talk twice a day, no matter where they were," Detective Laurel said. "So when Mrs. Nixon didn't answer her phone this morning or this evening, Mr. Nixon called Mrs. Phelps and Mrs. Kline to go over and check on their— "

Detective Shank came over and cut her off. "I don't mean to be disrespectful, Dr. Cross, Detective Sampson. But are you sure it's okay for the two of you to be here? I mean, isn't this kind of a conflict of interest?"

"We're here on orders," Sampson said. "Take us inside."

Shank, a tough, wiry guy who'd once served in a Marine Force Recon unit, didn't like it, but he understood orders. "Straightaway, sir."

Detective Laurel returned to the neighbors. We followed Shank into the house, which had been decorated by Pottery Barn and Toys R Us.

Shank told us there were no signs of forced entry, and although the house was in the disarray you'd expect with a young, affluent family, we saw no indications of a struggle as we moved down a short hallway to the type of kitchen you see in gourmet ads.

There were kids' drawings taped to the stainless-steel fridge along with a calendar page where the Nixons kept track of babysitters and doctors' appointments. It wasn't until we got past the stove that we saw evidence of a fight.

A kitchen chair had fallen over. A glass vase lay shattered on the floor by a breakfast nook. Beyond it was a family room. The television was on, blaring the news about the police presence currently building on Harrison Avenue in Friendship Heights.

The body of Katrina Nixon, who'd been a pretty brunette in her late thirties, was on the far side of the room, naked and slumped in an overstuffed chair. Her skin was bluish and coated in a thin white film. Her mouth was stretched wide, as if she'd tried to scream, and locked in rigor. Her eyes were open and dull.

The air reeked of bleach. The instrument of her death, a red and purple Hermès silk scarf, was wrapped impossibly tight around her neck.

A piece of plain white paper lay on her lap.

As I walked over to look at it, I felt as if something foundational was cracking inside me. I read the note and felt a chunk of myself break free and fall.

You messed up big-time, but don't sweat it, Dr. Cross, it read. *Ultimately, for his past sins, Mikey Edgerton got what he deserved when he rode old Sparky right into the great hereafter.—M*

CHAPTER 4

M.

I was still rattled when I pulled up in front of my house two hours later. The rain had stopped, and a breeze that was unnaturally warm for mid-March was blowing.

I saw Bree sitting on the porch swing with a light blanket around her. She patted the seat beside her, said, “True?”

I nodded and took a seat. “He signed it.”

She was quiet. Then: “You know the Edgertons are going to use this as evidence to prove that their son was framed and someone else was responsible.”

I sat back, exasperated. "Unless we tell the press about M, and the whole mess comes out."

"Nothing stays a secret forever, Alex," she said, stroking my head.

"That's what I'm afraid of," I said. "Then I become the story."

"You are his focus."

"I get that," I said. "But it's just..."

"What?"

"Confusing."

"Mikey Edgerton was guilty."

"I know that," I said, spotting something in our neighbors' dark front yard. "M's just playing his games. What's going on over there?"

"Scaffolds. Morse said they were doing it right, inside and out."

"More banging," I said, irritated. "They moved away for the year just so they wouldn't have to hear it."

"They're both on sabbatical."

"Lucky for them," I said, getting up. "I'm hungry."

"Nana's getting dinner ready for you. I'm going to sleep. I have a feeling tomorrow could be difficult."

I kissed her, told her I loved her, and went inside.

The television in the living room was streaming *Terriers*, currently the favorite show of my seventeen-year-old daughter, Jannie. The air in the front hall was perfumed with the scent of garlic, onions, and basil wafting from the kitchen.

The smells and sounds calmed me. I went into the front room, where Jannie was on the couch in her running sweats, dozing. A biology textbook lay open in her lap, but she held the remote for the TV.

"Hi, sweetheart," I said, giving her a little shake.

Jannie startled awake and punched the pause button. "Hi, Dad," she said sleepily.

"You sleeping, studying, or watching?"

"All three," she said, smiling through a yawn.

"You can't do all three."

"Most men can't, but most women can."

"Run that one by me."

"So, like, in class last week? We learned that the latest research says male minds are hardwired for single tasks. They learn best and do best when everything comes at them one at a time, you know, like one project and then the next. And it probably helps if they can move around. While they're studying, I mean."

"Okay. And the female mind?"

"Women are amazing!"

I grinned. "I'll agree with that wholeheartedly. But why?"

She used her index finger to draw imaginary circles around her head. "The female mind can focus on many things at once. My teacher said it's like juggling. Where men tune out everything but the one thing they're working on, women can hear it all, smell it all, and see it all. And get it all done!"

"Except when they're sleeping."

She laughed. "Okay, except when they're sleeping."

"I'll admit, you know your stuff. If you see your brother trying to multitask, please tell him about the male brain and stop him. Okay?"

"You think he'll listen?"

"Probably not," I said. I leaned over to hug her. "I missed you, baby."

"Missed you too, Dad," she said, and she yawned. "I don't know why I feel so tired."

"Get to sleep early tonight."

She nodded but seemed concerned about something.

As I was leaving the room, she called after me, "My first outdoor meet's Tuesday afternoon."

"Already in the calendar of absolutely must-dos," I said, heading into the kitchen.

My ninety-something grandmother, an avid

foodie, was stirring something in a deep pan on the kitchen stove.

"I don't know what it is, but it smells awful good in here."

"New chicken recipe," she said, tapping the spoon on the side of the pan.

"Dad!" Ali called from the room beyond the kitchen. "Check this out."

Nana said, "He's been dying to show you some mountain-bike video, and you won't eat until he does."

I held up both hands in understanding. My youngest child, Ali, was ten, smart as a whip, and always into something new. And when he got into something new, he was like a terrier—he wouldn't let go.

Ali's latest interest was mountain biking. It had actually begun last year when a friend had lent him one, and he'd asked for a bike for Christmas.

We made sure he got one because, unlike his older sister, Ali had never been known to exert himself physically if he didn't have to. But something about the bike had captured his imagination, and he rode it all the time now, even in the cold and snow.

Ali was on the floor, stretched out in front of his laptop, when I walked in.

"You're late," he said, sounding put out.

I held up my hands. "Beyond my control. You ride today?"

He nodded. "The usual way by the Tidal Basin."

Bree and I often ran that route. It was safe and well traveled. I'd okayed him to use it if he wanted to go out for a ride on his own as long as he got permission first and it wasn't too early or too late. "You wanted to show me something?"

He hit a key on his laptop. The screen came to life, showing the helmet-camera feed of a mountain biker poised high above a sprawling city.

"Where is this?" I asked.

"Lima, Peru," he said. "You won't believe it."

The guy riding the bike took off and immediately went down an impossibly steep, covered staircase. Then he shot out into sunlight and he was on a wall about two feet wide with a big drop on either side.

Crowds of people watched the rider skim along the wall to the end and launch into the air. He dropped a good twenty feet and landed on a dirt path on a hill so steep, I thought he was going to go over the handlebars and tumble to his death. But he punched the landing, cut left, crossed a narrow wooden bridge, hit another bump, soared again, and landed on another staircase. The insanity went on for a good four minutes before the rider pulled over and started laughing. The video stopped.

"Wasn't that amazing?" Ali asked.

"What was that?"

"Urban-downhill mountain biking!"

"Wow," I said. "A new sport every day."

"I'm going to do that someday," he vowed.

"Not if I have anything to do with it," Nana said from the kitchen. "Alex, your dinner's ready."

CHAPTER 5

INSTEAD OF FOCUSING ON EDGERTON'S execution, the strangulation of Mrs. Nixon, or the latest message from M, I savored Nana's fantastic pesto and chicken on black-bean pasta, a dish that I told her had to be a multiple repeat.

Ali wandered through, his laptop under his arm.

"Bed?" I asked.

He yawned and nodded. "Dad, do you have Wickr?"

"Uhh, I don't think so."

"It's this cool messaging app for, like, spies."

"Okay?"

"It has military-grade encryption," he said earnestly. "We could text each other and no one would know because it has this self-destruct feature."

"The phone self-destructs?"

"No," he said, his nose wrinkling. "The message. Or telegram, they call it. They vanish after a couple of minutes. Real good for spying, right?"

"If you're on your phone when you're spying, I would think so."

"You want me to put it on your phone? It's easy, and we could, you know—"

"Talk like spies?"

He grinned and nodded.

"Let me think about it," I said, and I kissed him good night.

"Dad? If urban-downhill became an Olympic sport, I think I'd be good at it."

I smiled at the way his mind swung from one obsession to the next. "I think you'll be good at whatever you love to do."

After Nana went to bed, I cleaned up and went into the front room. Jannie was long gone. I tried to watch a basketball game. When I went upstairs, it was almost midnight.

Bree was already dead asleep when I slipped between the sheets. Despite everything that had happened that day, sleep came for me.

But just as I was dozing off, I heard a dog barking in an irritating pattern: three deep barks, a pause, and then two or four barks of higher pitch. The window was open. I got up, closed it, and latched it, but that only muffled the barking.

This had been going on for almost a month now, but I hadn't had the time to find the owners and complain. And I was in no mood to do it that night either. I put in earplugs and turned on a white-noise app on my phone.

I closed my eyes. I didn't want it to, but my mind swung toward M and what I knew of him, all of it scanty and contradictory.

There was only one indisputable fact about M, I thought as I fell asleep—the note he'd left with the strangled corpse of Mrs. Nixon was not the first time he had directly taunted me.

It was the fourth time.

In twelve years.

CHAPTER 6

ALI CROSS SLIPPED INTO HIS father's bedroom around seven the next morning, a Saturday. Bree was already up and downstairs.

Ali went over to where his father lay snoring and shook his shoulder lightly. Alex startled and sat up, confused.

"Want to go for a run?" Ali asked. "I'll ride my mountain bike."

His father lay back on his pillow and groaned. "I hardly slept, pal. I don't think my body's going to be up for that this morning."

Ali was disappointed, but he kissed his dad on the cheek and said, "Get some sleep. We'll go next Saturday."

Alex smiled, and his eyes drifted shut.

Ali found Bree downstairs, drinking a coffee and dressed for work.

"You don't want to run either?" he asked.

"Not today," she said. "I have a desk to clear."

"I'm going to ride the usual route, okay? And I'll take my cell phone."

"Did you ask your dad?"

"He's in a coma."

Bree smiled in spite of herself. "I'll tell Nana where you are when she gets up."

Ali grinned. He hadn't expected to get approval so easily.

But then again, he was ten, almost eleven, wasn't he? And in the sixth grade, a full grade ahead of most kids his age. He knew how to take care of himself.

He got his mountain bike from the shed out back and set off. Although Alex Cross's younger son felt most at home with his head in a book or on the internet learning something new, he adored his bike, especially when he could launch off something. The front and rear shocks on the thing were amazing.

By the time Ali was past the Martin Luther King Jr. Memorial, heading south along the west side of the Tidal Basin, he'd found at least ten great jumps and had landed them all. He had the main path almost to himself.

As Ali was pedaling hard toward the Franklin Delano Roosevelt Memorial, he saw a man kneeling beside his bike to the right of the path. The man spun around and waved his arms, telling him to stop.

But it was too late. With his attention on the man, Ali had taken his eyes off the path. His front tire rolled over the shards of a broken bottle and blew out.

Ali veered off the path and crash-landed hard on the ground. It dazed him and knocked the wind out of him.

The man who'd waved at him rushed over. "Are you all right?"

"I'll be okay."

"Darn it, by the time I heard you coming, I couldn't warn you off the glass," the man said in an easy Southern drawl. "Got both my tires. Lucky I didn't bend a rim."

He was tall and very fit in biking shorts and a tight jersey that read U.S. ARMED FORCES CYCLING TEAM. He wore wraparound Oakley glasses and a Bell racing helmet over short, sandy-blond hair.

He helped Ali up, said, "I'm Captain Arthur Abrahamsen."

"Ali Cross."

"Nice to meet you, Ali Cross. Can I check the damage to your tire?"

"No, sir, I'll just walk it home. It's okay."

"You *might* ride it home," Captain Abrahamsen said, smiling, "if the tire's fixable. Do you mind if I take a look? I know a bit about this."

Ali hesitated, but then shrugged and nodded, thinking that it *would* be a lot easier to ride home than walk the three and a half miles pushing a bike with a flat tire.

"Can you kick the glass off the path while I see if it's salvageable?" the captain asked. "We don't want any more people getting flats or we'll have a convention."

"Sure," Ali said.

Abrahamsen lifted his bike's front fork and spun the tire.

Ali kicked the big pieces of glass into the grass with the sides of his sneakers. "You in the military?"

"I am, the U.S. Army," Abrahamsen said, still looking at the tire.

"Do you, like, race for them?"

"Sort of," he said. "I'm good enough to train with the team but not quite good enough to fly all over the world to ride for my country. Yet."

He said this with such conviction and enthusiasm that Ali couldn't help but smile. "That's awesome."

"Totally, as my nephew says," Abrahamsen said. "Here's your puncture."

He held the wheel in place and showed Ali where the glass had penetrated it.

"Is it fixable?" Ali asked.

"I might be able to patch it up so that it'll get you home. After that, you'll want a new tire and tube."

Abrahamsen went over to his own bike. "Can you carry your bike like this?" He picked up his bike and put his right arm through the frame and got it up onto his shoulder.

Ali nodded. He'd seen mountain-bike racers doing that when they had to cross impassable stuff.

"But where are we going? Don't you have tools and a patch kit with you?"

"Enough for one tire," he said. "Don't worry. I've got everything we need in the team van. It's parked down by the marina. You want a team sticker for your bike?"

Ali liked that idea. "I've never known a professional bike rider."

"And you still don't. Yet. C'mon, let's pick up

the pace. I have to be at a meeting at noon. And I imagine your mother will be looking for you."

"Nana Mama, my great-grandmother," Ali said, lifting his smaller bike onto his shoulder and very much wanting Captain Arthur Abrahamsen to think he was strong enough to carry it the whole way to the marina.

The captain smiled. "Great-grandmother? Do you want to give her a call? Tell her where you are and who you're with? Wouldn't want her to get worried."

Ali frowned, set his bike down, and slapped his pockets, looking for his phone. "I know I had it leaving the house."

"Here," Captain Abrahamsen said, handing him his own phone. "Call her and I'll look around back there, see if it fell out when you went down."

Ali took the phone and punched in the number while Abrahamsen went back to where they'd both crashed.

The phone rang and Nana picked up. "Hello?"

"Nana? It's Ali. I had a flat, and Captain Arthur Abrahamsen, he's a bike racer in the army, he's going to help me fix it. I'm on his phone."

"Well, that's nice of him."

"I'll be home soon," Ali said and hung up.

He turned around to see Abrahamsen crouched

near some deeper grass. The captain stood and held up a black phone. "This it?"

Ali breathed a sigh of relief. His father would have had a cow if he'd lost his phone. "Yes. Thank you."

They exchanged phones. Abrahamsen said, "Did you get your great-grandmother?"

"Yes."

"It's better that she doesn't worry, don't you think?"

Ali nodded, already getting his bike up on his shoulder again. "Much better, sir."

CHAPTER 7

I FINALLY WOKE UP AROUND nine on Saturday morning. After showering and dressing, I went downstairs and out onto the porch, looking for the morning paper. A van emblazoned with decals of men and women bicycling and the insignia of the U.S. Armed Forces pulled up in front of the house.

To my surprise, Ali jumped out. "Dad!"

A man in his early thirties climbed out the driver's side. He was wearing a sweatshirt that said U.S. ARMY over bike pants.

He and Ali climbed up the front steps as Ali said, "Captain Abrahamsen is almost on the U.S. Armed Forces bicycle-racing team! I got a flat. We couldn't fix it, so he offered to drive me home."

The captain smiled and stuck out his hand. "Arthur Abrahamsen, sir. You've got quite a boy there."

I shook his hand and smiled. "He is that. Thanks for helping him out."

"My pleasure," Abrahamsen said, and he chuckled. "He taught me a lot about a lot of different subjects."

"I hope he didn't talk your ear off."

"No, sir," Abrahamsen said. "Both ears intact. Well, let me get his bike out. He's going to need a new tire and tube, I'm afraid."

"We both hit broken glass and got flats," Ali said as Abrahamsen went over and opened up the rear of the van.

The van was filled with wheels, tires, and other equipment hanging off the walls.

"So, do you race full-time for the military?" I asked as he took out the bike.

"He trains with the team," Ali said.

"And even that's hardly full-time," Abrahamsen said, closing the van doors. "I'm busy over at the Pentagon and up on the Hill, so I try to squeeze in my training rides when I can." He brought the bike over.

"Well, thank you again," I said, and we shook hands once more.

The captain smiled at Ali. "It's always good to meet a fellow cavalryman."

Ali looked at him, puzzled.

"I used to be in the U.S. Army Fourth Cavalry," Abrahamsen explained. "Tanks. But I've always thought that in this day and age, cavalrymen should be on bikes instead."

"Mountain bikes," Ali said, smiling.

"Exactly! They're more like horses," Abrahamsen said, pointing at him and winking. "Take care, now. Nice meeting you, Mr. Cross."

"You too, Captain," I said.

Abrahamsen got into his van, waved, and pulled out into the street.

"He's a really nice guy," Ali said.

"Seems like it," I said, lifting his bike up.

"Do you think I could be in the cavalry someday?" Ali said.

"In a tank or on a bike?"

"Bike."

I paused and then said, "You can have anything your heart desires if you work for it."

CHAPTER 8

FOR THREE DAYS, I IGNORED the media's reports about Edgerton's execution and the accusations from his family that Katrina Nixon's murder was proof of Mikey's innocence. On Tuesday morning, I checked into the federal detention center on Mill Street in Alexandria, Virginia, not far from the Courthouse.

The sheriff's deputy returned my ID, said, "Dirty Marty know you're coming?"

"Mr. Forbes made the request for counseling himself," I said.

The deputy, a stout woman named Estella Maines, sniffed and said, "We'll bring him out to you, Dr. Cross, but I don't know why you bother."

"The hopeless idealist in me, Deputy."

Maines almost smiled as she buzzed me through.

I went to the booth, reminding myself that these kinds of visits were important for me. Despite the fact that I had a busy life as a contract consultant to DC Metro and the Federal Bureau of Investigation, I found deeper fulfillment in my role as a therapist.

Martin Forbes shuffled out a steel door and took a seat on the other side of a bulletproof-glass divider. In his mid-forties, balding, Forbes was an unremarkable-looking man except for a squiggly white line that ran underneath his jaw. That scar was the only reason I'd agreed to see him.

Once upon a time, I'd worked with Forbes at the FBI when he was briefly assigned to the Behavioral Analysis Unit. He was a junior agent then and as eager to catch bad guys as I was.

That eagerness had almost gotten Forbes killed, but it had saved the life of Ned Mahoney, my former partner at the Bureau. We'd all been investigating several violent murders in Arizona, New Mexico, and Texas that had smelled of a serial killer but turned out to be a crime syndicate covering its tracks.

Mahoney had gotten too close to a cell of the

Sinaloa drug cartel and was snatched off the street one night in Tucson. Forbes witnessed the grab, followed, and fought successfully to free Ned. Before he managed that, a cartel thug tried to slit his throat.

Forbes picked up the phone on his side of the glass. "I appreciate you coming, Alex."

"It's the least I could do."

"I'm innocent."

"I saw that you pleaded not guilty."

"I did," he said. "This is no legal bullshit move, Alex. I've been framed."

I sighed. "You said you wanted counseling, Marty. It's why I came."

"I knew you wouldn't come otherwise. I did not do this."

"You've got history, Marty. Your rep caught up with you."

Forbes flushed, but he calmed himself. "I was cleared on those shoots. Didn't you tell me that if you want to put out the fire, you've got to get close enough to burn?"

"That was Mahoney."

"Well, I am no vigilante. I don't know who pulled the trigger on those scum on the yacht, but as much as they deserved it, I sure as hell wasn't the one who did it."

I didn't reply for several moments, letting my mind tick back through the case as laid out in the news articles that had dubbed the former FBI agent Dirty Marty, a riff on Dirty Harry, a cop gone rogue, taking justice into his own hands.

Though Forbes had been cleared in those shooting incidents, the Bureau was concerned enough to rein him in; he'd been transferred from a senior investigatory position in Chicago to a desk job in crime analysis at Quantico. At the time, Forbes had been leading a probe into a sexual-slavery ring, a group of people who brought women and young girls and boys from underdeveloped countries into the United States through Canada or Mexico.

The twenty-four-month probe had penetrated the ring at low levels, enough to free more than fifty women enslaved as prostitutes traveling the country, guarded by violent pimps. Those freed women had identified two men and a woman as the likely masterminds of the ring.

Carlos Octavio, a Panamanian national fluent in eight languages, was said to work in tandem with Ji Su Rhee, a Korean woman who spoke nine languages. Octavio and Rhee bought girls, boys, and young women in lawless, impoverished countries. Gor Bedrossian, an Armenian with ties to U.S. and Russian crime syndicates, was believed to be the one who put the smuggling and distribution system together and enforced it all with an iron fist.

The problem for Forbes had been twofold. First, there had been no concrete evidence tying any of the three alleged masterminds to the enslaved women who'd been freed in various raids around the country. And second, the trio rarely, if ever, stepped foot on U.S. soil.

Before his transfer out of the field, Forbes had followed money trails, attempting, unsuccessfully, to trace them back to the ringleaders. A year after his transfer, Forbes took a two-month leave of absence to write a book about sexual slavery in the twenty-first century.

Prosecutors believed the real reason he took the leave of absence was to murder the suspects.

Six weeks after Forbes left to write his book, the U.S. Coast Guard boarded an adrift yacht called the *Harén*—Spanish for "harem"—off the coast of Florida. The bloated, headless bodies of six people, including Bedrossian, Octavio, and Rhee, were found aboard, all of them shot dead.

In compartments belowdecks, Coast Guard officers found sixteen teenage girls from Brazil, Cambodia, and India. They were all starving and dehydrated.

The girls later said the shootings had occurred four nights before. They'd heard a boat come alongside the yacht, which was not an uncommon occurrence. Usually that meant there was a buyer or a seller coming aboard.

Then the shooting started, at first slow and methodical, then more frenzied. They heard the other boat leave, and then there was nothing but silence for days. Because the yacht had been found adrift close to international waters, the FBI had been called in. The condition of the bodies had hampered the investigation but not thwarted it.

Each of the six victims had been shot at point-blank range from behind, right between the shoulder blades. Their heads had been removed with surgical precision.

The bullets were later matched to a gun Forbes had used when he'd been a field agent. The .40-caliber pistol was found in a closet at the West Virginia cabin where he'd gone to write his book. The FBI also found DNA evidence putting Forbes on the yacht.

"Alex?" Forbes said now, pressing his hand

against the bulletproof window. "Please, you've got to listen to me. I didn't do this. I was framed."

"By who?"

He hesitated. "I...don't know...I can't say for sure. He calls himself M."

CHAPTER

9

AT THREE THAT AFTERNOON, I climbed up into the grandstands above the track at Coolidge High School, still feeling like I'd entered some kind of twilight zone during my discussion with Martin Forbes.

M?

Again?

How is that even possible?

But those six bodies were…just like…

"Alex?"

I glanced over to see Nana Mama waving at me. My grandmother wore a wool hat and jacket and had a heavy blanket across her lap. The drizzle had stopped, but the air was still chill and dank.

Ali, next to her, was engrossed with something on his phone.

"How's our girl looking?" I said, sitting down next to them.

"Haven't seen her yet," Ali said without raising his head.

"Really?" I said, gazing at the track and field where athletes from three different high schools were warming up. "That's not like her."

"You notice she's been dragging?" Nana said. "She's not getting enough sleep."

"She's a seventeen-year-old girl. It's impossible for her to get enough sleep."

"Dad," Ali said, "can I borrow your phone? Mine died."

"To play a game?"

He looked insulted. "No, to read a book."

I handed it to him, said, "What are you reading?"

His thumbs flew over the screen of my phone as he said, "*Criminal Investigation: An Introduction to Principles and Practice,* by Peter Stelfox."

"Where'd you find that?" I asked.

"Online."

"You should be reading books that are more age-appropriate," Nana said.

"Age-appropriate things bore me," Ali said as he stared at my phone's screen.

My grandmother looked at me sharply, apparently waiting for me to say something. "I could use a little backup at times," she said.

Before I could reply, Jannie came out and started jogging around the track; she wore sweatpants and a hoodie, which was up. Normally, my daughter ran with a noticeable springiness in her gait, a bounce every time her foot hit the ground. It was almost like she was bounding. That natural stride had attracted the serious attention of several NCAA Division I coaches, all of them waving scholarships.

But as Jannie increased the pace of her warm-up run, I could see she was not striking the ground with the balls of her feet but farther back, toward her heels. It made her look awkward, and that was one thing Jannie never was on a track.

"She injure her foot again?" Nana Mama asked, concerned.

"I sure hope not," I said, standing and raising my binoculars to get a better look.

Jannie had gone through a difficult year after breaking one of the sesamoid bones in her foot. She'd had an operation, and it was touch and go for a time whether she'd recover fully. But she had, and she'd run some very impressive times during the indoor-track season.

Now, however, something was definitely off, though I didn't think it was her foot. Her shoulders were level, and her face showed no evidence of pain on the footfall.

But there just wasn't the spark you normally saw in her.

"She mention anything bothering her in school?" I asked Nana Mama after Jannie slowed to a walk, hands on her hips, head down.

"Straight As so far."

"Boys?"

Ali sniggered. "Jannie scares them away."

Bree arrived and sat down. "Did I miss her?"

"No," I said, watching my daughter again through the binoculars. She seemed distracted, almost listless, as she crossed the field toward her team.

I lowered the glasses and gave Bree a hug and a kiss. "Glad you made it."

"Me too," she said, and she smiled. "You texted that you had something bizarre to tell me?"

CHAPTER

10

I DID HAVE SOMETHING TO tell her, something almost unbelievable that Forbes had said, something with implications and ramifications far beyond the mystery of M.

"It's bizarre, and it's complicated," I said.

"What is?" Ali said.

"None of your business, young man," my grandmother said. "Why don't you read up on mountain bikes and how to fix them? Like Captain Abrahamsen said."

Ali cocked his head and smiled. "That's a good idea, Nana."

"We'll talk about it later?" Bree said to me.

"Yes. Most definitely."

I pushed my conversation with Forbes to the back of my mind and refocused on Jannie, who was scheduled to run the four-hundred and then the two-hundred.

In the last of her preparations for the start, Jannie seemed to shake off whatever had been bothering her. She went to her line in lane three, stutter-stepped, and then broke into a few loping bounds.

"That looked good," Bree said.

"Right there," Nana Mama said.

I said nothing, just watched Jannie go back to the line and take her marks. She coiled at "Set" and sprang at the gun.

Her arms chopped. Her knees rose and stabbed down. Each foot strike was light and elastic, and her stride was near perfect as she rounded the first turn.

"She's ahead!" Ali cried. "She's got this!"

Jannie did have it. Coming out of the turn, with the stagger compressing, she was in front of the others by a good five body lengths.

She kept that lead down the backstretch and as she entered the far turn, but at the three-hundred-meter mark, her head rocked back out of position, and she seemed to get lazy. And her breathing cadence changed.

A senior from another school passed Jannie coming into the final stretch. You could see Jannie wanted to respond. But she had no gas.

Another girl went by her, and a third. Jannie was fourth crossing the line, the worst finish she'd had since injuring her foot.

She slowed to a walk and then to a shuffle, her head down. I expected her to be devastated, but when she finally turned around, her expression was more bewildered than anything.

Jannie groped for something that wasn't there. Then her eyes rolled up in their sockets. She wobbled, staggered, collapsed forward onto the track.

"Jannie!" I roared. I sprinted down the stands and through the gate onto the track, where her coach and a trainer were already at her side.

They had rolled her onto her back. She had a scrape on her jaw where she'd hit the ground, but her eyes were open and searching.

"Dad?"

"Don't move, baby," I said. A physician, the mother of one of the other runners, came rushing up.

Dr. Ellen Roberts examined Jannie, who was becoming more alert. "Tell us what happened," Dr. Roberts said.

Jannie said she'd felt tired all day, even worse

than she'd felt the day before and the day before that. She'd fallen asleep twice in biology class and had to take a cold shower to wake up for the meet. She felt good at the start of the race and in the middle.

"But then I just lost everything," she said. "I don't know, I..." She closed her eyes. "Everything aches."

"I believe she has a fever," the doctor said. "Which doesn't surprise me."

"Flu?" her coach asked.

"I'm thinking Epstein-Barr, though we'll need to test her ASAP."

"Epstein-Barr?" I said.

"The virus that causes mononucleosis," Dr. Roberts said. "It's rampant at the school. If it's mono, I'm afraid your girl won't be running again for a good six weeks."

CHAPTER 11

"SIX WEEKS." JANNIE MOANED. We were back home after a trip to an urgent-care center, where the doctor had confirmed the diagnosis of mono.

Jannie was lying on the living-room couch under a blanket and looking forlorn. "Dad, that's almost the entire spring season. Gone. Just like last year. What am I, jinxed?"

I felt her heartache and frustration and said so, but she just started to weep.

"It's over," she cried. "No college coach will want me now. I'm cursed."

"You're sick because you've been burning the candle at both ends," I told her. "And I'm sure

D-One coaches have dealt with athletes with mono before."

She stared blankly at the wall.

"I just wanted it to all be good, Dad. Like, no question I was ready."

"I know. And I think you already are a no-question recruit to many coaches. They've seen your tapes and times. They know your potential."

She looked at me hopefully. "You think?"

"I do. The best thing you can do is follow Dr. Roberts's advice. Take those vitamins she mentioned, drink gallons of water, and get lots of sleep. You'll be better in no time."

Jannie seemed to surrender to the situation then. "Nana Mama's bringing me soup."

Bree came back from the health-food store with a buffet of vitamins, and the two of us went upstairs to change before dinner.

"So, about your meeting with Dirty Marty?" Bree called from the closet.

"He says he's not dirty," I said.

She stepped out of the closet, looked at me with a knitted brow. "And you believe him?"

"I don't know," I said, and then I told her about Forbes being contacted by M.

No one outside a very small circle in the law enforcement community knew about the notes

M had sent to me, and Forbes was certainly not part of that circle. We'd decided to hold that information back right from the start all those years ago.

"Doesn't mean Forbes couldn't have hacked into files at the FBI to learn about M," Bree said.

"Point taken," I said, and then I told her everything.

Forbes claimed M had contacted him first by untraceable e-mail from a server in Panama and later by text from a burn phone.

Forbes said M seemed to know the inner workings of the sex-slave operation Forbes had been trying to break and he offered to provide evidence and the location of the three ringleaders. Shortly after, M mailed Forbes documents detailing the purchase of a yacht in Panama and the aftermarket work done on it to create the prison cells belowdecks.

M lured Forbes to Florida, saying that he'd relay the yacht's location once it had entered U.S. waters to deliver its latest shipment of sex slaves. He also told Forbes to bring twenty-five grand with him and to take a room at a particular motel in Fort Lauderdale.

Forbes claimed that when he entered his room after dinner on the second day, there was a man hidden in the bathroom. He put a cloth over Forbes's face doused in what Forbes believed was chloroform.

"I went down, but I wasn't completely out," Forbes had said. "It was like I was paralyzed and looking at him in a nightmare as he dragged me up onto the bed and put an IV in my arm. Then I really went out. For good, and for four days."

"Four days?" I said. "No one found you in that motel room?"

"All I know is that when I woke up, I had a splitting headache, it was the afternoon four days later, and the money was gone."

"But you didn't report it to the police?"

He looked down and shook his head. "I should have, I know that now, but I was too embarrassed at the time. Here I'd gone off on a rogue investigation and I'd been played by a con artist."

"One who took your money and set you up to take the fall for killing six people."

He looked up angrily. "I didn't know that then. I was so disgusted with myself, I decided to just get in my car and drive back to West Virginia. I got there a day later and started to work on the book again. Two days after that, agents were at my door."

I thought about that for several minutes. "Did you have the forty-caliber pistol with you when you went to Florida?"

"No, I took my nine-millimeter, but I know what you're thinking: How did they get the forty? The guy who knocked me out or someone working with him must have broken into the cabin and found it. That's my only explanation."

"Except there were no prints on the gun other than yours," I said. "And they found hairs and skin cells matching your DNA on the yacht."

"He put that there to frame me!" Forbes said. "M or whoever he was."

"You told the Bureau all this?"

"Every bit of it, but they don't believe a word."

"Why's that?"

"The overwhelming evidence against me," he said in a bitter voice. "And who I said I thought M was."

"Okay?"

"You won't believe it either, Alex. I know I still don't. But I saw his face when I was in that cloudy nightmare state after the chloroform while he was working to get the IV in me."

I saw where this was going. "Are you saying you recognized him?"

Forbes chewed his lip, looked away, and nodded

so slightly that I knew he was doubting his own thoughts.

"Who was it?" I asked.

He took a deep breath and gave me an even gaze.

"An old friend of yours," he said. "Kyle Craig."

CHAPTER

12

IN OUR BEDROOM, AFTER I'D recounted the entire interview, Bree stared at me.

"Craig? That's impossible. Craig's been dead for years, Alex. You saw him die."

I nodded. "I did. Right in front of me. On our honeymoon."

Kyle Craig *was* dead. My nastiest opponent was long gone.

I'd wounded him, and rather than go back to prison, Craig had shot an oxygen tank, which blew up and burned him to bone and ash.

Sitting there on our bed, I tried not to see Craig die, but it was almost tattooed on my brain. All I had to do was close my eyes to see it.

"I figure Forbes was hallucinating," I said. "The effects of the chloroform triggering some deep memory of Craig."

"Or Dirty Marty made the whole story up," Bree said. "He somehow got wind of M and is now playing on your obsession with Kyle Craig."

I thought about that.

Marty Forbes had to have known how fixated I'd been on the FBI agent gone evil. Kyle Craig was a sadistic serial murderer who'd killed Betsey Cavalierre, my girlfriend at the time.

Bree came around and got into bed.

I climbed in beside her. "He could have been playing me. But for what? So I could help him get out of prison by convincing federal prosecutors that the man incinerated in front of me had risen from the dead and was now going around calling himself M?"

"Guilty men have come up with stranger stories," she said.

I turned off the light, thinking, *Then again, Craig used the alias Mastermind for a time, didn't he? Is he now M? Could he possibly have survived that blast?*

My rational mind said, *No. Absolutely not.*

After a few minutes, Bree was snoring gently. I started to drift off…

That dog began to bark again, and I snapped

wide awake. I was about to get dressed and go have it out with the owner at last when I heard tapping against the window and realized it had started to rain. I figured that would end the barking.

I was wrong. Twenty minutes later, I was still awake, and the dog was still barking in that damn repeating pattern.

Finally, I got up and climbed the stairs to my attic office. I closed the window behind my desk, turned on the light, and looked at the boxes stacked waist-high by seven bulging upright filing cabinets. Evidence of old cases, some solved, others not.

Though I did not want to, I knew where I needed to go—back to the beginning, back to the hunt for Mikey Edgerton, long before M had come into the picture.

I found what I was looking for in a box labeled KISSY at the bottom of the stack in the right corner of my office, where I thought I'd put it to rest forever. I set the box on the desk but hesitated to open it, wondering if I was wise to dig into this part of my past. A smart part of me said that it was wiser than not digging into it.

I pulled off the box cover, took out the first file, and almost immediately fell back in time.

CHAPTER 13

Twelve years before

IN A DRIVING RAIN ON a late May afternoon, John Sampson and I hurried north on Wisconsin Avenue toward La Cravate, an upscale men's-necktie store that catered to the rich and powerful in Washington, DC.

I carried a tie in a plastic evidence bag. The tie was silk and in a blue-and-red-paisley print, the kind you might see on a high-powered lobbyist on K Street. At least, that was the impression I got seeing it, brilliantly colored, crisp along the edges, and the knot near perfect around the neck of throttled twenty-six-year-old Cassandra "Kissy" Raider.

Two homeless men looking for a place to crash for the night had found Ms. Raider's corpse in a stolen and abandoned panel van in Southeast DC. She had been naked and spread-eagled on the floor, her wrists and ankles lashed with half-inch nylon webbing through eyebolts turned into the walls of the van, which reeked of bleach.

An autopsy found the killer had drenched Raider's body in a diluted bleach solution, which had destroyed any DNA evidence that might have been left after she was savagely and repeatedly beaten and raped prior to her strangulation.

At first, we treated the rape and murder as a one-off, and in the crucial first forty-eight hours, we focused on Raider's work at the Stallion Club, a strip joint in suburban Maryland, and on her ex-boyfriend, a biker from Roanoke, Virginia, who'd been convicted of some minor crimes in the past.

But when we ran the basic facts about the Raider case through the FBI's files, we got seven hits, including one in Boca Raton, Florida, and another in Newport Beach, California.

Like Kissy Raider, both victims had been petite, buxom blondes and single moms of young children. And like Kissy Raider, both women had been raped, beaten, and then throttled with a fine silk tie.

None of the ties carried a manufacturer's mark, which had us stymied for almost a week. But then Sampson started researching shops that specialized in high-end ties, and that was what led us to the Georgetown boutique.

We went inside and were greeted with the scent of some kind of essential oils misting the air, cedar and something I couldn't quite place. Whatever it was, it seemed to put me in a better mood, although that could have been due to just getting out of the pouring rain.

A fit, balding man in his forties with tan skin stood behind the counter. A second man was stocking the racks upon racks of men's neckties. He was as tall as the other guy but must have weighed close to three hundred pounds. But you wouldn't have known that at first glance; the tailoring of his suit hid it until he started moving.

The one behind the counter fixed us with a *What are you two doing in an upscale place like this?* stare and said in an English accent, "We take deliveries around back."

Sampson pulled himself up to his full height—well over six feet—and shot the man a surly look.

Then he dug out his badge and ID while I did the same.

"We're not here to make a delivery, Chatsworth," Sampson said.

I said, "We're homicide investigators with Metro PD."

The man behind the counter looked indignant and then sputtered, "My name is not Chatsworth, it's Bernard Mountebank, and we know nothing about any murder."

"Nothing at all," the other man said in a mild Southern accent. He was Nathan Daniels, he told us, and he and Bernard owned the shop.

"We didn't say we thought you were involved in a murder," Sampson growled. "We need your help."

"We hoped you could help identify this tie, gentlemen," I said, holding out the evidence bag. "The manufacturer, anything at all you can tell us."

That seemed to somewhat mollify Daniels, but Mountebank still seemed insulted by Sampson having called him Chatsworth. I thought it was kind of funny as well as justified, given that he'd taken us for deliverymen.

Mountebank didn't move, but Daniels ambled over to us. The fabric of his suit made swishing sounds as he came closer, interested now.

I handed him the evidence bag. He looked at the tie, then flipped the bag over.

"Can I remove it?" he asked.

"Only if you wear gloves," Sampson said, holding out a pair of disposables.

I made a note on the bag that we were opening it, put on my own gloves, pulled back the zipper closure, and handed him the tie, which was still knotted.

"Hmmmm," Daniels said, peering at the tie. He dug out his reading glasses so he could look closer. "Jacquard and Italian, for certain. Very nice indeed. Bernard, I believe this is a Stefano Ricci."

Mountebank seemed piqued when he said, "Are you sure?"

"No, I'm not," Daniels said. "You have a better eye for this kind of thing."

That seemed to please Mountebank no end and he quickly came over, giving Sampson a harsh glance as he passed. He donned gloves, studied the tie in some detail, noting the stitching and the weave.

"It would be easy to think this is a Ricci, but it's not," Mountebank said at last. "This is a limited-edition tie from Kiton in Naples, Italy. Very nice. Two, maybe three hundred, retail."

"For a tie?" Sampson said.

"If fashion were your thing, Detective, you would understand." He sniffed and returned the tie to me.

"Sell a lot of limited-edition Kitons?" I asked.

Daniels laughed. "That's a rather niche market."

"Did you carry this specific tie?"

Mountebank thought about that, then said, "You know, I believe we did. Last year. Sold it to one of our best customers."

"Who was that?" Sampson asked.

"Oh, I'm not at liberty to say. He's someone who values his privacy."

Sampson looked ready to swat the twit but said, "This is a murder investigation. We can come back with a warrant to tear this place apart and seize your computers."

Mountebank blanched. "Oh my. Well, Perry Singer, then."

His partner looked confused. "Perry?"

"Most definitely," Mountebank said, tilting his nose skyward. "He's a tie fanatic. He just might be your man, Detectives."

CHAPTER 14

NATHAN DANIELS LOOKED UP Perry Singer's address and reluctantly gave it to us. He lived on Cambridge Place in Georgetown, which was only eight blocks away. The rain had let up, so we decided to walk it.

Mr. Singer lived in a beautiful old Georgian townhome. The sidewalk and stoop were brick, as was the facade of the house. There was no doorbell on the dark green door, just a polished brass knocker with a carving of a rising sun above it.

Sampson struck the door with the knocker a few times.

A maid soon opened the door. We told her that we wished to speak with Mr. Singer, and she said he'd just stepped out and that we were lucky that he was in Washington at all rather than Palm Beach or La Jolla, where he also had homes.

Given that the two other rape-and-murder victims had been found a short distance from those two cities, we were now very interested in talking to Mr. Singer.

His housekeeper said he'd decided to take a walk after the rain let up and had headed to Georgetown Cupcake on M Street.

We hustled south and then west to the shop, which was full of kids just out of school and moms with younger children, all of them eager for cupcakes. There were only two men besides us in the establishment, each sitting at a table. One was in his thirties, wearing a gray suit that didn't fit him very well and a tie that looked like it might have been a clip-on. The other, who had his back to us, wore a sharply tailored blue sport jacket, khaki pants, and blue socks with white polka dots. His hair was jet-black and slicked back with some kind of pomade. This had to be Perry Singer.

When we got around the table, we discovered a man in his late eighties sipping an espresso and nibbling at a chocolate cupcake he held with shaky hands. He wore a starched white shirt and a bow tie that matched his socks. A fancy cane rested against his thigh.

He didn't seem to notice us even when Sampson muttered, "This is supposed to be our suspect? I've taken an intense dislike to Bernard Mountebank."

"The British have an odd sense of humor," I said. "Mr. Singer? Perry Singer?"

The old man started. "Do I know you?" he asked in a soft Southern accent.

We showed him our badges and IDs and told him we were working on a homicide investigation.

"Just tying up some loose ends," Sampson said. "Nothing to be alarmed about."

Mr. Singer shrugged. "Okay. How can I help?"

After showing him the tie in the evidence bag, I said, "Do you own one of these ties? It's a Kiton, the kind they sell at La Cravate."

He fumbled in his breast pocket, found glasses, and put them on. The old man studied the tie and then nodded. "I do own one. Or did. I haven't seen it in a while. Besides, this style of tie is almost out of fashion these days."

"But you said you haven't seen the tie in a while?" Sampson asked.

Mr. Singer seemed to find that confusing and then amusing.

"That's right, but who knows, it might be in my closet here or in Palm Beach or La Jolla. I have at least four thousand ties in my collection."

"So this *could* be your tie?" I asked.

"Well, I suppose it could have been stolen from me. But I most certainly did not tie that knot. It's a four-in-hand, and I've always preferred a Pratt or, if I'm feeling particularly jaunty, a Van Wijk."

Before I could reply, I happened to glance up to see FBI special agent Kyle Craig coming through the door. He spotted me and appeared taken aback.

I excused myself and went over. "Kyle?"

"What are you doing here, Alex?"

"Interviewing an octogenarian about his ties."

Craig curled his lip. "Perry Singer?"

That surprised me. "Yes."

"You sent over by the British guy?"

"Yep."

"I don't like that one, that Bernard."

"Neither does John. How are you involved?"

"Behavioral picked up the case now that there are three," he said quickly. "I was looking at pics of the ties and decided to go to the only tie store that was local."

"Great minds think alike."

"There anything to him being involved?"

I shook my head. "Mr. Singer owns a tie that matches the one used to kill Kissy Raider but says he hasn't seen it in a while. Although that doesn't mean anything; he evidently has four thousand ties spread across closets in three homes." I also told him about the knots. "Are the other knots four-in-hand?"

Craig shrugged. "I don't know the difference. I just do the one my dad taught me."

"The one Nana Mama taught me is a Windsor knot, I think."

"Dead end, then?"

I glanced over at Sampson and saw him shake Mr. Singer's feeble hand and then pick up the evidence bag.

"Sure looks that way," I said.

CHAPTER 15

WE WERE STALLED IN THE Kissy Raider investigation for another week, and then files and reports came back from labs and in response to requests we'd made to the FBI and various law enforcement agencies in Florida and California. I sat at my desk and read.

It was interesting to me that each of the three victims had had a bad relationship with the father of her child. Each woman had decided to go off on her own with her young son.

Althea Marks, the woman found in Newport Beach, had a six-year-old son. Samantha Bell, the victim found in Boca Raton, had a five-year-old boy. Kissy Raider's son, Max, was five when his mother was strangled to death.

Kissy's sister, Crystal, had come north almost immediately to claim her nephew. Crystal had been as forthcoming with information as she could be, given that her sister had run away from home at sixteen to be with Ricco, her biker boyfriend, who'd "treated her like crap and knocked her up."

Crystal said that once her sister had seen Ricco's true colors, she'd walked out on him and gone to a shelter to start a new life. And she was proud of it, even if she'd had to work in places like the Stallion Club to support her son.

I checked to see if the other two women had worked in strip joints, but they hadn't. Althea Marks had been a waitress in various restaurants for years; her last stint was at a burger joint in Laguna Niguel, California.

Samantha Bell had worked in everything from retail to construction to bartending at a Hooters.

To my surprise, the Hooters was in Laurel, Maryland. According to a report I got from the Florida detectives working the case, Ms. Bell had been in the Washington, DC, area three years before. She'd left the job at Hooters ten weeks prior to her strangulation.

I went back to Marks's file from the Newport Beach detectives and then to an FBI dossier Kyle Craig had sent over. I found her application to the burger joint and looked at what she'd listed as prior employment.

Five months before her death, Marks had left a job at a Hooters in Fairfax, Virginia, after spending nearly a year in the area.

Feeling like I might be onto something, I started digging madly through Kissy Raider's files. I found her job application for the Stallion Club, but she'd written *Not applicable* to the question about previous employment.

So I called Crystal Raider in Florida.

When Kissy's sister answered, I could hear kids yelling. "This is Crystal," she said wearily.

"This is Detective Cross."

"Yes?" she said, perking up. "Have you found him?"

"We're still hunting," I said.

"Oh," she said, disappointed. Then she asked anxiously, "How long will it take to find him? You don't know what it's like waking up day after day not knowing."

"Actually, I do know," I said. "My wife was murdered several years back, and her killer is still at large. Just like my wife's case, Kissy's investigation will take as long as it takes. We don't give up on capital crimes. Ever."

She sighed. "How do you live with it? Not knowing?"

"You learn to box it up and put it away until it has to be opened."

"I can't do that yet."

"I wouldn't expect you to."

Crystal sighed again. "How can I help?"

"Did Kissy ever work at a Hooters? I mean, before the Stallion Club?"

"No, I…wait. Yeah, maybe. I think she said she was there only a couple of weeks. Some creep kept hitting on her, so she quit."

"To go work at a strip bar?" I asked.

Crystal's voice was colder when she replied. "Kissy felt safe at the Stallion Club. They had bodyguards for the girls. Far as I know, that's not the case at Hooters."

"I'm sorry if I sounded snarky there. I'm just trying to understand the situation."

There was silence before she said, "Okay."

"Do you remember which Hooters she worked at?"

"I don't know. Somewhere around DC. How many can there be?"

CHAPTER 16

FOR THE RECORD, THERE ARE seven Hooters restaurants in the DC area, including one on Seventh Street in the northwest part of the District.

Sampson and I went there on a muggy June evening, but when we showed the manager a picture of Kissy, he said he'd never seen her before. We asked if he could search the Hooters chain for her, but he said we'd have to take that up with corporate in Atlanta.

It was nearly seven p.m., which meant it was highly unlikely that the Hooters' bean counters would still be at their desks, so we decided to go to the franchises in Laurel, Maryland, and

Fairfax, Virginia, where we knew for certain two of the victims had worked.

Alice Fox, the manager at the Laurel location, recognized Samantha Bell right away. "Sure," she said. "Got a young kid. Hard worker, that one. Why?"

Sampson said, "She was murdered in Florida."

"Murdered?" she said, horrified. "My God. You never know, do you?"

"No, ma'am," I said. "Why'd she leave?"

Fox frowned, said, "I think she had issues."

"Boyfriend issues?"

"A few weeks before she quit, she started insisting that someone always walk her to her car. She said she thought a guy was stalking her."

"What guy? A customer?"

She frowned again, thought a moment, then shook her head. "No, I don't think so. She would have said something about that, right?"

"You'd think."

"Sorry I can't help you more than that," she said.

"No, this helps," I said.

On the way to the Fairfax Hooters, we laid odds on the likelihood of a creep or stalker having shown up in Althea Marks's life. Sampson was calling it at three to two.

But I was thinking five to one when we went

through the front doors and saw well-endowed young women in tight shorts and white T-shirts ferrying drinks and food to ogling young men, just like we'd seen at the Hooters in DC and in Laurel.

A creep could definitely be stalking young women here, I thought while Sampson asked to speak to the manager. Peter Mason, the manager, came out and apologized when he was unable to identify Kissy Raider or Althea Marks from photos.

Sampson said, "Ms. Marks worked here. She put it on a job application."

Mason frowned. "How long ago?"

"Three years and a couple of months?"

He thought about that and then his brows shot up. "I was on paternity leave for ten weeks about then. Let me ask Stella. She's been here as long as I have."

Stella, the assistant night manager, didn't recognize the name Althea Marks, but when she looked at the picture, she said, "Aly. Yeah, she worked here, maybe six weeks. Good waitress."

"She say why she quit?" Sampson asked.

That seemed to make Stella uncomfortable. "What's this about? She okay?"

"No," I said. "She was murdered in Newport Beach, California, two years ago."

"Murdered?" she said in a bewildered voice. "Oh my God. She was right."

"Aly was right?" I said.

"I wanted to promote her or at least give her more shifts. But out of the blue, she came in and said she thought she and her son were unsafe here and that she was quitting. She wanted me to send her last paycheck to some PO box in California."

"Who was making her feel unsafe? A customer?"

She shook her head. "No. Anyway, I don't think so. We didn't have any incidents with her and a guy that I could point to. But you know how it is—people's lives are complicated. Especially for a young mom like that."

By the time we left, it was pushing ten, and Sampson was in favor of calling it quits for the evening.

"No," I said. "We're three for three on the victims thinking they were unsafe or being followed by a creep. We just need to find out where Kissy worked."

"You want to go to all four other Hooters on the list tonight?"

"One more," I said. "The one in Chantilly, and then we'll call it."

Big John wasn't thrilled about it, but he said, "Deal."

We had luck on our side.

Carol Patrick, manager at the Chantilly Hooters, recognized Kissy Raider the second she saw the picture of her.

Her face lost all color and she said, "Is Kissy okay? Please tell me that beautiful soul is okay."

CHAPTER 17

CAROL PATRICK BROKE DOWN IN a booth at the back of the Hooters where we'd gone to talk.

"Kissy told me he was a psycho," Patrick said through sobs. "She said she could see it in his eyes, and that she needed to run."

We told her to back up and give us what she knew. After she'd composed herself, Patrick said there'd been a guy in his thirties, real well dressed, who'd come to the restaurant several times and always asked for Kissy to be his server.

"He tried to follow her home one night," Patrick said. "Kissy said she drove her car crazy and lost him, but she was frightened out of her mind, said she needed to quit."

"Do we have a name?" Sampson asked.

"I don't think she knew for sure. She called him creepy Mike, I think."

"Mike," I said, writing it down. "No last name?"

"Just creepy Mike with the dead eyes. And he wore a toupee."

Sampson said, "He pay with a credit card?"

"No. That I do know. He paid cash and left her a big tip every time he was in."

"And that was how often?" I asked.

"She worked here only, what, three weeks? He might have been here four times."

"What about after she left?"

Patrick thought about that. "I don't see everyone who comes through the door."

"But you saw him?"

"I did. Twice."

"Did you get a good look at him?" Sampson said. "Enough for you to work with a sketch artist?"

"I guess. Sure, and..." Something seemed to dawn on her.

"What?" I asked.

"I'll be a son of a...I got someone you might want to talk to."

Patrick got up and came back with a Hooters girl in tow. Her name was Marlene Rogers. She was in her late twenties, five two, a buxom pretty blonde.

"She could be Kissy's sister, couldn't she?" Patrick said. "I've always said that."

We knew Kissy's sister, and she didn't look anything like Ms. Rogers, but there was no denying Marlene's resemblance to Kissy Raider, Althea Marks, and Samantha Bell. They were all of a type.

"Tell them, Marlene," Patrick said. "Tell them what you told me last week."

"I don't know," she said, twisting a strand of her hair. "It's just a feeling I've been getting."

"What kind of feeling?" I asked gently.

"Like I'm being watched. Like maybe someone is following me."

"Who?"

"I…I don't know for certain, but I'd swear it was this guy who came in for lunch about six weeks ago. Maybe longer."

"Sharp dresser," Patrick said. "Obvious toupee, right?"

Rogers frowned. "No toupee. He was balding. He was big and lean, and yeah, he had nice clothes."

"What did he talk about?" Sampson asked.

"Wanted to know all about me."

"What about you?"

"Like if I was married. And if I had a kid."

"Are you? Do you?"

"My husband died in Iraq, and I have a little boy. Eddie."

"How old?" I asked.

"Four."

Blond, busty single mother with a young son.

We asked her if she remembered anything specific about the guy other than that he was lean and a sharp dresser. She said that he made her uncomfortable every time she went to his table because he stared at her with this bright smile. "And his eyes were weird. Too blue to be real, like he was wearing contacts."

She didn't remember the exact date that he'd been in the restaurant, but it was definitely more than a month ago. Patrick said that, unfortunately, they didn't keep security-camera footage past thirty days. Corporate policy.

The waitress was more than willing to work with a sketch artist as well.

"That will help, thank you," I said. "One final question?"

"Sure."

"When was the last time you felt you were being watched or followed?"

"Like, every night since then. I'm always looking over my shoulder."

We gave them our cards and told Ms. Rogers to alert us if that customer came into the restaurant or if she saw him anywhere else in her life.

"You can call anytime," I said. "Day or night."

All the way home and even as I finally started to fall asleep, I kept thinking that if he was the same creep Kissy Raider believed was stalking her, he sounded very much like a predator.

And Marlene Rogers might be as close to bait as we were ever going to find.

CHAPTER 18

THE FOLLOWING NIGHT, SAMPSON AND I camped out in an unmarked squad car outside the Chantilly Hooters while Marlene Rogers worked her shift.

We were on the lookout for a big, lean balding guy or a big, lean guy wearing an obvious toupee, but we saw no one meeting either of those descriptions. I began to wonder if the waitress felt like she was being watched or followed because she'd been conditioned to feel that way.

I considered that idea. I'd been to a seminar earlier that year in which a speaker asked how many of the men in the room had felt physically or psychologically threatened during the previous month. Maybe four men out of the two hundred there raised their hands. When the two hundred women there were asked the same question, a hundred and seventy or so raised their hands.

I'd been shocked by that, and it had given me a new appreciation for what women, including Marlene Rogers, went through on a daily basis. I decided she'd probably been sexually harassed enough to know when a guy posed an actual threat, so if she said someone was following her, I believed her.

Around nine, Rogers, no longer in her Hooters uniform and with a heavy purse over one shoulder, came out the back door of the restaurant. She climbed into her Toyota Prius and drove out of the parking lot. No one followed her except us.

"She's headed to her mom's place to pick up her son," I said. "Let's go sit on her condo and make sure she gets inside, then we'll call it a night."

"Works for me," Sampson said.

Rogers lived in the upper right unit of a two-story, fourplex rental near the Walmart Supercenter off I-66. We parked across the street and down the block.

I used binoculars to scan the cars on the street but saw no one in any of them. Rogers rolled in ten minutes later, parked the Prius in her normal spot—nose in against a cedar hedge—and carried her sleeping son up the stairs and into the apartment.

We watched for a few minutes, and I was about to call it when Rogers came back out and hurried to her car. She opened the door, ducked inside, and emerged with her purse. Slinging it over her shoulder, Rogers turned to head back to her apartment.

A looming dark shape slipped from the cedar hedge, took two steps toward her, and grabbed her from behind.

CHAPTER 19

HE WAS BIG AND OUTWEIGHED Marlene Rogers by a solid hundred pounds at least, maybe more. He clamped a gloved hand over her mouth and wrapped his other arm around her neck.

He started dragging the waitress as we bolted from the squad car and ran down the street toward them. He'd taken her through the hedge by the time we reached her car.

We went through the hedge, guns drawn, and found ourselves on a lawn behind the parking lot of another, larger apartment complex.

He was maybe fifty yards away, dressed in black from his boots to his face mask and hood. Rogers had stopped squirming, and he was hustling her toward the open side door of a beige panel van. We sprinted at him, me slower and more off balance than Sampson but refusing to stop.

Still not seeing us, he turned, keeping the waitress in front of him, and tried to pull her back into the van. But when he did, she dug in her heels and drove herself backward, going with his momentum. It threw him off balance, and he let go of her mouth long enough for her to scream and strike at his ribs with her elbow.

He grunted, swore, reached behind.

"Police!" Sampson shouted, gun up, coming between two parked cars about thirty yards away from them. "Let her go!"

The man put a Glock to Marlene's head. In a flat voice, he said, "If you want her to live, you let me go."

"Let her go *now!*" I said, coming at him from a slightly different angle.

"Stay where you are, or I'll kill her," he said. "I've got nothing to lose. I swear I'll kill the bitch out of spite."

Before we could say anything in response, a shot rang out, then another.

Sampson and I dived for cover.

But we needn't have.

The big guy wasn't the one who'd fired the gun.

One bullet went through his right shoulder, which caused his arm to buckle and sag, and the second round struck him four inches higher, entering the side of his neck.

He went limp as a rag doll and let go of the gun and Marlene Rogers. Then he fell backward and landed half in and half out of the panel van.

The waitress let out a shriek and ran. I tried to grab at her from my knees as she passed. "You're okay!"

"No, I'm not!" she screamed. "I have to make sure Eddie's safe!"

She got by me and tore toward the cedar hedge, sobbing hysterically.

Sampson and I lurched up and got into combat shooting crouches, still on high alert, guns aimed toward the darkness where the two shots had come from.

FBI special agent Kyle Craig stepped from the shadows, right hand and service weapon hanging at his side, his open left palm raised in salute and surrender.

CHAPTER 20

"GOOD THING I CAME ALONG when I did," Craig said, sounding matter-of-fact rather than smug, "or that young lady would have been dead. Or one of you."

Our astonishment was complete as we lowered our pistols.

"Jesus, Kyle," Sampson said. "Where did you come from?"

"Back there," he said, walking toward the body. "I've been watching this guy. But I had no idea what he was going to do even after he disappeared through that hedge."

"Wait," I said. "You've been following him?"

"Last night and all day today," Craig said.

"You know who he is?" Sampson said.

"Definitely," Craig said, holstering his weapon, getting out a flashlight, and shining it on the dead man's face. He removed the mask and said, "Pal of yours, Sampson."

We gaped at Bernard Mountebank, the shop owner who'd given us the runaround when we asked about the tie.

"What?" Sampson said, dumbfounded.

"Right?" Craig said, sounding pleased with himself.

Hearing sirens in the distance, no doubt summoned by Craig's shots, I said, "How did you get onto him?"

"I knew he was bad from the get-go, kind of smelled it, especially after he sent us all to see that old man at the cupcake shop. So I dug into him a little. He's not Bernard Mountebank, and he's not from England. Meet Gerald St. Michel, suspected serial sex offender from the British Virgin Islands."

He told us St. Michel had entered the United States after obtaining a green card by marrying a woman from Northern Virginia. St. Michel hadn't said anything to her about his criminal past, nor did he mention that in his application for permanent-resident status or in his dealings with his business partner Nathan Daniels.

But Craig had found documents through an FBI database that showed St. Michel had changed his name to Mountebank a year before leaving the Virgin Islands. Craig had contacts on the islands who put him in touch with a police detective there.

"He hadn't heard that St. Michel had gotten resident status," Craig said. "No one had ever contacted the BVI about him. If someone had, the detective would have said that St. Michel was a suspect in several sexual assaults down there, often of female tourists."

The detective believed St. Michel had abducted five different young women over the course of seven years. In each case, he'd kept the woman as a sexual slave for three days, then drugged her and let her go.

"He always wore a mask," Craig said, gesturing at the one he'd set by the dead man's head. "And he was careful to clean the women up. But the detective said there was no doubt in his mind that St. Michel was his man."

"You think he's the one who killed Kissy Raider?" Sampson asked.

"He's looking awful good for it to me," Craig said.

I took a flashlight from my pocket and shone

it inside the van, where there was a kit waiting: strips of duct tape for his victim's mouth and ankles, hanging above a pair of handcuffs linked through a bracket welded into the van's wall.

"He had it worked out. Looks just like what happened to Kissy," Sampson said.

"But it's not," I said. "Kissy was restrained by nylon webbing and eyebolts."

"Close enough," Craig said.

"Maybe," I said, opening the passenger door of the van.

The dome light had been turned off, but I beamed my flashlight under the seats, across the dash console, and into the glove compartment.

Then, as the first Fairfax County Sheriff patrol cars pulled into the parking lot, I went through St. Michel's pockets. I found nothing.

"Is it the same guy?" Sampson said after I'd taken a step or two back from the scene.

"I don't know," I said. "If it is, where's the bleach solution? More important, where's the tie he was going to strangle her with?"

CHAPTER 21

Present day

EVENTUALLY I PUT AWAY THE files in the attic and went back to bed. The next day, operating on less than five hours of sleep, I managed to see several private clients in my basement office. But in the gaps between appointments, my mind slipped repeatedly into the deep past, replaying how Kyle Craig had appeared out of nowhere to shoot Gerald St. Michel.

But no nylon webbing. No eyebolts in the van wall. No bleach. No tie.

A dozen years later, I could still feel the instinctive response I'd had to those discrepancies in the pattern, could still remember how I left the crime scene with lingering doubts that St. Michel was our serial rapist and killer.

But as Sampson kept saying, St. Michel had targeted a blond single mom who had a young son and worked at Hooters. What were the odds of two different killers sharing the same target profile? Pretty slim, and that and the fact that there were no new attacks for a while had allowed me to dismiss my doubts.

Then a man grabbed a young blond woman late at night in Falls Church, Virginia. He used a necktie to bind her hands and threw her in a panel van. She managed to escape when he stopped at a light and was able to give police a rough description of her assailant.

I was lost in thought when a knock came at my office door, and I shot up about a foot in the air, I was so startled.

"Yes?" I said, frowning because I was done with patients for the day.

"Alex, I'm baking brownies," my grandmother said, opening the door. "And Ali's home from school."

Brownies. I glanced at my watch. Half past four. A good time for a break.

"I'll be right up," I promised, and I shut down my laptop.

When I entered the kitchen, the smell of baking brownies was incredible.

"Don't you go looking in that oven," Nana Mama said. "I've got them on a timer."

"I wouldn't dream of it," I said, pouring myself some orange juice, but I desperately wanted to open the oven and breathe in the aroma of my grandmother's heavenly brownie concoction, which had three different kinds of chocolate and chopped walnuts and pistachios.

Ali came into the kitchen and put his school bag on the counter. "Hi, Dad. How long, Nana?"

"Ten minutes. Anyone can wait ten minutes."

He started to protest, but I said, "Rule number one: Listen to Nana. Rule number two: See rule number one."

"Sound advice," my grandmother said, walking up behind me, turning on the light in the oven, and crouching to look through the glass.

The front doorbell rang.

"I'll get it!" Ali said, and he darted off.

I decided to go back down to my office and finish writing a note on one of my clients, and I was about to ask Nana to send down a fresh brownie when they were done when I heard Ali say, "Hi, Captain Abrahamsen!"

"Isn't he the nice man who brought Ali home?" Nana Mama said.

"One and the same," I said, leaving the kitchen for the front hall. The captain was on the porch in his U.S. Army dress uniform. He was chatting with Ali through the screen, saw me, and straightened up.

"Mr. Cross," he said, smiling.

"Captain," I said, then I looked at Ali. "Aren't you going to let him in?"

Ali opened the door.

Abrahamsen wore laminated badges that I recognized as Pentagon and U.S. Capitol passes. He held up a plastic shopping bag, then stepped inside and said, "I had to be up on the Hill for a meeting, and I thought Ali might be able to use these for his bike. They're surplus."

Ali took the bag and looked inside. "Whoa!"

He pulled out a knobby tire wrapped in rubber bands, a small bicycle pump, a tube for the tire, and a patch kit.

The captain grinned at Ali and then looked at me. "He really should have the patch kit with him if he's off riding by himself."

“Good point,” I said. “Do you know how to use it, Ali?”

My son shrugged. “Sort of. I watched someone do it on YouTube.”

Abrahamsen said, “I’ve got twenty minutes. Get your bike. I’ll show you.”

“You won’t get dirty?” Ali asked.

“Not if you do the work.”

Ali looked at me, and I bobbed my chin. He took the porch steps two at a time and disappeared around the corner.

“I wish I had his energy,” Abrahamsen said, then he laughed. “He reminds me of my stepbrother. Willis is ten too.”

He pulled out his wallet, thumbed through it, and came up with a picture of himself kneeling by a towheaded boy in a Little League uniform.

“Where’s he live?” I asked, seeing palm trees in the background.

“Southern Cal,” Abrahamsen said. “With my dad and his second wife. Love that kid.”

“What do you do for the army?”

“Now?” he said. “I brief folks up on the Hill. Liaison work, mostly.”

“And you bicycle.”

The captain grinned. “My orders do include training rides three times a week.”

"Lifer?" I asked as Ali came puffing up the porch stairs, bike over his shoulder.

"If the work stays challenging, I could put my twenty in."

"Captain?" Ali said.

"Be right out," he said. "Can I use your latrine?"

"Sure," I said. "Right down the hall, through the kitchen, and on your left."

"Thank you," he said. He walked by me and almost bumped into Nana Mama, who had appeared with a plate of warm brownies.

"I figured you'd want some, Captain Abrahamsen," she said.

Abrahamsen laughed. "You must be Nana Mama."

"The one and only," I said. "The captain needs to use our bathroom."

"Through the kitchen and on the left. I'll put these on the porch for you all."

My cell phone rang. FBI special agent Mahoney. "Ned," I said.

"Pack an overnight," Mahoney said. "And get to Reagan National Airport."

CHAPTER 22

FOUR HOURS LATER, MAHONEY AND I pulled into the driveway of a beautiful home in Shaker Heights, Ohio.

Diane Jenkins, a forty-two-year-old mother of two, had vanished thirty-seven hours before. Her husband, Melvin, owner of a string of home-nursing companies, said his wife had failed to pick up their daughters after school. The girls and their father had tried to reach Mrs. Jenkins for hours but their calls went straight to voice mail.

Jenkins went to the Shaker Heights police to file a missing-person report on his wife that same evening. The police said they had to wait to investigate until Mrs. Jenkins had been out of contact for a minimum of twenty-four hours.

Finally, Jenkins remembered his wife had an active OnStar membership for her Cadillac. Diane's vehicle was located outside a low-income housing project fifteen miles from home, a place his wife had no reason to be. When Jenkins drove to North Royalton, Ohio, he found the car had been stripped.

Then Jenkins received a call from someone using a voice-distorting device. The caller demanded five million dollars in a cryptocurrency called Ethereum in exchange for the safe return of his wife. Jenkins had forty-eight hours to pay it.

Despite being warned not to by the kidnapper, Jenkins called the FBI. He'd managed to record the ransom conversation. A transcript of the recording had made its way to Mahoney's desk, which was why we were knocking on the Jenkins's front door.

A Cleveland-based FBI agent named Andrea Rowe let us in.

We found Melvin Jenkins, a wiry marathon runner in his late forties, looking emotionally exhausted. Mentally, however, the man was sharp, alert, and direct.

His wife had last been seen eating lunch in downtown Shaker Heights with a friend who was having a hard time after her husband's recent death in a car crash. They'd parted with plans to meet again the following week.

"She said Diane was going to the library, where she serves on the board, and then to pick up the girls," Jenkins said. "She never made it to the library."

"Do we know what time her phone was turned off?" I asked.

Special Agent Rowe said, "Two thirty-two p.m., approximately forty minutes after she left the restaurant."

"Where did it go dead?" Mahoney asked.

"Near the Brecksville Reservation," Jenkins said. "It's a forested hiking area not far from where her car was found."

"She go there a lot?" Mahoney asked.

"A lot? No. I mean, she'd been there," Jenkins said. "We've all been there."

"But she hadn't mentioned plans to go there?"

"No."

"Could we hear the ransom demand?"

Jenkins nodded and fished his phone out of his pocket. He thumbed the screen, and an androgynous, digitally altered voice came on.

"I am the only one keeping your wife alive, Melvin," the voice said.

"Who are you?" Jenkins demanded.

There was a pause before the voice said, "If it helps, you can call me M."

CHAPTER 23

YOU CAN CALL ME M.

That was the line that had eventually led to Mahoney and me getting on a plane to Ohio. It was the same line that rang in my head long after we heard Diane Jenkins's crying at the end of the recording and begging her husband to pay the ransom.

"Five million in Ethereum?" Mahoney said.

"I had to look it up," Jenkins said. "One of those cryptocurrencies. You have to go through a whole legal process that takes like a month before you can even transfer money into an exchange to buy Ethereum."

Special Agent Rowe said, "He's right, sir. There's no quick way to get the approval for that much in crypto in the time Mr. Jenkins has to gather his resources."

I said, "Unless we get someone high up in the Treasury Department to approve it."

Mahoney said, "We don't usually encourage people to pay ransoms, but I can ask—if that's what you want to do, Mr. Jenkins. I mean, if you have that kind of money."

"Not liquid," Jenkins said. He hesitated, then added, "But I might be able to get it from a line of credit my company has. I could use it as a loan and then repay it."

"I'll give someone a call. Do we know which crypto exchange you're going to use?"

"Kraken?" Jenkins said.

Ned nodded and left, and Jenkins looked at me and said, "Can I get you some coffee, Dr. Cross? I was about to make some."

"I'll go with you," I said. "I've been sitting too much."

I followed him down a narrow hallway hung with pictures of Jenkins, his kids, and his wife, a handsome brunette with a big, genuine smile. I hesitated in front of a picture of Diane Jenkins alone on a cliff above tropical water somewhere.

She looked radiant, and I could not help thinking, *Why is M asking for a ransom for her? He's never done anything like this before. Why does he need the money?*

"She's beautiful in that photograph," Melvin Jenkins said. "And never happier. That's Fiji. It was her dream to go there."

"Did you take the picture?"

He nodded.

"You can feel her love as she looks out at you," I said.

Jenkins's chin quivered. He nodded again and turned away, sniffling.

We went into a kitchen with low ceilings, dark beams, and a cozy atmosphere. He seemed to find solace there and made us a pot of coffee.

My phone made a weird dinging noise. I pulled it out and saw a message on the screen: Hi, Dad!

Then it vanished. I frowned and stuck the phone back in my pocket.

"Are you married, Dr. Cross?" Jenkins said, pouring coffee into a cup for me.

"I am, sir."

"Kids?"

"Three," I said. "Where are your daughters?"

"At my sister's house. I didn't want them to be here if news of the kidnapping leaks. There'll be a media circus, and I don't want them exposed to that kind of thing in any way, shape, or form."

"I don't blame you. I've been there, and they try to eat you alive to get ratings."

"Oh, I know," Jenkins said. "Diane used to be an on-air reporter, but she got disgusted with it all and quit."

"She sounds like one tough lady."

"You have no idea," he said with a smile that quickly weakened. "Has this M done other things? I mean, does he come up in your databases, a kidnapper named M?"

"He does," I said.

"Okay," Jenkins said, brightening. "So he does let them go?"

I didn't want Jenkins to lose hope. To get through the next few days, he was going to have to be stronger than he'd ever been, and I worried about weakening his spirit in any way.

But in the end, I told him the truth. I've found that lying to people, even with good intentions, comes back to haunt you one way or another. Besides, a man like Jenkins would want to know who and what he was up against.

After I finished, he stared down at the wooden floor and then up at the beams.

"This was Diane's idea," he said, gesturing around. "She designed it to look like her grandma's farm kitchen, which was where she was happiest as a child."

"It's beautiful," I said.

"I think so," he choked out. "My girls...I...I don't know what to tell them."

Jenkins broke down and hung his head.

"Mr. Jenkins, you have to stay positive," I said, putting my hand on his shoulder. "There's always a possibility that M will change his pattern."

Jenkins stiffened. "*You're* what this is all about, aren't you, Dr. Cross? I mean, M leaves these notes for *you.* He knew you'd find your way to this case."

"I think that's fair to say, Mr. Jenkins."

"So my Diane's a pawn in some twisted game you're playing with this guy?"

"It's not a game I entered willingly. It's a game I was sucked into."

"For twelve years?" he said. "Who does that? Why you?"

"I don't know."

My phone made that odd dinging noise again.

I did not move a muscle.

"Is he going to kill my wife in order to punish you?" Jenkins asked.

"I can't answer that. But I do know that this is the first time he's requested money. That's a good thing. Money is traceable."

"Not those cryptocurrencies," Jenkins said. "I've

read up on them in the past day or so. They're untraceable. That's why China banned them."

"*Mostly* untraceable," I said. "FBI experts are on their way from Quantico, and they're brilliant with anything cyber. If anyone can track the flow of the ransom money, it's them."

My phone dinged a third time.

"Excuse me," I said. I walked out into the hall and pulled the phone from my pocket in time to see It's me, Dad! Ali! Go to Wickr on your phone and message me back. We can be spies!

CHAPTER

24

BY THE FOLLOWING EVENING, as the deadline for the ransom payment approached, I had put aside the extreme irritation I'd felt on learning that Ali had put the Wickr app on my phone without my permission.

I'd checked the app out on the web and saw it was legitimate, but I told Ali he'd better ask me in the future before he put anything on my phone and emphasized that there was to be no "spying" when I was on duty. Ever. He promised, and after a few "secret" messages between us over breakfast, I was able to turn my full attention to the Diane Jenkins case.

An FBI contractor and eccentric tech genius

named Keith Karl Rawlins had flown in along with his handler, Special Agent Henna Batra. I'd worked with them before and considered them a formidable team. As I sat in the Jenkinses' kitchen that night, I felt like we had a decent shot at finding our way to M and to Mrs. Jenkins.

Rawlins, who went by the nickname Krazy Kat or, sometimes, KK, was dressed in green parachute pants, sandals, and an embroidered purple shirt that matched the color of his hair—or some of his hair, anyway. The FBI forgave his free spirit because, with dual PhDs from Stanford and another from MIT, the man was beyond a wizard at a keyboard.

"We good?" Mahoney asked, glancing at the wall clock in the Jenkinses' kitchen.

Rawlins sat at the breakfast counter chewing his lip and looking at three different laptops set around a much larger screen.

"If historical data reverts to the mean, we have a real chance," Rawlins said.

Special Agent Batra, a petite woman in her thirties, sat by him. "We would if this were a cash transaction," she sniffed. "Crypto is an entire paradigm shift."

"Paradigm shift," Rawlins sniffed back. "How Y-Two-K of you, Batra."

"He could be anywhere," she snapped.

I understood the conflict. Historical FBI data going back to the 1920s strongly suggested that kidnappers interested in money usually remained close to where they'd snatched their victims. Based on interviews with serial kidnappers, investigators knew there were many reasons why. The biggest was to avoid a long drive that might trigger a police stop. Better to take a victim somewhere quickly and make the ransom demand from there.

Being close to the victim's home also helped when the kidnappers moved to pick up the cash payment. But with cryptocurrency, that seemed less important.

Still, Rawlins had set up digital traps in the operating system of cell towers around Cleveland and in the park where Mrs. Jenkins's cell phone had gone silent. He'd also buried digital tracking bugs in the metadata surrounding the Ethereum currency.

Jenkins's iPhone buzzed and rang. On the screen was UNKNOWN NAME, UNKNOWN NUMBER.

"Here we go," I said, tugging on wireless headphones linked to Jenkins's phone.

"Hello?" Jenkins said.

The voice was the same as in the recording—flat, sexless, hollow.

"Are your hands clean, Mr. Jenkins?"

"I don't understand."

"Did you notify the FBI?"

"You told me not to."

"Answer the question."

"No."

"You're lying, Mr. Jenkins."

"No, I—"

A different voice came over the phone, one that was not distorted. Diane Jenkins began to scream in agony. "No! No! Melvin! What have you done?"

There was a weird heavy noise, like something slamming, and then we couldn't hear her anymore.

"That was your wife's wedding and engagement rings coming off, Mr. Jenkins. Along with her finger."

The horror on Jenkins's face was complete.

"But I have the money!" he cried. "The Ethereum. Isn't that what you wanted? Please, just tell me where you want me to send it. Give me the account number."

Several seconds passed and then M said, "Dr. Cross? You're there, aren't you?"

I shut my eyes a moment. After twelve years, he was talking to me directly. I knew I wasn't hearing his true voice, but before I answered I prayed I could hear his soul.

"I'm here, M."

We all heard a sigh of pleasure. "I thought so."

I said nothing.

He laughed. "It's rather funny, isn't it? After all these years, you and me? Like pen pals who've never met but are profoundly connected. Am I right, Alex?"

"It's been a one-way conversation so far."

"Certain things are worth waiting for. And planning for. And anticipating. And now here we are. Talking. At last."

"Mr. Jenkins has the ransom money. Do you want it or not?"

"Oh, I want it," he said. "So here are the rules. If you've bugged the transfers, Cross, debug them. Now. I will know if the transaction is being traced. Once I've received the money, I'll tell Jenkins where he can find his wife."

Then he rattled off a sixteen-character code of letters, numbers, and symbols.

"Send the crypto to that account at the Kraken exchange within the hour. If the Ethereum is not in that account by ten p.m. eastern, well, until next time, Dr. Cross. And I'm sorry for your loss, Mr. Jenkins."

The line died.

We all looked at Rawlins, whose eyes were darting from screen to screen.

"Well?" Mahoney said. "Did you get him?"

"I'm stripping out the obvious bugs," he said.

"I knew you wouldn't catch him local," Batra said.

There was an audible ding from the laptop closest to me. Rawlins finished typing, glanced at that screen, and started clapping.

"And yet, Batra, I did just catch him local," he said.

CHAPTER 25

THE NINETY-ACRE SCHULTE FARM sat half a mile off Mennonite Road, just shy of Mantua, Ohio, which was no more than twenty miles east of where Diane Jenkins had vanished. M had stayed on the line toying with me long enough for Rawlins to get a fix on the burn cell somewhere on that farm.

Mahoney and I had left Special Agent Batra to oversee the transfer of the cryptocurrency and sped toward the farmhouse. We'd called for more agents, hoping to surround the place, but they were still a solid thirty minutes away when we pulled over on the shoulder of Mennonite Road and killed the lights.

I checked my watch. It was 9:44 p.m. Sixteen minutes to go.

Mahoney called Batra and put her on speakerphone.

"How long do you want me to wait to make the transfer?" she asked.

"Till two minutes to ten," he said.

We climbed out of the vehicle, got tactical vests, semiautomatic rifles, and night-vision goggles from the trunk, then set off toward what had been an active dairy farm up until three years ago. The owner had died, and the surviving Schulte children did not wish to milk cows for a living.

The homestead had been platted for a subdivision, put up for sale at an astronomical sum, and empty ever since. At least, that's what we'd gleaned from looking at the property on Zillow.com.

"Perfect for him," I said. "They have to keep the heat and electricity on for prospective buyers, and it's remote enough no one's going to hear Diane screaming."

"He's no dummy," Mahoney said, climbing over the steel gate that blocked the dirt road into the farm.

I did the same and then tugged on the infrared goggles. Instantly the drive was lit up brighter than twilight. We went fast to the clearing. The house was dark.

"Money just moved," Batra said over the earbuds we wore.

"Which means he's going to move soon," Mahoney said.

But we stood there watching the farmhouse for twenty minutes before Batra said, "He's got the five million, and Rawlins says it's already been split and transferred on. The good news is he's staying with it."

"Let's go," Mahoney said.

Guns up, we ran to the front door of the farmhouse, turned the handle, and found it unlocked. I pushed the door open and eased inside. There was furniture covered in plastic in rooms off a central hallway, and a kitchen that was bare.

Thinking about that heavy slamming noise we'd heard on the phone, we considered the possibility that he had her in a basement room or out in the barn. We checked both but found nothing.

We didn't figure out why until we discovered a small device with a blinking light plugged into a socket in the main bedroom. Rawlins informed us we were looking at a repeater.

M had called the repeater from his burn phone, and the repeater, in turn, had called us. As we trudged back to the car, the skies opened, and it began to pour.

"Son of a bitch," Mahoney said. "He played us."

"Perfectly," I said, going to the passenger door. "We just have to hope he was serious, that he'll get the five million and let Diane Jenkins go."

Mahoney clicked the remote to unlock the car and turn on the interior lights.

That's when we saw blood on the backseat, a severed finger with an engagement ring and a wedding band, and the decapitated head of a woman, brunette hair hanging across her face.

CHAPTER 26

MY STOMACH LURCHED, AND I had to turn away and compose myself for several moments before I found my cold professionalism.

"He was right here," I said. "This whole area is a crime scene."

"Fat chance we'll find anything in this rain," Mahoney said. "Is it her?"

I forced myself to stare through the rain-streaked window at the severed head, the blood, and the finger, then I put on gloves and opened the rear passenger door.

"The rings are Mrs. Jenkins's," I said, tasting acid at the back of my throat. "I recognize them from a picture in their house."

Mahoney opened the other rear door and peered in at the head, which was closer to him. With gloved hands, he gingerly brushed back the hair from the corpse's face and sighed.

She was Asian.

"I don't know whether to be happy or sad," Mahoney said.

"Why kill another woman?" I said, studying her face.

"I have no idea what this guy's play is," Mahoney said. "Wait, are those gummy bears in her mouth?"

I leaned forward, feeling sickened all over again.

"Full of gummy bears," I said. Then I noticed something white under the dead woman's head. I reached over and shifted it over.

A folded piece of paper fell into the blood. I grabbed it before the blood could soak in and unfolded the sheet. On it was a laser-printed message.

You didn't think it was going to be simple, did you, Cross?

Well, this is not simple. It won't ever be simple. Not from a mastermind like me.

You know, if you hadn't tried to trace me, maybe I would have set Mrs. Jenkins free. But you did try to trace me, and now I just don't know what to think or do, and I suspect neither do you.

We'll just have to see, you and me.

M

"What does it say?" Mahoney asked.

Before I could reply, I saw the headlights of several large vehicles bearing down on us. They slowed and stopped not twenty yards away, their high beams lighting up the car and the interior from behind.

Mahoney threw his forearm up to shield his eyes, yanked out his ID and badge, held them up, and yelled, "FBI! Turn those damn lights off!"

The lights dimmed, and I could see three television satellite trucks.

A platinum-blond woman barely five feet tall launched herself out of the nearest rig with a cameraman right behind her.

"Is it true?" she demanded. "Is there a head in there with gummy bears in the mouth? And a finger? Is it Mrs. Jenkins? And who is this mysterious M?"

CHAPTER 27

MAHONEY PULLED HIMSELF UP TO his full height and rushed right at her, saying, "Move. Now. Back up your perimeter. This is a crime scene, and I want it sealed immediately!"

The reporters retreated as the young woman said, "We have a right to answers."

"No, you have the right to ask questions," Mahoney said, getting right in her face. "I decide whether I'll answer them. And I'm more likely to answer them if you give me a little slack to take care of a dangerous, fluid situation. Okay?"

Her jaw relaxed, and she nodded. "Okay. Lisa Sutton. Channel Six News. We'll move back, but I'm assuming my questions have answers."

Mahoney threw up his hands. "Assume all you want, Ms. Sutton. Just get away from my crime scene. Now!"

The reporters backed off a few more steps, and Mahoney got on his phone to notify the local sheriff and get a forensics team dispatched.

I went to the car and looked at the finger and at the head of the Asian woman. Who was she? Why put gummy bears in her mouth?

And what the hell was it with M and the damned gummy bears?

My thoughts raced backward twelve years to the first time I'd gotten a message from M.

I suddenly saw myself and John Sampson climbing out of an unmarked car south of tiny Rupert, West Virginia.

We'd pulled off a muddy road and parked up against a chain across an overgrown gravel drive that led into thick woods. There was a NO TRESPASSING sign hanging from the chain. A faded FOR SALE sign dangled from a pine tree.

"What's with the damn bugs?" Sampson grumbled, waving his hands at the clouds of blackflies and mosquitoes that swarmed around our heads.

"Cheaper than guard dogs," I said, swatting the back of my neck.

"Doesn't look promising, does it?"

I gazed beyond the chain and saw no tire tracks or footprints of any kind.

Sampson said, "We could have asked West Virginia State Police to take a look around before we drove for four hours to get here."

"I don't like other people doing my work," I said, and I stepped over the chain.

Sampson hesitated. "We don't have warrants."

"Since when have you leaned Boy Scout?" I asked and then gestured at the FOR SALE sign. "We're thinking of buying a fishing camp to retire to in our old age."

"I'm a little too young for retirement."

"Don't you watch those financial-adviser commercials?" I said. "It's never too early to think about retirement."

Sampson pursed his lips, shrugged, and then stepped over the chain. Cicadas buzzed from thickets on both sides of the two-track, and somewhere ahead crows were squawking.

I kept studying the mud, hoping to see some indication that a vehicle had come in here recently. But there'd been thunderstorms in the area for the past three days, and other than our own prints, the wet ground appeared undisturbed.

"Doesn't exactly feel like a setting for romance," Sampson said.

"Different strokes," I said.

We were there looking for a missing thirty-seven-year-old woman named Arlene Duffy. Duffy ran a successful chain of day-care centers and worked ferociously hard. She always had a jar of gummy bears on her desk.

Although single and, according to her staff, not dating anyone, Duffy had left work early the day of her disappearance and bought a merry widow corset at a Victoria's Secret at a mall in Falls Church. Her car was still parked there eight days later.

Security tapes from the mall revealed Ms. Duffy getting into a black Chevy Tahoe. The windows were tinted. The license plates were doctored.

But using computer-image enhancement programs, we'd been able to make out the sticker on the bumper of the vehicle. It said SPELLMAN'S LIVE BAIT AND TACKLE.

Sampson and I came to an overgrown clearing with a lake beyond it. There were several boarded-up cottages in the tangle of thorny vines that choked the place.

Sampson pointed to the biggest building, which had a caved-in front porch roof. Hanging by a single nail, a rusty sign said SPELLMAN'S LIVE BAIT AND TACKLE.

We walked down to the water.

"Place is hardly developed at all," I said. "Just a few cabins way over there."

"You're saying this *could be* a retirement investment?" Sampson asked as crows began to quarrel somewhere in the woods.

"Gorgeous spot," I said, seeing a crow dive-bomb into the weeds on the far side of the old fishing shop. Another one came screaming in behind it, and then they both came out angry over something.

I walked that way, found a game trail, followed it for fifteen yards. Then I stopped and called out to Sampson.

He came over quickly and peered at the colorful mound in the trail in front of me. "Gummy bears?"

CHAPTER 28

"WHAT THE HECK'S A PILE of gummy bears doing there?" Sampson asked.

"Exactly," I said, squeezing one. "And they're fresh."

"I don't get this."

"Arlene Duffy always kept a jar of these on her desk, remember?" I said, gazing down the game trail. "There are more of them up there."

Sampson and I stepped off the trail and walked parallel to it through the thorns and vines, seeing a gummy bear or two every few feet. We soon left the clearing and entered a thicket.

The light was dimmer, but I could see a crow on its side, quivering, on the trail ahead of me. There were gummy bears all around the bird, which seemed to be suffering some kind of seizure.

"Those candies are poisoned," I said, gesturing at the crow. "Some of them, anyway."

We found another dead bird and then a third before we reached a second, smaller clearing in the forest. A single decrepit cabin slouched there, overgrown by climbing vines, moss, and saplings.

The gummy bears led us toward the cabin, but when the breeze picked up and changed direction, the candies no longer mattered.

"Jesus," Sampson said, pulling out a handkerchief and covering his mouth and nose. "I think there's camphor in the car if we need it," he said.

I mouth-breathed as I walked up onto the ramshackle porch, already hearing the blowflies. I got out the small flashlight I always carry and flicked it on.

The plank floor was buckled and covered in dead leaves, trash, and the odd gummy bear or two. I stepped gingerly inside, hoping to God the floor didn't give way.

The boards grumbled but held as I took another step, then a third.

I swung the flashlight toward the buzzing flies. The beam passed over an old woodstove and the ruins of a couch before illuminating a headless corpse lashed to a chair. The head rested on a table beside her.

"It's her," I called out, feeling depressed and angry. "Arlene Duffy."

"Shit," Sampson said. "You're sure?"

"She's wearing the merry widow," I said, playing the light over her. "And he cut off her head, Meat Man–style."

"You're kidding," Sampson said, no doubt remembering the gruesome details of a case we had worked a decade before.

"I wish I were," I said, taking a step toward her. She'd been dead for at least two days and was putrefying in the heat. Despite the cloud of flies, I could see the gummy bears stuffed in her mouth. A note written in lipstick was pinned to her chest.

I've done the world a favor, Alex Cross, it read. *This bitch was a molester and pornographer. She used drug-laced gummy bears to subdue her victims. Check the jar on her desk. And arrest her assistant. If she didn't know, she suspected.—M*

CHAPTER 29

Present day

MORE THAN A DECADE AFTER that message and four days after M managed to put a head and finger in the back of our car in Ohio, I entered the visitors' center at the Alexandria jail for my scheduled meeting with Martin Forbes.

I didn't fully trust Marty Forbes's alibi tale. I still believed he could have found the reference to M in files at Quantico and then cooked up everything else, hoping to lure me in to help him.

Forbes was smiling when he entered the booth on the opposite side of the bulletproof glass.

"I read the papers," he said. "I see it's out in the open now. M is messing with you, isn't he, Cross?"

"He sent a note."

"What did it say?"

"I'm not at liberty to discuss that."

That pissed off Forbes. "You don't trust me. This is my life."

"I know it is, and no, I don't trust you. Not entirely. That's just the way it is."

He stewed over that for a while and then said, "I'm a smart guy. I was a good agent, a good investigator."

"I'd agree with that."

"Then use me," Forbes said, tapping his head. "I do nothing but sit around all day. Who was the woman? The head?"

"We don't know yet."

"C'mon, Cross, let me in. I can help."

I thought about it and decided to let him in on some of it. I read him a copy of the note M had left us.

Forbes listened, gazing off into the middle distance.

"He called himself Mastermind," he said after a few moments. "Craig's alias."

I shook my head. "M didn't call himself Mastermind. He said that he *was* a mastermind."

"Still. That's something."

"It's not," I insisted. "Craig's dead. I saw him blown apart and consumed in flames. This guy's using words he knows will yank our chain. It's misdirection."

"I know what I saw," Forbes said.

"While you were drugged," I said. "It could have been a hallucination. Or M wore a disguise to look like Craig."

I could tell Forbes was not convinced, but he let the issue drop and said, "He called the media. That's a bold move."

"Very bold," I said. "And now they know he has a name. Or a letter, anyway."

"Is the story getting traction?"

"The media doesn't know the extent of it all yet," I said. "Not by a mile."

"What does that mean?" he said, studying me.

I considered telling him about the earlier notes from M but then decided to keep that close. "Your story, for one," I said.

"It's going to come out," Forbes said. "I've told the Bureau about this."

That was news to me, but before I could question him, he said, "And I told you and my attorney."

"That's a good thing," I said. "But I'd appreciate

it if you kept a lid on that until it comes out in court. If he wants you in here, there's a reason."

He stared at me, then shook his head in disgust. "You're not here about me at all, Cross. I had it wrong. You're not the straight shooter I thought you were. You're in it for yourself, same as M, same as everyone else. Meanwhile, I sit and rot."

Before I could reply, he slammed down the phone, glared at me, and then got up and walked away.

CHAPTER 30

NANA MAMA MADE COUNTRY-STYLE short ribs with jasmine rice and homemade coleslaw that evening. She'd slow-cooked the ribs, and the meat was sweet and spicy, falling off the bone. It was so good that no one spoke for a full ten minutes.

Jannie pulled her robe tighter around herself and sighed. "I don't feel any stronger after that, but I sure feel better, Nana."

My grandmother got up and threw her arms around my daughter.

"You are getting stronger," Nana said. "Those vitamins are in there working. They just haven't turned the tide yet."

That only made Jannie morose. "My friend Jeanette had it, and she said it took her six weeks before she wasn't falling asleep all the time. And this kid, Connor Bartlett? He got it twice. Twice!"

"Stop," I said. "Jeanette and Connor are not you. And they were not on this vitamin regimen."

She rolled her eyes. "They make my stomach feel rude."

Bree said, "The doctor said to take them with food, and if you take them, drink a lot of fluids, and sleep a lot, you *will* start feeling better next week."

"Maybe sooner," I said.

"Or later," Ali said.

I glared at him.

"What?" he said. "No two people react to an illness the same way. It said so in the *Washington Post* the other day."

Not wanting to belabor the point, I said, "Why don't you start clearing the table."

"It's Jannie's turn."

"She's sick," I said, and I looked at my daughter. "Shouldn't you be on a couch under a blanket drinking water?"

Jannie got up, hugged Nana, kissed me on the head, and disappeared.

Ali still wasn't moving.

"I'll help you," I said.

"So will I," Bree said, grabbing her plate and glass.

We worked as a team while Nana watched *Jeopardy!*

"Dad," Ali said. "I've been reading about that guy M in the papers, and I Googled some stuff about the investigation."

"You did? Why?"

"Because you're involved."

"You know I can't talk about open cases."

"I get that. But you know what I think?"

I sighed. "What's that?"

"I think he's a copycat. M. I mean, he leaves a beheaded lady in a car just like that guy you caught a long time ago, the Meat Man, and—is M the one killing people with neckties? Like Edgerton?"

I stared at my ten-year-old. We hadn't mentioned the similarities between Meat Man's murders and those committed by Mikey Edgerton. "What makes you say that?"

He raised his eyebrows. "Well, I read that, like, right after that man Edgerton was executed, someone killed a woman just like he'd done it, with a necktie. And then the head of that lady, just like the Meat Man did it. He's a copycat, isn't he, Dad? M?"

I glanced at Bree, who appeared concerned.

"Good theory," I said. "And a well-thought-out one, but I can't talk about open cases."

Ali looked disappointed, but then he noticed the time. "That's okay. There's a big bike race in Italy on ESPN in, like, ten minutes."

Quick as a blink, Ali was back to being my son, fixated on his latest obsession.

"Did Captain Abrahamsen teach you how to use the patch kit and how to change the tire?" I asked.

He brightened. "Yeah. I got it pretty quickly once he showed me how. He's a really good teacher. Can I go riding with him one day?"

"Doesn't he bike fifty miles a day?"

"Not always. Sometimes he and the team train on mountain bikes, so they're climbing up and down steep single tracks but not for that long. That's what we'd do."

"Did he ask you to ride with him?"

"No, I asked him. He said maybe. I think I'd learn a whole lot from him fast."

"He said maybe."

"He'll say yes."

Later that night, when Bree and I were in our

bedroom, Bree said, "I don't think it's good that Ali spends so much time reading about crime and murders on the internet. He's ten."

"Ten going on sixteen some days," I said.

"Maybe intellectually, but he is still a young boy emotionally. It can't be good for him to be thinking about killers and sadists at his age, can it?"

"Well, no. Not in the kind of detail he's interested in."

"So what are you going to do? Ban him from looking at those websites?"

"How? He's got a phone, a laptop, access to computers at school. If he wants to go there, he probably will."

I could see she was going to protest, so I held up my hands.

"I'll talk to him, though. I promise. And we'll keep up the bicycling. He's really taken to it in a way I didn't expect."

Bree softened. "Ali's not just a brain—he's got one of the biggest hearts I know. As big as yours, Alex, and I don't want his heart…I don't know… polluted with crime? Not at this age. Not when he can still find wonder in a mountain-bike ride."

I started laughing, and she broke into a grin. "But you see what I'm saying?"

"I do," I said, leaning across the bed and hugging her. "And I love that you love him as much as I do."

"How could I not?" she said, snuggling into my arms. "He's part of you."

CHAPTER 31

THE DOG STARTED BARKING AROUND one that morning, sharp, insistent, in that same irritating, sawing pattern.

That did it. I couldn't take another sleepless night, so I got up, got dressed, and went out to find the dog.

But I couldn't find the dog.

When I stepped out on the front porch, the barking sounded like it was coming from the back of the house. But when I walked around to the alley, I could have sworn I heard the dog barking to the south.

I went south, but the sound seemed to be moving away. All of a sudden, it stopped. Then it started again, and I had the animal pinpointed.

He was on the back porch of a small, unlit house a little more than a block and a half away, across the street from the Caseys, old friends of my grandmother. I could see the shape of him up there, barking, a small dog for the size of its voice, a terrier of some kind.

I was just about to go to the front and knock when a door opened to the rear porch, and the dog vanished inside.

I stood there waiting for ten or fifteen minutes to make sure the dog was not going to reappear, then I went home. As I climbed the stairs, I told myself to get some sleep.

But at the bedroom door, I realized I was wide awake. I decided to go down to the kitchen, maybe make one of those magnesium drinks that are supposed to help you sleep by working on your adrenal glands or some such nonsense.

Instead, I found myself climbing to the third floor and thinking about how perceptive Ali had been to theorize that M sometimes acted like a copycat. Would I have come up with that at his age?

I doubted it. At ten years old, I was all about sports and trying to fit in at school after Nana Mama brought me up to Washington, DC, following the death of my mother. No, there had been too much turbulence in my life at that age for me to have reasoned like Ali did.

I flipped on the light in my attic office and sat at the desk. Bree was right. It *wasn't* good for a boy of ten to be fixated on dark criminal behavior.

And yet, there was a part of me that wanted to brag about him.

Here Ali was, only ten, and on his own he'd figured out something that had completely eluded the reporters who were writing about M and Diane Jenkins. They hadn't seen the connection between her kidnapping and Arlene Duffy's death years before or between the decapitated head and the Meat Man. But Ali had seen it.

How did that happen? Where was the insight?

After a few moments of pondering, I grew concerned, thinking about the possibility of Ali digging further and deeper, especially into the case of Mikey Edgerton.

Who knew what he'd find if he was given the chance?

My attention swung to another corner of my office and other stacks of boxes containing my old investigative files. Where were they, the Edgerton files?

I wasn't sure, and for some reason that made me

a little flustered. I got up from behind the desk and went over to look. They weren't where I expected them to be, with Kissy's old files, and I started to panic.

What if Ali came up here and looked around in the files? What if he took them to his room and is studying them? How perceptive can a ten-year-old be?

But then I lifted up an old army blanket and found them, four boxes, each marked M.E.

Part of me wanted to lower the army blanket back over the Mikey Edgerton files and leave them alone, just as I had for years. But the idea of Ali finding the files forced me to put the blanket aside and grab the boxes.

When they were restacked next to my desk, I considered what to do with them. Why did I even still have them? I should have burned them all years ago, turned the secrets in those files to smoke and ash.

But I had not.

John Sampson had done that with his. He told me so two months after Edgerton's conviction, said he took them to a friend's cabin in the Poconos and fed the files one by one into a roaring fire. Put it all behind him.

Try as I might, I couldn't do it, although I couldn't have said exactly why.

Something had stopped me from destroying the evidence of guilt as well as the evidence of innocence in those boxes. It wasn't shame or contrition on my part, because I felt none whatsoever when it came to Mikey Edgerton.

So what was it?

I stared at the boxes and told myself to go back to sleep. But deep inside, another voice was telling me there might be answers in the boxes, clues that could lead me to M.

Or doom me.

Once I'd thought that, there was no pushing ahead. I threw the blanket over the boxes and left.

CHAPTER

32

MY CELL PHONE BUZZED, SNAPPING me awake. I picked it up and saw a Northern Virginia area code and an unfamiliar number. I thought about letting the call go to voice mail, but then I answered. “Alex Cross.”

“Mr. Cross, this is Captain Arthur Abrahamsen. I hope you don’t mind that Ali shared your number with me.”

“Not at all,” I said, sitting up. “How can I help, Captain?”

“Ali has been asking to go on rides with me, but honestly, sir, the training runs scheduled over the next few weeks will be tough on me, let alone on a ten-year-old.”

"I pretty much told him that," I said.

"Sure, and thank you, sir. But, anyway, I mentioned Ali to a friend of mine, and he pointed me to a kids' riding group called Wild Wheels. You can look them up on the web. There are several chapters locally, one of them geared toward mountain bikers. I was thinking, with your permission, I could go to one of their evening rides with Ali. That way we could kill two birds with one stone—he gets to go for a ride with me, and he gets introduced to more age-appropriate friends and training partners for the future."

"I appreciate that. Let me take a look at the website and show it to him," I said. "But it sounds as if he'd like it. Especially riding with you."

Abrahamsen laughed. "He's a ball of fire."

"He is that," I said. "And thank you for taking an interest in him."

"It's the least I can do for someone with as much passion for the sport as Ali has. Next Wild Wheels ride is Thursday, seventeen hundred hours, in Rock Creek, which works for me. I'm on recovery that day, training-wise."

"Okay, we'll get back to you."

"Look forward to it," he said, and he said goodbye and hung up.

I looked at the phone for a moment, then looked over and saw Bree's side of the bed was empty. I glanced at the clock and groaned. It was almost nine.

But before I got up myself, I called Ned Mahoney. "Do me a favor?" I asked.

"Depends."

"Can you run a U.S. Army captain named Arthur Abrahamsen? Works as a liaison between the Pentagon and the Hill."

"Why?"

"I don't know. Abrahamsen's a big road racer, sponsored by the military, and he's taken an interest in Ali. I just want to make sure he is who he says he is."

"For you, Alex, anything," Mahoney said.

I took a shower and was dressing when my phone rang.

"U.S. Army captain Arthur Abrahamsen, defense intelligence liaison to the House Armed Services Committee. West Point graduate. Two tours in Afghanistan. Heck of a bicycle racer. Your kid's lucky he's taken an interest."

"Thanks, Ned."

"What are uncles for?" he said and hung up.

I put on my shoes, feeling a little down. I appreciated someone of Captain Abrahamsen's caliber helping Ali, and I'd had male coaches and teachers who'd been big influences on me. But there was also a certain sadness in realizing that Ali, my baby boy, was moving to a time where he'd rely on me for guidance less and less.

My cell phone rang again. This time it was Keith Karl Rawlins.

"The Ethereum stopped moving," he said.

"Okay," I said. "Where is it?"

"In two hundred and fourteen accounts spread out all over the world. Some of it has been downloaded to so-called hard wallets, but I have the codes for them. Not a Bitcoin of it has been spent, though. As far as I can tell."

"So it's just sitting there?"

"Correct."

"We know who owns the accounts?"

"Shell companies of one sort or another. I haven't been getting far in that regard. But I might have something else for you. There's an idea I've been toying with, and I wanted your input. Can you come to the lab at Quantico?"

CHAPTER

33

LESS THAN THIRTY HOURS AFTER I spoke to Rawlins, John Sampson was driving us down a winding backcountry road in western Virginia's Shenandoah Valley, not far from the village of Graves Mill. I had an iPad in my lap and was studying an OnX Maps app that showed the land on both sides of the road, the property boundaries, and the names of the properties' owners.

We'd gone past a couple of new subdivisions before entering farmland interrupted by fingers of timber spilling out of the Blue Ridge Mountains.

"Beautiful country," Sampson said.

"Perfect place for a troll to build his troll hole."

"Mahoney said he calls it an anthill."

"I read the reports. Sounds more troll than ant to me. His property line is coming up in a mile."

"Left or right?" Sampson said.

"Right side for three miles and west all the way to Shenandoah National Park. It's a big piece. Seven hundred and fifty-some acres."

"He's got the money to do whatever he wants."

"And get away with it," I said.

It was the money, almost thirty million by some estimates, that had brought the landowner to our attention. Or at least, the money was part of what made him stand out for us. Or what helped us sift him out from the others.

Not long ago, it had felt like our investigation had ground to a halt. Then I'd gotten that call from Keith Karl Rawlins.

When I got to Quantico, the FBI contractor asked me if I'd done a behavioral profile of M. The question surprised me because, strangely, I had not, even though creating those kinds of profiles was what I had done at the FBI.

Why hadn't I considered doing a profile before?

Before I could come up with an answer, Rawlins proposed writing an algorithm designed to sift for the *kind* of person M most likely was, based on my behavioral assessment. But he added that he didn't want me to do the assessment the way I normally did.

Instead, the computer wizard asked me, John, and Ned to create a string of search words that described our suspect in as much detail as possible. We did, starting with *wealthy*.

Given the scope of what we believed M had been involved in, including tracking down and killing the human traffickers, the three of us agreed that he had to be rich. But why would he ask for ransom for Mrs. Jenkins? We couldn't answer that but left the *wealthy* filter in there nonetheless. *Cold-blooded* was another term we wrote down, along with *forward-thinking* and *amoral*.

We came up with a total of thirty-seven distinctive traits that summed up our understanding of M. I have to admit that much of what Rawlins did with those words afterward went right over my head. But his digital sieves began to sift, and eight hours later he had a list of fourteen possible candidates.

We'd narrowed it down to the five who lived within a day's drive of one of the murder scenes. Two of those we discarded almost immediately; they were old men and in jail for prior heinous crimes. The third and fourth men were only mildly interesting.

But the fifth man? The more we dug into his past, the more he looked like the jackpot suspect we'd been searching for.

CHAPTER 34

JOHN AND I PARKED AT the pull-off into a field that was roughly two hundred yards from the north-west corner of the sprawling property. Mahoney parked behind us and got a drone and a laptop from his trunk.

"This legal without a warrant?" Sampson asked.

"Long as the drone's high enough," the agent said. "We're just having us a look-see."

He gave the remote an order. The little heli-copter blades started spinning, and soon the drone lifted off.

I said, "If Dwight Rivers sees it, he'll probably get his shotgun and blow it out of the sky."

"I hope he does," Mahoney said. "Then we'd have probable cause to enter."

"A person can't just shoot a gizmo that's spying on him?" Sampson said.

"Not if it's high enough," Mahoney said.

"Which means you wouldn't want to take it to court," I said.

"No comment," Mahoney said, watching the drone soar over the treetops, heading southwest.

My cell phone buzzed with a Wickr text from Ali. I read it in a glance.

Going riding with Captain W and the Wild Wheels!

I grinned and texted back, Have fun! Text me when you're home!

A thumbs-up emoji appeared and vanished. I put my phone back in my pocket. We crowded around Ned's laptop on the hood and saw what the drone was seeing: the woods, several logging roads, then a fast-running creek and a meadow with at least fifty big solar panels in it.

Mahoney had the drone climb to four hundred feet as it flew over the solar array and then over a lone pine tree in the meadow that looked scorched; maybe it had been hit by lightning, because its crown was gone. A nest big enough for an eagle had been built in the remaining branches at the top, but it looked abandoned.

Then Ned altered the camera angle, and we saw what looked for all the world like a giant, squat anthill rising out of the meadow several hundred feet beyond that pine.

Nearly sixty feet tall and covered in green vegetation, the anthill had to have been two hundred feet wide. At the top, it was less than fifty feet across and it had waist-high defensive walls around the perimeter and concertina wire above.

"Heck of a high ground," I said.

"Rivers evidently planned it that way," Mahoney said as the drone took us high above the anthill.

We could see over the defensive walls now. Three satellite dishes were bolted to the roof of a tan and green railroad container car that jutted out of the top of the anthill, like a ready-made bunker atop a bunker.

"How many containers inside the hill and belowground?" Sampson asked.

"Our sources say at least thirty more, all connected and laid out according to some plan only Rivers seems to grasp," Mahoney said. The drone moved past the anthill and various pieces of heavy excavation machinery sitting idle by a serpentine dirt road and continued on to a beautiful house on a knoll above a pond.

The home was all stonework, wood beams, and

glass; it had a broad flagstone terrace and a carriage house with a three-car garage. It was the kind of trophy property that might grace the cover of a pricey real estate brochure.

"This guy Rivers is smart, huh?" Sampson said.

"Wharton MBA," Mahoney said. "Self-made man. *Mucho dinero.*"

"Right, so then what is it? I mean, what makes a guy like that, a guy who has it made, all of a sudden crack and go full-on survivalist?"

"They call themselves *preppers,* John," I said. "Doomsday preppers."

CHAPTER 35

I'D HEARD OF DOOMSDAY PREPPERS going to extremes so they'd be ready to meet the coming apocalypse. People spent minor fortunes on food, fuel, and crop seeds to be used to eke out a life after Communists or zombies or whatever future plague they expected had laid waste to society.

But according to the dossier Mahoney had shared with us, few of them had spent as much on their preparations as Dwight Rivers had. He'd apparently made big money in the sale of TRUAX, a global security firm that had been founded by a group of seasoned ex-military men and women. He'd been the company's business brain.

Based on FBI interviews with local machine operators and builders, on UPS and FedEx delivery records, and on multiple eyewitness accounts, Rivers had gone on a mind-boggling spending spree from the moment he bought the estate. During the first two years, he'd overseen the excavation and placement of the subterranean container cars and the construction of the upper anthill. The third year, a steady parade of contractors, electricians, and plumbers had finished the interior.

That's when the supplies started rolling in, enough for Rivers and a small army to survive for a long time after the apocalypse. He had three thousand-gallon gasoline tanks buried in the field near the anthill, and the solar panels fed big battery banks somewhere inside it.

All of this had gone on below the FBI's radar initially. Then Rivers began buying assault rifles, scores of them. He filled an underground armory with the weapons and enough ammunition to defend himself for a long, long time. But even that did not catch the federal government's attention.

That happened when Rivers's name came up in the course of a joint FBI and Bureau of Alcohol, Tobacco, and Firearms investigation into a ring of former soldiers and mercenaries selling contraband weapons, including grenades, shoulder-mounted rocket launchers, and claymore mines.

When BATF and FBI agents interviewed Rivers, he denied knowing anything about those kinds of weapons. When they'd asked to inspect the anthill, however, he'd refused, citing his constitutional rights.

Without cause, the Feds could do nothing but wait for Rivers to make a mistake. And Sampson, Mahoney, and I couldn't do much but survey the area with a drone.

Mahoney saw no activity inside the property and turned the drone around. I scanned the rest of the dossier. A few facts caught my attention.

Rivers had been divorced twice. The records of those proceedings were sealed, but FBI agents had contacted his ex-wives. They said he had a violent streak and that he liked to read about and pontificate on big murder cases, especially those involving serial killers.

His ex-wives said that he often made fun of police, said most of them were idiots who could be manipulated and fooled by a clever criminal.

Rivers had come to the attention of law enforcement prior to the weapons investigation only twice, both times for accusations of sexual assault. The victims said Rivers had drugged and raped them. But tests were inconclusive, and the multimillionaire denied everything, even provided alibis for his whereabouts during the alleged assaults.

Rivers was in his late forties when he bought the estate, and he had spent much of his time there with a steady string of younger girlfriends. One of them, Cora James, twenty-seven, had spoken to an FBI agent.

She said Rivers was a manic-depressive who could be charming and brilliant one moment and vicious and paranoid the next. He was also ultra-secretive, especially about the anthill.

"It gave me the creeps how he'd go out there from the house," she'd said. "Like, okay, it could have been just like Dwight said, a place to be safe if things got out of control. But I couldn't help thinking that it could have been a prison, you know?"

When asked why she would say that, Cora James said she had gone down by the anthill one night when Rivers was inside. There were air vents in the side of the bunker.

"I thought I heard a woman crying in there," she said.

James said she became frightened and confronted

Rivers about it. He'd laughed and said she'd heard the squealing of a dumbwaiter he'd installed.

He'd even volunteered to take her on a tour of the bunker, but something about his body language had made her uneasy, and she'd declined. Rivers tried to monitor and restrict her movements after that.

"I waited until he went to town for groceries a couple of days later, and then I got the heck out of there on foot," she'd told her interviewer.

The drone landed and Mahoney picked it up and took it back to his vehicle.

I closed the file and stared off into the distance.

"What are you thinking, Alex?" Sampson asked.

I struggled a moment, then said, "If Rawlins's algorithm is right, if Dwight Rivers is M, then I would love to see exactly what he's got going on *inside* of his anthill."

CHAPTER

36

MAHONEY QUASHED THAT IDEA the second he heard it.

"I tried to get search and wiretap warrants through two federal judges this morning," Mahoney said, putting the drone in his car. "Both turned me down. Having an anthill filled with legally bought guns is evidently not enough to warrant a search."

"Someone's got to go in there," I insisted.

"Not without cause, Alex," he shot back. "If Rivers is your M, we want to get him clean, fair and square, no fruit of the poisonous tree, no giving him a way out of a prison cell or a death chamber."

I stewed on that after Mahoney got in his car

and headed back toward Quantico in the waning light.

"We done?" Sampson said, sliding into the driver's seat. "Gonna be dark soon, and we are a ways from home."

"Not yet," I said, looking through binoculars across the field toward the gravel road that led past Rivers's driveway.

"C'mon, Alex," Sampson said. "Without a drone in the sky full-time, we're not surveilling this guy. We're just looking at trees."

"Unless we go into the trees."

"Jesus, you heard Ned."

"What if Rivers has a woman in there, John? What if *he is M,* and he's got Diane Jenkins in there?"

"What if he does?"

For a long moment, I felt conflicted, but then I didn't.

"I'm going in there," I said and yanked the door handle.

"If you're going, I'm going."

"No, you stay here. You're still on the job. I'm a contract employee who's not under contract at the moment."

"Which means what?"

"I'm a civilian. The rules are different for me

than they are for someone who's full-time law enforcement."

"Yeah, try that one in court. You'll just be some burglar looking at ten years."

"Hopefully, it won't come to that. If I'm not back in an hour, use the Find My Friends app and come get me."

I shut the door before he could protest and set off across the road to Rivers's property with just enough light to see. Mahoney's drone had sailed over the woods in seconds, but it took me ten minutes to reach the north edge of the meadow.

I could make out the solar panels, the anthill, and, beyond them, Rivers's house. There were lights on.

I trained my binoculars on the windows that overlooked the pond and the meadow but I saw no movement. Was he even in there? Or was he inside his bunker?

I didn't give myself time to think about answers to those questions; instead, I broke out of the woods and ran toward the anthill as fast as I could.

When I was within fifty yards of it, I got down on my belly and used my binoculars to study the exterior. Though the outside walls weren't completely vertical, no one was climbing that thing without equipment. I remembered several workers quoted in the dossier had said that the entrance to Rivers's bunker was on its southwest side.

I crouched and skirted the perimeter until I could see a recess in the side of the anthill with a padlocked steel door that looked like something you'd find on a navy ship.

I spotted a camera above the door.

That wasn't good. I studied the camera and the angle it was aimed at, then moved west again. When I was out of its range, I went to the side of the bunker and sneaked back toward the entrance.

When I got closer, I squatted down, grabbed some loose damp soil, and spit in it to make it muddier. With my back to the wall, I edged along the anthill until I was underneath the camera.

Then I reached up and smeared the lens with the dirt.

I noticed a humming noise coming from the other side of the door. A generator? Then I caught a faint squeal. Or was it a cry?

I pulled my shirtsleeve over my hand to prevent fingerprints and tugged on the padlock. To my surprise, the hasp was not fully engaged. The lock opened.

Either Rivers had made a mistake or he planned

to come back soon. I prayed it was a mistake, removed the padlock, and turned the hatch wheel. It spun easily, as if it had recently been greased.

The door swung quietly toward me.

I stepped inside and saw a short hallway lit by dim, red overhead lights leading to a metal staircase. The humming was louder now; it was definitely some kind of machine running.

I hesitated and then walked far enough to my right to look up at the house with the binoculars. No one on the other side of those windows that I could see.

I went back, set the padlock in the latch, stepped inside, and pulled the hatch door snug behind me.

CHAPTER 37

AFTER WAITING A FEW MOMENTS to let my eyes adjust to the dim red light, I crept down the hallway toward those stairs. I paused there, remembering reading in the dossier that at least twenty-five container cars were buried belowground and that there were five or six above in the cone of the anthill.

The stairs both up and down were unlit. Below me, the stairs dropped into darkness, and that gave me a claustrophobic feeling even when I turned on the flashlight and shone it down the shaft.

The workers who'd helped Rivers build the anthill had described it as a maze belowground, the kind of place you could easily get lost in. And at the back of my mind, there was the nagging possibility that the padlock had been left open on purpose because the prepper was coming right back.

My cell phone buzzed. A Wickr text from Ali: Home! So much fun! Captain W is a beast on a mountain bike!

I hit the thumbs-up emoji, wrote, Working. I will call you later.

Then I stood there, straining to hear if someone was calling for help, but I heard nothing except that hum, which seemed to boil up from below. I glanced at my watch. Twenty-two minutes had passed since I'd left Sampson.

I decided to climb. I flicked on my little flashlight, went up a flight, and found small doors, one on either side of the landing. Both were unlocked.

The container car on the left held shelves stocked deep with food supplies. The one on the right was set up as an emergency medical facility and had a safe that I assumed held medicine.

I climbed up another flight and found two more doors. The container car on the right was the armory. The place smelled lightly of oil and solvent. There were at least eighty assault rifles in racks and three hunting-style rifles with scopes.

The container car on the left was an ammo dump, with crate after crate of 5.56x44mm NATO surplus ammunition. I looked around and saw a crowbar but recognized the futility of trying to open every crate to see if it held anything but bullets. There were just too many.

I went up the next flight of stairs and found a fifth container car, this one with three workstations and an array of computers and monitors, all dark except for two set up on a bench in a corner.

Those two screens were each split into four quadrants that showed real-time feeds from security cameras. It was obvious which feed came from the camera over the door: you couldn't see a thing because of the mud I'd smeared on it. The next three feeds on that monitor seemed to be from cameras fixed high on the anthill; they showed various angles of the darkly shadowed meadow.

Had I been seen? No, I decided.

The next feed was a wide-angle shot that showed the road to the house and the machinery parked there. The last two cameras were trained on the house, one aimed at the front, one aimed at the back. Nothing moved behind the windows, which were not shuttered or draped.

There were no more stairs, but a fixed ladder led to the last container car, that bunker on a bunker that stuck out of the top of the anthill. It was not lit inside, and I had to use the flashlight again to look around.

It was then that I saw that slits about six inches tall and three inches wide had been cut at intervals in the upper walls of the container. Shooting ports.

And there was a sliding window cut into the wall facing the house. I peered through it, noticing that a metal flap could be lowered across it for protection.

There was a small door that allowed access out to the roof of the anthill. I opened it, looked out, and saw a winch bolted to the side of the container car with coils of rope on the roof below it. That puzzled me until I saw a low metal gate in the waist-high defensive wall that surrounded the roof.

The gate was almost three feet across and I realized Rivers must use the winch and rope to bring things up the side of the anthill.

I stepped back into the bunker and was taking one last look around Rivers's little citadel when I happened to glance through the window back toward the house. Even though I was two hundred yards away, I saw something move up there.

I spun around, clambered down the ladder to the room with all the monitors, and ran to look at the feed from the cameras facing the house. Nothing. But on the feed showing the road and the excavation equipment, I saw something. The camera picked up the motion and shifted to some kind of infrared lens.

Dwight Rivers was walking fast down the hill and carrying a shotgun.

Then he broke into a run and sprinted toward his doomsday bunker.

CHAPTER

38

I BOLTED DOWN TWO FLIGHTS of stairs and stopped, breathing hard, knowing I would not be able to get out of the bunker before Rivers got to the hatch.

I desperately did not want this to go sideways. *Will he notice the padlock isn't closed?* I thought as I pulled out my pistol. *Will he come searching for me?*

My breathing slowed and I heard metal scraping against metal. The padlock being opened? Or snapped shut, sealing me in here?

The hatch wheel turned. I eased deep into the shadows on the landing.

The hatch swung open. No flashlight beam. And no sounds for several long, gut-wrenching moments.

"Done playing games," Rivers said in a low, gravelly voice, slurring his words. "Time for follow-through. Time to commit, baby."

I crouched and looked down through the risers of the metal staircase into the hallway that led out. Was there someone with him?

"Time to commit, baby," he said again, and I heard the hatch swing shut. "Only those who commit get the goodies in life."

No response. I decided he was probably talking to himself. He chuckled, and I knew for certain he was drunk when he began walking in a wobbly line toward the staircase.

I saw the barrel of his shotgun first and raised my pistol ever so slowly.

The faint glow of the radioactive tritium in my rear and front sights found Rivers. He paused at the staircase, glanced upward, and for a terrible moment I thought for sure I was going to have to shoot defensively.

But then he looked away and chuckled again. "Everything you dreamed, baby. Here it is, yours for the taking…" He trailed off as if he'd fallen into a trance and stood there, unsteady on his feet.

Then Rivers threw back his head and howled like a wolf two or three times before stopping and beginning to laugh hysterically at some inner joke. When the echoes of it died, he leaned over the railing of the staircase and called down into his underworld.

"Can you hear me down there, Maxine?" he shouted. "Can you?"

He paused and listened, as did I. But no sound came back up the shaft.

Rivers set the gun against the rail, reached into his pants pocket, and came up with a flask. He opened the flask and drank from it. When he was done, he laughed softly and roared down the shaft again. "You'll hear me soon enough! You better get running, girl, cause Daddy's coming down there to find you!"

The doomsday prepper snatched up the shotgun and started down the stairs, increasing his pace until his footsteps sounded like someone pounding on a door. They got farther and farther away, and the moment I could no longer see him, I crept down the stairs and padded fast to the hatch.

I paused, listening, and heard him howl again and then open a door several stories belowground. The humming noise grew louder, but only for a second.

Part of me wanted to go after him. Part of me wanted to know if there was actually a woman named Maxine down there. Was this the woman who Rivers's old girlfriend had heard crying through the anthill's air vents?

Was Maxine down there?

I wanted to find out, but I'd pushed my luck already. I checked my watch. I'd been gone fifty minutes.

I left, shut the hatch, kept to the shadows, and made it to the tree line without incident. Ten minutes later, I exited the woods to see the silhouette of Sampson standing there on the dirt road.

"I was just coming for you," he said.

"Sorry I'm late. Let's get out of here."

We were in the car and a good mile down the road before I told John what I'd seen and heard inside.

"You think he's got someone down there?"

"Could be," I said. "But no way to prove it for the moment."

"So what do we do?"

I chewed on my lip for several moments before saying, "We follow Rivers everywhere he goes outside the compound. And when—"

My phone dinged in my pocket. I pulled it out, saw a Wickr text from Ali: Dad, Nana wants to know when you'll be home for dinner.

The message vanished, and I typed back, On my way, Mr. Bond!

CHAPTER 39

I WAS THE FIRST ONE up the next morning.

By the time Nana Mama showed up in her blue robe and slippers, I'd already made coffee, broiled bacon in brown sugar, and scrambled eggs.

My grandmother stood there and eyed me as I poured coffee for her, then gave my food preparations the once-over. She picked up a piece of bacon and bit into it. "That's good."

"Everything's better with bacon and sugar," I said and gave her a kiss. "Go on, sit down. I'll serve you this morning."

Nana cocked her head. "Well, what's come over you?"

"Just remembering some advice you gave me back when the kids were young. You know, about making meals family time."

She smiled and went willingly to the table. I served her and then Bree when she came down, and we all caught up with one another's lives. Ali arrived next, once again babbling about his ride with the Wild Wheels.

"There were twelve kids, four my age, all boys, and, my God, Captain Abrahamsen is an amazing mountain biker. We were riding in Rock Creek Park, and he hopped his bike over a log like it was nothing!"

"You said that last night," Nana Mama said. "Twice."

"And I still can't believe it!"

Jannie came down a few minutes later, her comforter wrapped around her. She yawned, sat in her chair, and stared at the vitamins I'd put in a cup by her plate.

She wrinkled her nose. "There are too many. They make my stomach feel gross."

"You're supposed to take them after you eat."

"You look better," Bree said. "I think those vitamins are working."

Jannie seemed about to argue, but then she nodded. "You know, I do feel better. This is the first morning I even wanted to get up. I don't feel great, but it's nothing like last week."

"See there," I said, glancing at Bree with gratitude. "Eat something and take the vitamins. By this time next week, who knows how good you'll feel?"

I was happy to see her eat eggs, bacon, toast, and a banana. Then she took the vitamins and washed them down with orange juice.

When she was done, Jannie turned to her great-grandmother and said, "Can you look at that essay I did for Mrs. Schultz?"

Nana's eyebrows went up. "You already wrote it?"

"Well, like, a draft," she said. "Last night before I went to sleep."

"You are feeling better. I'd be glad to."

Bree helped me do the dishes while Ali went upstairs to get dressed for school.

"You and John going back out there?" she asked. "To Rivers's place?"

"After we buy a drone," I said.

"Who's paying for that?"

"At the moment, I am."

She said nothing for several moments, just put dishes in the washer. Then: "You're that convinced Rivers is M?"

"He's smart enough. He's got money enough.

His ex-wives and girlfriends think he's controlling to the point of violent. And there's something about that anthill. It's a perfect place to hold hostages."

She barely nodded.

"What is it?" I asked.

"I don't know how much longer I can let you have Sampson," she said.

"As long as you can."

Bree studied me. "You getting obsessed with this?"

"In a good way."

"Promise me something?"

"Anything."

"At least once every four or five hours, stop for a moment and take the thirty-thousand-foot view of the situation."

"Perspective."

"Not a bad thing."

I took her in my arms and kissed her. "Not a bad thing at all."

CHAPTER 40

BY EARLY AFTERNOON THAT DAY, Sampson and I were back in that cut field northwest and across the road from Rivers's acreage. I got out the drone I'd bought at a hobbyist store in Fairfax, Virginia.

"You know how to use it?" he asked.

"Twenty-minute lesson from the young lady who sold it to me," I said, thumbing on the power for the remote. The drone was painted in desert camo, the main reason I'd bought this particular model. I followed her directions and then gave the drone the command to fly. To my delight, it lifted off right away, climbed seventy feet, and then came almost straight back down to a soft landing.

"I think I like this thing already," I said. "You seeing its camera feed on the laptop?"

"Very clear images," Sampson said, sounding impressed. "But I don't get it, Alex. What are we going to do, just have it hover over his place until the battery is dead?"

"I did buy extras." I sent the drone up again. "But I don't know if we'll need them."

"What's that mean?" Sampson said.

"Hang with me, old buddy," I said. I had the drone climb to three hundred feet and then head southeast toward Rivers's property, meadow, and doomsday bunker.

Nothing appeared different from the afternoon before. I flew the drone well past the solar panels, the anthill, and the house before starting to circle.

As the drone approached the bunker on its way back, I dropped it quickly down to one hundred feet. It flew right over the top of the anthill to that scorched pine tree where an eagle had built its nest. I twitched the joystick, brought the drone directly above the nest, and aimed the camera inside. "Definitely abandoned," I said. "Not even a feather."

"Alex, you're in Rivers's airspace."

"Something's off," I said, and I eased the drone down to four inches above the nest, pivoted it one hundred and eighty degrees left, then cut the power. The screen blurred for a second as the drone sagged into the nest. The lower part of the screen was obscured by a wall of twigs and leaves, but the upper part clearly showed the anthill and the ground surrounding it.

"You're serious?" Sampson said.

"Malfunction," I said.

"We're just going to leave it there?"

"Better than flying it for hours on end. And it saves a ton of battery life."

"What if Rivers sees it?"

"Why would he? It's painted camo."

John stared at the screen for several moments before throwing up his hands in surrender. "Can you turn the camera toward the house?"

After several fumbles, I moved the camera left almost forty-five degrees so it was aimed at the house, up there on the knoll above the pond. "We could have used a zoom function, but it's not bad," I said.

"And now what? We sit?"

"Well, I'm going to sit and eat."

CHAPTER 41

THE FIRST SPRINKLES OF RAIN fell. Sampson grabbed the computer off the hood. We got inside the car and ate our lunches, which we'd bought on the way, and watched the screen. I changed the drone camera's angle every so often.

We saw nothing for nearly three hours. The rain picked up, and although the camera lens on the drone had a protective hood, we were getting droplets on the feed. Then we saw a dark panel van pull into the driveway by the house.

The driver got out, ran toward the house, and disappeared. A few moments later, he got back in the vehicle and drove down toward the anthill.

The wind blew rain at the camera, making everything blurry when the van rolled past the excavation equipment and stopped by the anthill. The driver climbed out a few minutes later, his rain hood up, carrying what looked like two big, heavy toolboxes.

He vanished behind the bunker, reappeared for a moment near that recessed hatch door, then disappeared inside.

"Workman?"

"Looks like it," I said. "I wish we could read what it says on the side of that van."

I considered whether to start the drone and fly it closer, but I doubted my ability to fly the thing in a gusting wind.

Five minutes later, the driver exited the anthill, returned to the van, turned around, and disappeared down the drive. Another vehicle, a green Jeep Cherokee, followed a few minutes later.

"That's Rivers," I said, starting our car. "He's on the move."

"What about the drone?"

"I'll put it to sleep. It's not going anywhere."

We never saw the van leave the estate, but Rivers popped out in his Jeep a few minutes later. We followed him eight miles to a building-supply store in Madison, Virginia. Sampson went in and watched him buy a bow saw, a box of trash-compactor bags, a roll of plastic sheeting, rubber gloves, and bleach.

"Bleach?" I said when Sampson told me.

"And a bow saw," he said. "And everything else a creep might need if he was intending to kill someone and get rid of the body."

We followed Rivers home, trailing him at a distance. The rain was easing up when he disappeared down his driveway. We returned to the cut field, reconnected to the drone camera, and saw him in front of the hatch door getting his purchases out of the car.

Rivers went inside his bunker and did not come out. It got darker, and darker.

"I've got to get that drone out of there," I said, using the remote to turn it on.

For a few tense moments, I thought I'd blown it because when I tried to get the drone to lift off, it would move and the camera tilted as if a leg was snagged on a stick in the wall of the nest.

But then I brought the drone backward a bit and it broke free. In the fading daylight, I flew it back and landed it by the car.

"Ned's right. This is an amazing piece of machinery," I said, picking it up and bringing it to Sampson, who'd opened the trunk.

"So is a bow saw in its way," Sampson said. "Maybe enough for cause."

I set the drone in the trunk and closed it. "Doesn't feel enough," I said.

I heard my cell make that infernal Wickr ding noise. Ali was probably trying to find out when I'd be home for dinner.

I walked to the driver-side door as I tugged out my phone. "John," I said, "we're going to need something more compelling than—"

I looked at the screen and froze.

Hello, Cross,

At this very moment, I'm murdering a not-so-innocent.

But where am I, Dr. C.? Wherever could I be?

By a River?

Or somewhere deep underground?

M

CHAPTER

42

"HE'S IN THERE!" I YELLED as I jumped into the driver's seat and fired up the car.

Sampson climbed in. "Who is?"

I tossed my phone at him. "M! Read it! He's killing someone right now."

Before Sampson could reply, I mashed the gas pedal down.

We slid, bounced, and threw mud before the rear tires caught the gravel road and got some traction. I spun the wheel, straightened, and slammed the car into drive.

"Where are you going?"

"The anthill," I said, stomping harder on the gas. "He's in there."

"M's in the anthill?"

"Read the text, John! He's played his hand."

"There's nothing on the screen!"

I pounded the steering wheel. "Because the messages self-destruct!"

"What?"

"Wickr!" I shouted as I raced toward Rivers's driveway. "It's an app that Ali put on the phone. Messages vanish forever after a few seconds, but I'm telling you, M said he was murdering someone and he taunted me. He texted, 'Where am I, Dr. C.? By a River'—with a capital *R*—'or somewhere deep underground?' "

"It said that?"

"Signed M."

"Wait, Alex! You think he knows we're here?"

"No. No way," I said, hitting the brakes and skidding into Rivers's driveway.

"But what if M's somewhere completely different?"

I shouted, "What would you rather risk, John, an innocent woman's life or breaking a law with the best of intentions?"

He said nothing, but I glanced over and saw he wasn't happy at all. "How are you going to explain going in there if you've got no proof of that message?" he asked.

"As best I can," I said, driving past the house and parking by the excavation machinery. "Let's go," I said.

Sampson hesitated.

"Are you telling me you don't believe I saw that message?"

He shook his head. "No."

"Then let's do this, oldest friend and partner."

"Shit," he said, opening his door. "You don't play fair."

"Not when someone's life is at stake."

I got out, my pistol drawn and my flashlight cupped beneath the barrel.

"How many ways in and out?" Sampson said as we hurried around the bunker.

"Only one that I know of," I said, slowing as we reached Rivers's green Jeep.

I shone my light through the side windows, saw files on the seat and keys in the cup holder.

There was no padlock on the hatch. Sampson covered me while I turned the wheel and pulled the door open. Hearing that hum belowground again, I led the way to the staircase.

I paused, listening, but heard nothing except that hum. I'd just decided to take a step down when I thought I heard a faint wail from far below us.

"You hear that?" I whispered.

Sampson shook his head. "What?"

"Could have been a scream or a cry," I said, and I started down with more conviction and more speed, Sampson behind me.

We stopped at the first landing but found two padlocked doors.

On the next landing down, one door was not locked, and it opened. We looked into a container car set up as a kitchen and pantry with two tables and chairs. It smelled of cat urine from a litter box by the door.

There was a second door at the far end of the galley, but we didn't check it. I was sure that shrill sound had come from somewhere deeper in Rivers's anthill.

The single door off the third landing opened as well. Instantly the humming sound was louder. I spotted a light switch and hit it. We were in the bunker's power plant of battery packs and electrical motors fed by the solar arrays in the field above.

There were two other doors off the power plant, but I decided to wait to explore them, reasoning that I could not have heard the scream or whatever it was over the sound of the motors.

"I'm not liking this, Alex," Sampson said.

"We'll go down to the bottom, one more level, then work our way back up."

He seemed to struggle with the idea and then shrugged. "We've come this far."

"That's my man."

"What the hell do we do if we encounter Rivers?"

"Depends on what he's doing and who he's with."

"I'm saying I don't want to have to shoot in here. The walls are all steel."

"Then we won't shoot," I said and started down again.

There were two doors off the bottom of the staircase. The one on the left opened into a container car that held an elaborate water-filtration system and pump.

As we moved to the door on the right, we heard a loud clang on the other side.

"Someone's home," I muttered, raising my pistol and lifting the latch.

CHAPTER 43

THE DOOR OPENED INWARD AND revealed a lit workshop with neat racks of supplies on one side and workbenches and lockers and cabinets on the other. There was no one in the long rectangular space, and the steel door at the far end was ajar.

"Let's move," I whispered. "He slammed that door on his way out, but it didn't catch."

Single-minded, I started through the workshop, intent on getting to the opposite end and through that door as fast as possible.

Sampson grabbed my shoulder before I could go through.

I spun around, confused and annoyed. John looked stricken as he pointed to a workbench by the lockers. The bow saw was on it. Beside it, there was a reciprocating saw coated in blood and gore. There was blood on the floor below the bench and drops of blood leading toward a locker that was half open.

We walked over a few feet, enough to see a man's severed head on the shelf inside the locker. He was Caucasian, late thirties or early forties. His dull eyes stared out, and his mouth was frozen open.

We heard another clang, this one above us somewhere.

"Our boy's getting out of Dodge," I said. I twisted around and ran through the second door, Sampson right behind me.

We entered a short hallway that had a metal ladder bolted into one wall. I shone my light up it and saw that it climbed into a shaft of corrugated steel that looked like a culvert.

In the flashlight beam, dust and dirt swirled.

"He went up," I whispered, holstering my pistol and getting on the ladder. "Go back to the staircase, make sure he doesn't get out of here that way."

Sampson didn't argue and went back toward the workshop as I climbed up into the shaft, the flashlight in my left hand. The culvert was big enough to let me through but not so large that it quelled the dreadful feeling of claustrophobia that threated to overtake me the higher I got.

Gritting my teeth, I focused on each rung in the ladder and kept climbing. Twenty feet up, the ladder went through a hole in the floor of another short passage connecting two container cars. When I got up into that hallway, I heard the electric motors on the other side of a door and almost got off the ladder.

But there was still dust and dirt floating down from above.

I kept climbing up and through another short hallway, past a door I felt sure led to the kitchen, and up again into a third shaft. Sweat dripped from my brow when I stuck my head up through the next level, the one that had been locked shut on the stairway side.

The door on my right was not locked, and my curiosity soared as I wondered what Rivers might have in there. But the door to my left was closer.

I lifted the latch, tugged the door open, and felt air rush at me. For several moments, I was confused because of the strength of the breeze and because I wasn't looking into another container car but down a long, low-ceilinged tunnel.

In my flashlight beam, I could see fresh scuffing and handprints in the dust on the tunnel floor. They headed deeper into the passage, which jogged left after fifty feet or so, preventing me from seeing any farther.

My gut response was to crawl after Rivers, keep following him until I caught him.

But my mind seized on the wind hitting my face.

This tunnel leads out. It's another exit. It has to be.

A voice inside me told me to stop for a second and try to orient myself above and belowground, try to imagine where the passage might go.

Northeast, I thought. *Away from his Jeep, toward… the house?*

Well, it made sense, didn't it? Wouldn't a doomsday prepper want private and secure access to his bunker?

A split second later, I made my decision. Crawling a quarter of a mile in a tunnel like that would take time, and I could go faster if I covered that distance outside.

I jumped back on the ladder, dropped down a level, and ran through the kitchen and out the door to the stairwell. Charging up the stairs, I figured that Sampson and I could get to the car and then up to that house fast—maybe not before Rivers, but very soon after.

When I reached the hallway that led to the main exit, Sampson was by the hatch door with a sour look on his face.

"Son of a bitch locked us in. Please tell me there's another way out."

CHAPTER 44

MY FIRST THOUGHT WAS that tunnel. But how had Rivers gotten out to come around and lock us in? Was there an exit before the house?

Then I remembered something. I scrambled up the staircase yelling, "Follow me!"

I bolted up the three flights and climbed the ladder into the upper container car, the one that jutted out of the roof of the anthill. I pushed open the door and shone my light on the winch bolted into the side of the bunker and the ropes coiled below it.

By the time Sampson reached me, I'd found the winch control in a toolbox inside the bunker. I tied a loop in one end of the rope and hooked it to the quarter-inch steel winch line.

I handed the control to John, took the coil of rope, and moved to that low gate in the defensive wall. I unlatched it, opened it, and threw the rope over. As I'd suspected, it didn't reach the bottom.

"Play me out as I go," I said, turning to face him.

I started a modified rappel down the steep side of Rivers's bunker. The vegetation covering the bunker's side actually helped my footing, and I moved much faster than I'd thought I would.

Sampson uncoiled a good twenty feet of the winch line until the rope below me reached the ground. By the time I got there, John was on his way down.

I sprinted to our car, jumped in, turned the key in the ignition, and got nothing.

Nothing!

Jumping out, furious, I ran back. Sampson was almost down.

"He disabled our car," I shouted as I went past him.

When I reached Rivers's Jeep, the keys were still there in the cup holder. I snatched them up, found the right one, stuck it in the ignition, and felt like cheering when the engine turned over.

Sampson jumped in beside me, drenched in sweat, his hands bleeding. "That cable tore the hell out of me!" he said.

"Hold on somehow," I said as I threw the Jeep into gear.

I mashed the gas pedal down and kept cranking the wheel to get around the base of Rivers's bunker, then whipsawed it back the other way to avoid our dead car and the machinery. Once I hit the little road that led to the house, I straightened the car out and roared up the hill.

Just as we passed the pond, headlights went on up by the house.

A black Porsche sports car came peeling out of the garage.

For a split second, our headlights caught the car broadside before it accelerated up the drive.

Dwight Rivers was hunched behind the wheel, and when he glanced our way, he looked terrified.

"Get him before he hits a highway!" Sampson yelled.

I understood and kept the gas floored as much as I could, weaving up the driveway, trying to keep Rivers's taillights in sight.

The Porsche blew through the mouth of the driveway and drifted across the gravel road as Rivers skillfully kept up his speed.

I knew I couldn't do that, so I slammed on the brakes and still almost rolled the Jeep on the county road. By the time I got the SUV straightened out, Rivers was well ahead and accelerating toward a curve.

"We won't catch him," Sampson growled. "He's going eighty at least."

"Call the sheriff," I said as I lost the Porsche's taillights. "He's heading back toward Madison."

Sampson grimaced but used his bleeding, sore hands to dig in his pocket for his phone. He needn't have bothered.

When we rounded the curve, there were no taillights on the straightaway heading east. Rivers had lost control and rolled and then flipped the car over a stone wall into a cornfield. The sports car was on its roof in the mud, headlights still on and aimed across the field. We skidded to a stop.

"Call 911!" I said as I jumped out.

I vaulted the rock wall and sprinted toward the wreck. The engine was bucking and backfiring when I got close enough to kneel and shine my light into the sports car. It had a full roll bar, which definitely saved Rivers's life.

He was hanging upside down, caught by his safety belt and the airbag, bleeding, unconscious, but definitely breathing.

I smelled gasoline.

"Alex!" Sampson yelled. "The gas tank!"

"I know!" I shouted. I threw myself onto my

belly in the mud and wriggled to get my head and shoulders through the window.

"Turn the engine off!" Sampson said.

"I can't reach the button," I said. "Gimme your knife."

A second later he handed me an open folding knife. I reached up and slashed at the airbag and the safety belt until I got Rivers free.

I held his unconscious body with one hand and told Sampson to pull me out by my feet.

As I got free of the wreckage, I smelled gas again. I knew we were only seconds from disaster.

Sampson and I grabbed Rivers by his arms and pulled him out and away from the wreck.

Just as we did, a human head rolled out of the car, and then the Porsche exploded and went up in flames.

CHAPTER 45

NED MAHONEY WENT BALLISTIC AFTER I laid it all out for him outside Rivers's bunker, late on the night of the crash.

"There's no copy of the message he sent?" Mahoney asked, suspicious.

"I told you, it disintegrated, Ned, but it's burned in my brain."

"That won't do it!"

"Put my decades in law enforcement and my reputation behind it, and it will. And the heads we found? We were meant to find them, just as I was meant to see that Wickr message, Ned. Rivers or M did all this by design. It's clear as day he's imitating not only Mikey Edgerton but also the Meat Man."

"He might be, but nothing about this is clear to me," Mahoney said. "Make your statements, then go home and sit until I *can* see things clearly. In the meantime, I've got a crime scene to run."

I wanted to argue, wanted to stay and look for evidence, but I did as he asked.

We drove back to DC in silence. Sampson wanted to drive, despite his wounded hands.

I sat in the passenger seat trying to stay awake, but my eyes kept closing. As I dozed, I saw the severed head in the locker, then the second one tumbling from Rivers's Porsche, then the head M had put in our car the week before.

My chin hit my chest, and I woke up, groggily thinking, *He's doing the Meat Man, just like Ali…*

In my dreams, I relived what had happened more than a decade ago in West Texas.

There was a tornado watch in effect that sweltering afternoon. The wind was already starting to pick up.

Lightning flickered on the darkening western horizon, and distant thunder rumbled when Randall Peaks and I climbed over a locked cattle gate and walked up a dusty lane through sagebrush and live-oak thickets. We were way out in the boondocks, somewhere northwest of Lubbock, Texas.

"There rattlers around?" I asked.

"No doubt," the Texas Ranger said.

Peaks carried a nickel-plated Colt Python revolver in a leather holster on his hip and wore a starched white shirt, a bolo tie, a straw hat, and tooled cowboy boots despite the fact that it all made him stand out like a sore thumb in the foliage around us.

"What do we do if we see one?" I asked.

"Jumping's a good idea," Peaks said as we came to a second gate. "There she is."

I looked over the gate into a large, dusty, and overgrown industrial yard. At the back of the yard, there was a two-story wooden structure with a corrugated-steel roof maybe four hundred feet long. You could see a sign in faded paint on the side of the clapboard building; it read KING PROCESSING.

"This is where they happened?" I asked. "The first two? The parents?"

Peaks nodded. "Dale and Lucy King. They ran a one-stop shop for cattlemen clear to the panhandle. Slaughterhouse and meatpacking. Real successful in its day."

By then I had been working on the Meat Man case for more than ten months. My involvement had begun when a decapitated naked male was found in a panel van abandoned in an empty lot in Southwest DC.

A headless corpse I'd seen before, but not one with segmented black lines drawn with a felt-tip pen all over its torso, arms, and legs.

Two weeks after that, a second body was found in a car trunk. Female this time, she too was covered in similar segmented black lines, which we finally deciphered as the kind of cutting guide a novice butcher might use to take apart a cow and turn it into steaks and chops.

We ran a crime bulletin on the decapitations and the diagrams and quickly got hits from seven different states, including Texas, as well as three foreign countries.

It turned out that eleven decapitated bodies scored with similar diagrams had been found during the prior seven years, and two had been found nearly thirteen years before.

"Nothing bombproof to tie Tanner Oates to it?" I asked.

Peaks shook his head, then pinched some tobacco and stuck it between his cheek and gum. "Oates was the Kings' foster kid for a while, but that was years before. And he had a solid alibi. Until she conveniently died in a wreck a couple of years later."

"But you think Oates is the Meat Man?"

"I do," Peaks said, and he spit. "Whatever he's calling himself these days. You want to see where it happened?"

"Came all this way to get a better handle on him."

We climbed the second gate and crossed through weeds as the winds whistled.

"How are we gonna know if there's a tornado coming?" I asked.

"Hopefully, we'll see it first," Peaks said, spitting tobacco again as we came to a chained and padlocked door. "If we hear it before we see it, we're out of luck."

"You're full of good news."

"Just factual."

On the door was a notice stating that the property was condemned and a sign warning against trespassing. The Ranger ignored both, grabbed the lock, and spun the combination he'd gotten from the bank in Lubbock that had foreclosed on the property.

Peaks pushed the door open. As we flipped on our flashlights and went inside, the wind began to gust, no longer whistling but moaning and howling through the eaves of the old slaughterhouse.

CHAPTER 46

THE ABANDONED PROCESSING PLANT HAD been mostly stripped for salvage by then and was awaiting demolition.

"Oates work here as a child?" I asked.

"Where he learned the trade. From nine to fifteen, I think."

"It's close enough," I said, following him as he jumped over a channel cut in the floor that Peaks said had been used to sluice out blood and animal offal.

You'd think a place like that would still stink. But it didn't. It was just dusty and dirty, and it made me feel more than a little claustrophobic.

We reached an old metal staircase, and the winds outside seemed to ebb. As we climbed, I caught the sound of something humming that I attributed to a change in wind direction because it was quickly smothered by new gusts that shook the walls.

I imagined the place as a teeming operation and I tried to see Oates in it based on what I'd read in the disturbing files Peaks had shown me.

As soon as Tanner Oates was born, he'd been abandoned in an alley in Galveston.

It would be a gross understatement to say the Texas foster-care system let Oates down. When his speech did not develop past grunting and whining, his first foster father, sick of the noises, began to beat him.

In turn, the boy began to lash out like a raging wild animal, which only provoked more abuse.

It wasn't until he was nearly nine that he was finally diagnosed as profoundly hard of hearing. He wore bilateral hearing aids from that point forward and was eventually transferred to the care of the King family, who taught him to speak and read. His IQ, it turned out, was near genius level.

"This is it," Peaks said now.

We'd reached the landing, and he pushed open the door to a large empty office. He gestured toward the corner.

"Mr. King's body was there in a pool of blood. His wife's corpse was laid perpendicular to him. Both headless. The heads are still missing."

"Like all the rest of them," I said. "They're his trophies."

"Skulls by now," Peaks said.

"You said we could look at the Kings' old house."

"I said I'd ask."

The Ranger pulled out his cell phone, looked at it. "No bars. Let me try outside."

"Where the tornado's coming," I said, following him out.

"True enough," he said, and he dropped down the stairs.

I paused to take it all in, tried to imagine what Oates could have experienced there that caused him to saw off the heads of the only people who'd ever been good and kind to him. I failed.

By the time I reached the bottom of the staircase, Peaks was stepping outside. I half expected to see the door torn away by the gusts, but then, as before, the wind died down.

And I heard that humming noise again. I realized it was coming from the other side of the wall where I was standing. I flashed the light around and saw another door, right below the one upstairs.

I went over to it as the gusting rose again and tried the knob. It turned.

I pushed it open, went inside, and saw the source of the hum: a Honda generator pushed up against a hole that had been cut in the back of the building to vent the machine's exhaust. A heavy-duty extension cord ran from the generator and into a jumble of old boxes, trash, and debris left behind by the salvagers. I followed the cord to a large, dark windowless room also crammed with junk.

I flashed my light around into the shadows and then back along the electric line that ran to a large, filthy white box. I crossed to it, kicking aside cans and other trash, and realized I was looking at an old lift-top freezer.

I raised the lid and a powerful strobe light went on, blinding me. But not before I'd seen at least a dozen frozen human heads stacked inside the cold locker.

I staggered backward, dropping the lid, and threw up my arms to block the light, which seemed to be coming from the wall right behind the freezer.

Over the wind, I thought I heard something a split second before someone very powerful grabbed me around the neck from behind.

CHAPTER 47

THE MAN HAD HIS MASSIVE forearm pressed so hard against my windpipe, I thought he would crush it. His head was jammed tight next to mine, so even over the wind, I could hear his high-pitched wheezing and grunting.

I am not a small man by any means, but Oates dragged me backward as if I were no bigger than a child as I choked and clawed for my weapon. He slashed my right wrist with a blade of some kind, and it went through flesh and tendon right down to the bone.

I moaned in pain. He grunted with pleasure and dragged me back another few feet.

"I don't care who you are," the Meat Man said in a weird nasal voice. "You don't come into my house without an invitation."

I felt him square his feet as if he meant to use that blade again. A deep, instinctive will to survive took over. So did all my years of training.

I dropped my chin hard against his forearm, dug in my heels, and drove myself back. It threw him off balance, and that gave me just enough leverage to twist left and drive my elbow hard into his solar plexus. It knocked the wind out of him, and his grip on me eased enough that I was able to break free of his hold.

The strobe was still going, and there was still a bright blob in my vision as I jumped away from him. I attempted to draw my pistol left-handed, but I tripped and landed on a paint can, breaking one of my ribs.

I heard Oates shouting at me over the roar of the wind outside, and I knew he was coming. I started scrambling away on all fours, thinking, *Get some space. Get the gun. Shoot him.*

Then I felt something slam into my calf and cut right through the meat of it.

The gaping wound was agony. I grabbed at it as I rolled over.

I could see him standing above me in the pulsing light of the strobe, which revealed the bloody meat cleaver he held.

Oates was grunting and wheezing so hard it sounded like a pig with asthma. He seemed ecstatic as he raised the cleaver high over his head and started to swing it down at the center of mine.

A shot went off.

Oates jerked, screamed, and let go of the cleaver in midswing.

I heard it slam into something six inches behind my skull.

Another shot rang out.

The Meat Man jerked, stumbled, crashed against the freezer that held the severed heads of his victims, and then sprawled lifeless in the trash.

Peaks ran to me, grabbed my hand, and pressed it hard against my gaping calf wound, which was spurting blood. Then he tore off his starched white shirt, ripped it in two, and wrapped one piece tight around my calf and the other around my wrist. When he was done, he said, "Let's get you help."

"What about him?"

The wind outside had gone beyond the roar of

crashing surf. It sounded like a freight train blazing at us down a tunnel.

"Jesus," Peaks said.

"What the hell is that?"

"Twister! It's coming right at us!"

CHAPTER 48

THREE DAYS AFTER THE RUN-IN with Dwight Rivers, as I entered George Washington University Hospital, I thought about the Meat Man and the tornado. Even all these years later, I was still awestruck at the way it had passed within two hundred yards of me and Randall Peaks, tearing apart outbuildings but leaving the slaughterhouse untouched.

I spotted John Sampson coming down the hall toward me and waited for him.

"Mahoney tell you anything?" I said.

"Just to be here. Sixth floor."

Since the night we found the head in Rivers's

bunker, we'd been kept completely in the dark about the case. All we knew was what we heard from the media reports, which were sketchy because Mahoney's team was keeping a tight lid on the details.

The night before, I'd been watching a piece on the local news that featured the Shenandoah County sheriff and a Virginia State Police captain, both of whom were angry about being excluded from the Rivers investigation, when I got a text from Ned telling me to be at the hospital at nine the next morning.

Mahoney was waiting outside a hospital room for us. "His attorney's in there."

"Seeing things clearer?"

"Clear enough that you're here, but do me a favor?"

"Anything."

"Next time you get a self-destructing message from M, simultaneously squeeze the sleep button and the home button on your phone. It will take a screenshot and put it in your photos folder."

"Really?"

"That's what Rawlins says to do."

Before I could tell Mahoney that I was grateful for his show of confidence, Sheila Cowles, Dwight

Rivers's attorney, came out of his room. A tall, skinny woman in her forties, Cowles adjusted her blazer and said, "I advised him not to speak to you until he's feeling better. But he wants to talk to you so he can give you his version of events sooner rather than later."

"What we wanted to hear," Mahoney said, and the three of us followed her inside.

Rivers was in a hospital bed with the back raised slightly. Monitors chirped around him. An IV ran into his left arm. His right ankle and lower leg had been broken badly in the crash and that leg was in a cast. His face was swollen, but not enough to obscure the deep blue, intelligent eyes that scanned us as we entered.

Mahoney and Sampson held up their badges. Ned identified me as an FBI consultant.

Rivers studied me, then said, "You the one who saved my life?"

He'd bitten his tongue in the crash, so it was a little hard to understand him, but I nodded.

"Thank you," he said.

"You're welcome."

Mahoney turned on the video app on his phone, set it in a little stand on a cabinet facing the patient, and said, "Your attorney says you want to talk."

"Want to help. Any way I can."

That surprised me. What was Rivers's game? The right play would be silence, wouldn't it?

Mahoney said, "Mr. Rivers, before you say anything, you should know you have the right to remain silent."

"I know. But I did not kill anyone."

Sampson said, "Sir, we found the decapitated head of an unidentified male in the third subbasement of your bunker, and another head—an unidentified Hispanic male in his forties—fell out of your Porsche after you crashed the car."

"I heard that. I didn't know it was there."

Rivers claimed he'd spent much of that day in his basement office in the house, working on his computer and engaging in a series of phone and FaceTime meetings with executives at companies in which he invested. He said he was on the phone when the dark panel van appeared in the rain and stopped at his garage.

Rivers said he got so many deliveries that he kept a sign on the inner garage door that told drivers to leave packages there if they were addressed to him but put the packages in the front hall of his bunker if they were marked *Prep.*

"So you just leave that bunker open?" Mahoney asked, incredulous.

"During the day. Wouldn't get any work done if I didn't. Never been a problem before. I live in rural America, you know? People leave their houses unlocked here."

Sampson said, "What was the delivery?"

"I don't know exactly. I buy a lot of things online. And there's a bunch of locals who work for me."

"Building your anthill," Mahoney said.

He stiffened. "Free country. Man's got a right to spend his money any way he wants."

I wanted to press Rivers on that, try to get him to talk about the paranoia that seemed inherent in spending a fortune to build a doomsday fortress in western Virginia, but before I could, Ned said, "You have security cameras on the driveway."

"Two motion-sensor cameras at the drive entrance, one near the garage. They feed to a server in my house office. All the others feed to hard drives in the anthill."

"Do we have your permission to look at them?" Mahoney said.

I squinted. *Permission?* Two heads had been found. The FBI must have already looked at those feeds. They must have already torn Rivers's bunker apart.

Rivers said, "You are free to look at any and all of my security recordings."

"Can you tell me what you think we'll see when we look at the hours in question?"

CHAPTER 49

RIVERS SAID THE RECORDINGS SHOULD show that, shortly after four that afternoon, in a rainstorm, he left his property to go to Madison to buy a bow saw to prune apple trees, bleach to disinfect a part of his anthill that had become rodent-infested over the winter, and plastic tarps for a paint job he had planned.

Rivers said he returned to the estate and drove directly to his bunker with his purchases, exactly as we'd seen on the feed from my drone camera. He went inside the bunker and saw three shipping boxes in the front hall by the hatch door.

He left them for later, climbed to the third floor

of the upper bunker to make sure his security cameras were all working, and then went down to his workshop three floors belowground.

"That's when I saw the reciprocating saw covered in blood and..." Rivers trailed off, sounding subdued. "And then that...that head."

He closed his eyes for several moments. "I've never been so rocked in my life."

Rivers claimed he stood there on wobbly legs for a long time, staring at the head and trying to figure out who'd put it there and what he should do.

"Then I heard people coming down the staircase," Rivers said, "coming to the door to the workshop, and I figured they were the killers, the ones who'd put the head there, and they were coming for me."

He said he ran for the exit at the opposite end of the workshop, got to the ladder, and scrambled up it to get to the tunnel to his basement in the house.

I closed my eyes for a second when I understood that we had chased him out of that workshop. We had been the people coming down the staircase.

I said, "Is there another exit from that tunnel?"

"No," Rivers said. "Why?"

I'd been thinking about the fact that we'd been

locked inside the anthill, and I hoped to pin that on Rivers, shake up his story. "Just trying to get the lay of the land," I said.

Rivers said that when he reached the basement of his house, he considered calling 911, but then he decided it was smarter to go straight to the sheriff's office in Madison.

"I got in my Porsche, pulled out of the garage, and there they were," he said. "Headlights right in my eyes and coming hard from the anthill. In the Porsche, I knew I could outrun them, but I took that turn too fast for the slick road and flipped the car." Rivers grimaced. "That's all I know. I mean, I'm surprised I'm even alive."

I felt my stomach churn. I'd been the one chasing him, not whoever put the head in his subbasement.

His attorney cocked her head and gazed at Sampson and then me. "How was it that you came upon my client so soon after the crash?"

"They'll answer that in due time, Counselor," Mahoney said a little too quickly. He looked at Rivers. "Where do you think those heads came from?"

Rivers took a sip of water through a straw, said, "I've been thinking about that. It had to be that delivery driver or someone else who came onto my property while I was at the hardware store. Look at the tapes."

"We will," Mahoney promised. "Any reason someone would want to frame you, Mr. Rivers? Enemies?"

"Two ex-wives? Three or four angry ex-girlfriends? Actually, nah. They might want to cut my testicles off for whatever reason, but I can't see any of them sawing off people's heads to get at me."

I said, "Who's Maxine?"

Rivers frowned. "My cat?"

"Your cat?" Sampson said.

I closed my eyes again.

"Yeah," Rivers said. "She lives in the anthill and kills the mice. She can be a real pain, though. Almost impossible to catch when I need to give her her medicine."

Rivers's attorney was taking notes and studying us. "I've got a question for all of you."

"If we can answer, we will," Mahoney said.

She said, "This is connected to that woman's kidnapping in Ohio, isn't it? Diane Jenkins? There was a head left in an FBI car there during a ransom drop. The agents weren't named, but it was you, wasn't it, Special Agent Mahoney?"

"And me," I said, looking at her evenly.

Nodding, Cowles said, "So is this the work of the mysterious M?"

Rivers said, "Who's M?"

"We can't answer that question because we don't know," Mahoney told Cowles.

"But the cases are related?" the attorney said.

"Yes," I said.

She straightened. "I knew it. Why would M put two heads on my client's property? And, again, why were you in the area at all, Dr. Cross? Detective Sampson?"

"Counselor, this is a complicated federal investigation—" Mahoney began.

"But the truth alone will set us free," I said, and I held up my hands, palms out. "Mr. Rivers, Ms. Cowles, you deserve to know exactly what happened, regardless of the consequences to me."

CHAPTER 50

IF I'D LEARNED ANYTHING FROM Nana Mama, it was this: If you've screwed up, admit it and face the consequences. If you've crossed the line, admit it and face the consequences. If you've had lapses in judgment or viewed something with eyes full of prejudice, admit it and face the consequences.

"Any other course of action is deception and cover-up, which only makes the consequences worse for you in the long run," my grandmother told me when I was a boy. "Deal with the mess you've made, Alex, and move on."

Nana Mama's advice had been proven true time and again, so I followed it once more in Rivers's hospital room. Over the next twenty minutes, I laid out the bones of the story, from the earliest contact by M to the Wickr message I'd gotten moments before Rivers discovered the severed head in his subbasement to following him and rescuing him from the wreck of his sports car.

"We still thought you were M. Luckily, we got to you before your car exploded."

"Lucky?" Rivers's attorney said. "My client would not have crashed if you hadn't chased him. He would not have run in the first place if he hadn't heard you and Detective Sampson coming down the staircase. And my client's rights would not have been violated if you hadn't broken into his private bunker—*twice*—Dr. Cross."

I held up my hands. "All true. In my defense, I was hoping against hope that I'd find Diane Jenkins or evidence of her in Mr. Rivers's bunker."

"No, you were hoping you'd find evidence that my client was M."

"That too, no doubt about it," I said, and I looked at Rivers, who was studying me. "I have been chasing M for years, Mr. Rivers. M has taunted me, threatened me, and generally run circles around me, Detective Sampson, and Special Agent Mahoney. Please forgive me for being obsessive, but my heart was in the right place. I did not want anyone to be strangled or decapitated or held against her will by M ever again."

Cowles made a snort of derision and said, "Nice try. Look what happened to my client after you let your obsessions get the better of you. I'm smelling lawsuit."

"So much for coming clean," Mahoney said, looking disgusted. "I guess we're done here."

"No," Rivers said. "And there will be no lawsuit."

"Dwight—" his attorney began.

"No lawsuit, Sheila," he insisted. "Even if they hadn't been behind me, I would have been going way too fast for the road conditions. If they hadn't been chasing me, I might be dead."

"Well, that is absolutely not the way I see it."

Rivers fixed his eyes on me. "He's your Professor Moriarty, isn't he, Cross? This M?"

I got the reference to Sherlock Holmes's ultimate nemesis and shrugged. "You could say that," I said.

"Holmes became too obsessed with Moriarty. Because of that, he almost died."

"I remember."

Rivers watched me closely. "I don't know whether to be flattered or disgusted by the fact that you thought I could be M—or, rather, your computers did."

"I apologize for the computers' and my actions."

He laughed. "One thing I learned in the tech world is that you never apologize for a computer's performance. It did what its programmer told it to do. Nothing more. Nothing less."

"Dwight," his attorney said. "I think that—"

His eyes brightened. "You've got him now, don't you, Dr. Cross? M? He has to be on the security tapes. You're close, aren't you?"

"If M was the deliveryman, we are. I hope so."

Cowles chewed her lip.

"But how did M know you were watching me? How did he know to put the heads in my workshop and car and then alert you?"

"I don't know."

Rivers beckoned to his attorney. He whispered so softly, she had to bend closer as he repeated his words. She listened, then glanced at me and nodded.

Cowles came over to me, whispered, "Take your phone out of the room and shut it off."

CHAPTER

51

I PULLED OUT MY IPHONE, looked at it, then glanced at Rivers. He nodded.

I went out of the room and shut it off, then asked the nurse at the nurses' station if she could watch it. When I returned, Rivers said, "I'd put your phone in DFU mode if I were you."

"What's that mean?"

"It kills any hidden app a hacker might have installed to access the mike and camera on your phone. Google it. DFU."

I nodded, feeling invaded, creeped out, spied on, and determined to figure out if and how M hacked my phone and who knew what else. But how?

A nurse came in to say she had to take Rivers for a scan.

"We'll leave you to it," Mahoney said, and he motioned Sampson and me toward the door.

I stopped at the nurses' station and got my phone, and then we went down the hallway and into the elevator.

"You've already looked at Rivers's security tapes," Sampson said when the doors closed behind us and we began to descend.

"Every one of them," Mahoney said. "They all jibe with what Rivers said."

"You see the deliveryman?"

"From multiple angles. And you can't get a look at his face in any of them."

"The van?"

"Tinted windows. No markings. Stolen plates."

"So it was him," I said. "M."

"We might have had him if you hadn't put mud on the lens of the camera above the door to the bunker," Mahoney said. "All we could see was his shape when he made the deliveries and when he came back to lock you inside."

I puffed up my lips and blew out my breath. "Blunder."

"Yep."

The elevator doors opened.

We exited and went outside.

"I think Rawlins should look at your phone, pronto," Mahoney said.

"Agreed," I said. "I'll get it to him today."

Mahoney hesitated and then gazed at me earnestly. "Rivers could have sued your ass off, and he would have won, Alex."

"He still might if Cowles has her way."

"The FBI doesn't like its contractors getting sued."

I felt myself flush. "Understood. It will never happen again. I promise."

"Even the best of us have bad judgment from time to time," Mahoney said, then he shook my hand and left. Sampson, who had been strangely quiet, said he was heading to his office to finish up some work.

"We okay?" I asked.

Sampson closed one eye before he nodded slightly. "We're okay, but I'm not exactly happy. You could have gotten us worse than sued. What you did could have cost me my job."

My stomach dropped because I knew deep down he was right. "I'm sorry, John."

"I know. Just give me a little time to process, okay?"

The best friend I've ever had shot me a sad smile, then turned and lumbered away.

I watched him until he disappeared around a corner. I decided to walk home, mull things over, empty my head before a visit from yet another college track coach trying to recruit Jannie.

As I walked, I did my best to take my mind off Sampson, thinking that if Rivers was right, if M had slipped spyware into my phone, he was probably tracking me right now. Or he would have been if I hadn't turned the phone off.

Feeling somewhat invisible for the moment, I started asking myself how it was possible for M to have gotten into my phone. According to the Wickr website, all anyone had to do to contact me on the app was call my phone. As long as I had the app, the message would appear.

I supposed there were any number of ways he could have gotten my number, but it didn't explain how he'd figured out a way to track me and maybe listen in when I talked. Had M gotten close enough to me to clone my phone when I was using it? But when? And where?

It was maddening to think that M was staying three steps ahead of me. Or was he three behind, following me?

A wave of paranoia pulsed through me, and I couldn't help but look around to see if I was being tailed. There were people on the sidewalk behind me and on the other side of the street. But none were obviously watching me or acting suspiciously.

I took a few short detours to make sure no one was following me, and by the time I reached the National Mall, I was sure I was alone. As I cut southeast toward Fifth, I decided I'd better call Rawlins and have him come to my house. I just wouldn't say anything that would indicate our suspicions.

I turned my phone on, called him, and left a message asking him to call me on my landline at home. My regular messaging app showed two texts, one from Jannie reminding me to be home early to meet the coach and one from Nana Mama asking me to pick up a quart of milk.

I wondered if M could be monitoring my texts and was about to turn the phone off again when it dinged. A Wickr message appeared on the screen.

Stewing in a nasty kettle of fish these days, aren't you? Or should I say, a kettle of fish heads? Get it? Fish heads. Fish heads. Eat 'em up, yum!

Enough fun. Now things get interesting, Cross. This will all make perfect sense soon.

M is for...

Before the message could disappear, I did what Mahoney had told me to do: pressed the sleep button and the home button at the same time.

The screen flashed just before the message vanished.

CHAPTER 52

THE SCREENSHOT WAS STILL THERE in my photo album when Keith Karl Rawlins came to my house to get my phone. I met him on the porch and handed it to him when he knocked on our front door around six thirty that evening.

"Think you can find out how he's tracking me?" I said.

"No doubt," Rawlins said after looking at the screenshot. He powered the phone down and put it in a lead-lined bag. "The trick is to do it in a way he won't notice."

"Can you do that?"

He shot me a condescending look and said, "Blindfolded."

"Rivers said I should put it in DFU mode, but I have no idea what that means."

"Stands for 'device firmware update,'" he said, nodding. "It will get the bug out, but I want to take a look at the little nasty before I do that."

Rawlins left. Ali rode up on his mountain bike, soaked with sweat and grinning.

"Good ride?" I asked.

"You can't believe what some of these kids can do."

"Not Captain Abrahamsen?"

"He wasn't there. He had a long ride with his team."

"Go take a shower. The coach is coming to see Jannie after dinner."

"Do they have mountain-bike scholarships at Texas?"

"I have no idea. Shower."

We were just finishing the dinner dishes and Jannie had gone upstairs to send in her homework when the doorbell rang. I answered to find a tall, lean woman in her late thirties wearing a blue pantsuit and carrying a briefcase.

She smiled, stuck out her hand, and said, "I hope I'm not too early."

"Not at all, Coach Wilson. We're honored. Please come in."

Coach Rebecca Wilson ran the prestigious women's track team at the University of Texas at Austin.

"I appreciate you making time for me, Dr. Cross," Coach Wilson said.

"Anyone interested in Jannie gets our time," I said as I showed her inside.

Wilson had competed in the heptathlon in college. She'd twice been the NCAA Division I heptathlon champion, which was what had brought her to our attention.

To date, Jannie's biggest accomplishments had all been on the track, but a private coach who'd taken an early interest in my daughter had long argued that her broader athletic abilities suggested she could go farthest in the heptathlon, the most demanding of women's track-and-field events. Coach Wilson, we hoped, might be able to give Jannie an alternative to pure running in college.

"Smells good in here," the coach said while I hung up her jacket.

"My grandmother made apple pie for you."

"One of my favorites," Coach Wilson said. "And one of the reasons I get up every morning and go for a long run no matter where I am."

"I imagine these recruiting trips are demanding."

"When you're interested in the best, you have to put in the time. Is Jannie here?"

"She's just upstairs e-mailing in some homework," I said, leading her into the kitchen, where Nana Mama, Bree, and Ali were waiting.

After hearing that Texas did not offer cycling scholarships, Ali left to watch a video of mountain bikers in a race out west. Jannie came down as we made introductions and small talk. She looked better than she had in a long time, though she'd definitely lost weight and her eyes were still a bit sunken.

Coach Wilson studied my daughter as she smiled and shook her hand. "It's a pleasure to meet you finally, Jannie."

"You too, Coach Wilson," she said. "We appreciate you coming all this way."

"I imagine you've had quite a few coaches travel a long way to see you."

Jannie smiled softly. "Yes, ma'am. A few."

"Oregon?"

"Yes."

"Who else, if I may ask?"

I said, "Arizona, University of Southern California, and Duke."

"Very impressive for a junior. Offers from all of them?"

I said, "Verbal offers."

"But nothing on paper? No letters signed?"

"We're still listening to all that the world has to offer her," Nana Mama said. "Like you said, she's still a junior."

Wilson seemed to like that. She turned all business and pulled out a legal pad.

"I've seen your race times when you were a freshman and the two sophomore races, and I've reviewed the impressive videos," she said. "That ESPN highlight where you broke your foot in the four-hundred. How is the foot, by the way?"

Jannie glanced at me before saying, "Better than new. Doesn't hurt at all."

"Good. Glad to hear it. Dr. Cross, do you have a physician who will attest to the strength of her foot?"

I frowned. No one had ever asked that before. "I'm sure we could get the orthopedic surgeon to write something to that effect, but isn't it really how she feels?"

"To a great extent, of course," Coach Wilson said. "But we're considering a substantial investment of time and scholarship money in your daughter. We just want to make sure we're making a sound decision. I'm sure you understand."

Before I could answer, she turned back to Jannie. “I’ve heard you’ve been sick.”

“Mono,” Jannie said. “But I’m feeling a lot better.”

The coach scribbled something on her notepad, looked up. “Do you get sick a lot, Jannie?”

CHAPTER 53

JANNIE LOOKED AT ME. So did Nana Mama and Bree. The conversation wasn't headed where any of us expected.

I shrugged, said, "She doesn't get sick any more often than my other children, right, Nana?"

"Correct," my grandmother said. "Why are you asking that, Coach Wilson?"

Wilson smiled and set down her legal pad and pen. "The heptathlon is tough, physically and mentally. Two days, eight events. And training for the heptathlon is tougher still because it is an absolute grind-fest."

"Explain that," Bree said.

Wilson reached into her briefcase and pulled

out a thick spiral notebook. "This represents a year of heptathlon programming for my current athletes. Every day, they've got a job to do, three hundred and sixty-five days a year."

She went on to describe the training blocks—weights, plyometrics, and agility in the off-season, endless sessions of training and technical work leading up to competition, and hours of maintenance and recovery while performing.

"Do you see how that could wear out a young woman?" Wilson asked. "Do you see how someone could break down in this kind of pressure-cooker environment?"

"I do," Nana Mama said. "Is there time scheduled for studying in that book of yours?"

"Absolutely," Wilson said. She hesitated a moment and then said, "I'm going to be straight with you, and I hope the other coaches you are talking with are being straight with you as well. At least as far as competing in the heptathlon at the highest level, and by that, I mean at a level that could lead you into an Olympic stadium someday..."

"Okay?" Jannie said.

The coach put her hand on her chest. "It is my belief that from a training perspective, you will be better off if you take the bare minimum of academic requirements."

"What?" my grandmother and I both said at once. We didn't like that.

Wilson held her hands up. "Hear me out. During my NCAA career, I kept my academics to a minimum and filled that extra time with training. The courses I did take, I devoured. As a result, it took me five and a half years to graduate from college, but I did so with the highest honors. I also had two national championships under my belt and a shot at the Olympic Games."

We all chewed on that for a bit.

Jannie looked at me. "I think that kind of makes sense, Dad. I mean, I admit I've been worried about how training and school work at the next level."

"And you're right to be worried," the coach said. "I know how things can stack up on a young lady if she's trying to be both a world-class athlete and a full-time student."

After a few moments of silence, Bree said, "I can see it helping. The reduced workload in school, I mean. If she decides to compete in the heptathlon."

"What if she just runs?" I asked.

"If she just runs, she should be a full-time student, but at this point it probably won't be at the University of Texas."

That took us all aback.

"So you're not interested in having Jannie run for UT?" I asked.

"I could change my mind, but not as of today."

"I'm confused," Nana Mama said. "She's got five other great schools with great track programs making her offers."

"I know, and I'm not making her an offer today."

We were all quiet. Jannie sat forward. "You're not making me an offer to run track or you're not making me an offer to train for the heptathlon?"

"Both, and I'm going to tell you why," Coach Wilson said calmly and kindly. "I've watched videos of you when you were a freshman and I've talked with your coaches, and I have rarely seen anyone as gifted as you. You were a unicorn with limitless potential. But then you broke your foot."

Irritated, I said, "We've told you the foot is fine. And she dominated at her last few indoor meets."

"Believe me, I've been watching. But here's my quandary. Since Jannie's freshman year, she's run in only nine meets, and only one was outside. And here she's coming into the spring of her junior year and she's got mono, so the likelihood of her getting fit enough to really show me something outdoors this spring season is slim, at least as things stand. And as far as I know, she hasn't competed in any field events."

"Ted McDonald, an independent coach, has had her training in every heptathlon event for the past three years."

"I spoke with Coach McDonald. It's largely why I'm here."

Nana Mama crossed her arms. "To tell her she's not getting a scholarship from Texas? You could have done that on the phone."

Coach Wilson smiled. "Actually, I'm here to encourage Jannie to do whatever it takes to fully recover and then get fit enough to race in a short series of invitational meets happening around the country this summer. I or one of my assistants will be at every one of those races, and we'll be able to see if the unicorn is still in there.

"If Jannie is interested in the heptathlon, which is my preference, she should do more than just run at the invitational meets. I'd like to see her compete in at least two field events—the long jump, say, and the javelin. But it's her choice. If I like what I see in those meets, I'll be back with a full five-year-scholarship offer *in writing* as well as an in-depth training plan for her to follow."

Coach Wilson said goodbye and left a few minutes later, and we gathered in the kitchen.

"She was sure different than the others," Nana Mama said. "They were falling all over themselves to get Jannie."

Acting defensive, Jannie said, "Maybe I should just call up the coach at Oregon and tell him I'll take his offer."

"That would be the easy way, Jannie," I said. "But you know Coach Wilson wasn't dissing you. She was challenging you."

"To prove I'm worthy?" Jannie said.

"That's kind of the point, isn't it? To show you're more than worthy?"

"I guess," she said with little enthusiasm.

"You didn't think this was going to be easy, did you?" my grandmother asked.

"It felt that way with the other coaches."

"Nothing worth achieving is done without effort, young lady."

Jannie sighed and walked over to hug her great-grandmother. "You're right, Nana. How is it you're always right?"

"Not always," Nana said. "But often enough."

CHAPTER

54

I GRABBED A HOODED JACKET and went out on the front porch. It was in the low sixties, as beautiful a March evening as I'd ever seen, with air that smelled like flowers.

But my heart felt more than a little heavy when I sat in Nana's porch swing.

Bree came out and sat beside me.

"We never know, do we?" she said.

"What's that?"

"What twist or turn will be thrown our way."

"Jannie?"

"Yes. She's still digesting. You okay?"

"I'm fine with it."

"You don't look fine."

"Sampson," I said, and I told her all about it.

When I finished, Bree said, "He was right. And he was right to tell you."

"I know, and I feel lousy now...but in the heat of the moment, I did what *I* thought was right."

She leaned over and put her arm around my shoulders. "You took action to move toward danger. That's more than ninety-nine percent of the population would have done."

"It was worse than just moving in the wrong direction, Bree."

"No, it wasn't. Unless you intentionally dragged Sampson into a situation that could have cost him his job?"

"No."

"There, then," Bree said, and she hugged me tight. "Briefly lost at sea. No shipwreck. A little navigation issue. That is all."

I smiled. "My life as a voyage?"

She laughed and kissed me on the cheek. "Something like that."

"Thank you," I said, and I kissed her back.

"For what?"

"Believing in me."

"Always and forever, Alex Cross."

I felt a whole lot better about me and Bree, but

me and Sampson were still off. That conflict must have shown on my face because Bree said, "You need to see John."

"You are a perceptive thing, aren't you?"

"It rubbed off from someone I know."

"I'm going to drive over and knock on his door. Make this right."

Bree patted me on the chest and said, "If it will help you sleep."

"It will."

"Go on, then," she said. "I'll still be up."

I got in the car, flipped on the headlights of our old Mercedes, and pulled out onto Fifth.

A headlight beam slashed across my rearview mirror. I glanced back and noticed that a small black SUV had pulled out half a block behind me.

I drove to Sampson's home, a route I could do blindfolded, or at least without consciously thinking about it, which was good because my mind was on other things that night.

I had the screenshot of M's last message on an old phone in my pocket, but I didn't need to pull it out to remember it. The first three or four lines, the taunting tone, and the fish-head stuff were designed to get me anxious, to remind me that M was bizarre and unpredictable and actively plotting against me. He was trying to keep me under pressure, but I could avoid it by simply not dwelling on those parts of his message.

Those last few sentences were harder to shake.

Now things get interesting, Cross. This will all make perfect sense soon.

M is for…

I decided he was playing a game based on dwindling time, attempting to get me to burn mental energy as I tried to anticipate his next move. But there was more.

"He knows the whole M-thing bothers me," I murmured as I slowed for a yellow light turning red on Pennsylvania Avenue. "What it stands for. Who he really is."

Out of habit, I glanced in the rearview and saw five cars in the other lane—a service vehicle, a pickup truck, a minivan, a white Jeep, and a small black SUV.

The light turned green. I drove on toward the Beltway, the circuit of highways that girdle the nation's capital, and my mind once again returned to that last sentence: M is for…

Moriarty.

That just popped into my head, an idea left over from the talk with Rivers earlier in the afternoon.

And then, even though I knew it was impossible, I couldn't help but think...

Mastermind.

M is for Mastermind. Kyle Craig's alias.

Driving onto I-295 north, I dismissed the idea that Craig was somehow still alive, still playing some long and deadly game with me. But someone *was* playing a long and deadly game with me. Or was this all like a cat with a live mouse, the feline batting at the rodent with his paw every now and then, entertaining himself before the kill?

A horn blared behind me, startling me from my thoughts. I glanced in the rearview mirror and saw the delivery truck in the lane next to me veer off toward the East Capitol Street exit, revealing a black BMW SUV behind it.

It could have been another black SUV, a sheer coincidence, but my instincts screamed that I was being followed by someone.

I decided to test my instincts, and I stomped on the gas as I entered a curve.

When I came out of it, I scanned the highway ahead, saw it was nearly empty, then glued my attention to my rearview mirror.

The BMW roared out of the curve before I thought it would, in my lane now, right behind me, a total abandonment of the sophisticated tail job.

Whoever was driving no longer cared about being spotted.

He was coming after me.

And he was coming fast.

CHAPTER 55

I SPED UP AS I snatched my pistol from my shoulder holster and set it on my lap.

The BMW kept coming, headlights on high.

My left hand went to the side-view mirror control; I flipped it to the right and eased off on the gas pedal. The SUV closed the gap as we passed the Minnesota Avenue Metro stop.

He tried to come right up on my bumper, his high beams filling my car. But then I twitched the control on the passenger-side mirror.

Two years before, my older son, Damon, had been backing up in a crowded parking lot and grazed a telephone pole with that mirror. The accident bent the mirror mount slightly, which, we discovered, had a strange usefulness: if someone came up behind you with his headlights blazing, you could tilt the mirror up and in, and the other car's right headlight beam would be reflected back at the driver.

Which is exactly what happened. When the BMW was about fifteen feet off my bumper, its right high beam reflected off the mirror and shone dead in the driver's eyes.

He threw a hand up and hit the brakes as I goosed the Mercedes's accelerator. I opened a gap of sixty yards passing Eastland Gardens.

But I was so shocked at what I'd just seen, I barely noticed.

In the split second before the driver threw up his arm and hit the brakes, I'd gotten a look at him: a man in a dark suit and tie, black gloves, mid-forties, tinted glasses, sandy-blond hair, and the unmistakable nose, cheekbones, and prominent chin of disgraced and deceased former FBI special agent Kyle Craig.

The mental images of Craig throwing up his arm to block the glare were so vivid they almost blinded me to a panel van coming off the ramp from Maryland State Highway 50.

I hit the brakes, and the van swerved, horn honking, just in front of me. We barely missed colliding.

When I was sure we were not going to hit, I looked frantically in the rearview and side-view mirrors, trying to see the BMW. But it wasn't back there.

Indeed, there were no headlights anywhere close behind me. Impossible.

I clawed at the passenger-side mirror control and this time aimed it wide to the right. I caught flashes of the BMW running dark under the highway lights and coming up alongside me so fast, I got rattled.

I knew I should pull an evasive maneuver, hit the brakes, and let him pass. Instead, I rolled down the passenger-side window and kept glancing over, trying to see Craig through the tinted windows even as I knew beyond a shadow of a doubt that the man was dead and gone.

The panel van hit the brakes in front of me. I had no choice but to do the same. The BMW shot forward and passed into my headlight glare.

The driver-side window rolled down. I couldn't see his face, but I sure heard his voice. It seemed to boom back at me.

"M said you'd never learn, Cross!"

Then his gloved hand came out of the window and whipped something sideways and back at me.

A blue balloon burst off my windshield, coating it with dark liquid and blocking my view.

I hit the brakes hard and swerved right, praying I could see something of the road in that bent side-view mirror. When I got over on the shoulder, I was gasping, sweating. Whatever liquid was in the balloon was now smeared across my windshield, and my headlights looked like they had a copper tint.

I almost pressed the spray button on my wiper control, but something stopped me. From the glove box, I retrieved my Maglite, then I got out on the passenger side to avoid being run over by passing cars.

The BMW and the panel van were nowhere to be seen as I stepped up next to the front quarter panel and shone the flashlight on my windshield. The liquid was a deep, dark red and already setting up into a tacky gel in the cooling breeze.

I touched some, rubbed it between my fingers, and then sniffed enough of a copper odor to know the blood was not fake.

CHAPTER 56

JOHN SAMPSON LOOKED AT THE windshield in his flashlight beam.

"You drove over here trying to see the road through that?" he asked, gesturing to the small area I'd cleared directly in front of the steering wheel.

"I didn't want to tamper with the evidence any more than I had to."

"Why blood?" Ned Mahoney asked.

Ned had been working late downtown and came over as soon as I called. We were in Sampson's driveway. An FBI forensics unit was on its way.

"No idea," I said.

"You get a look at the guy who threw the balloon?" Mahoney asked.

"Yeah. You're not going to like it. I certainly don't like it."

Sampson said, "Lot of that going around."

I paced away from the car, still wrestling with what I'd seen, then I turned and gazed at the two men I trusted most in life.

"The man driving that car looked just like Kyle Craig."

"Oh, c'mon, Alex," Mahoney said, groaning. "Get over it. The man is dead."

Sampson said, "You killed him, Alex."

"I know! I know! At the very least, whoever was driving that BMW had an uncanny resemblance to what I imagine Craig might have looked like... had he..."

They both reacted with squints.

"Come again?" Sampson said.

"That's it," I said. "That guy looked like a pre-op Kyle Craig who'd aged. You know, like when we take photographs of people and have computers age them? But think about it. The real Craig had his face completely rebuilt by that plastic surgeon in Florida so he could impersonate an FBI agent before I figured it out and killed him."

They were quiet for a moment.

Then Mahoney said, "Unless that wasn't the real Craig you killed."

"My head aches," Sampson said. "Is that even possible?"

"No," I said. "It *was* Kyle Craig who died that night. The guy I saw *could have* been him *before* the facial work. Even his voice sounded like Craig's."

"What, you had a chat during a car chase?" Mahoney said.

"He yelled out the window so loud, it could have been amplified: 'M said you'd never learn, Cross!' He had the same kind of drawl Craig used."

"And then he threw the blood balloon at you?" Sampson said.

"Correct."

"What the hell is this sick bastard up to?" Mahoney said.

"Sick *bastards,* plural," Sampson said. "If Pseudo-Craig is to be believed, then *M told him* you would never learn."

"Pseudo-Craig," I said, and I smiled. "I like that. And correct."

To my relief, John smiled back.

The forensics team showed up and peeled off and bagged several strips of blood before giving us the go-ahead to turn on Sampson's hose and wash off the rest.

"You don't think I'm nuts, do you?" I asked Mahoney.

"About seeing Craig? Nah. You say you saw someone who could have been his pre-op older brother, I believe you. Now I have to go home and get some sleep."

"I appreciate it, Ned."

"Anytime, my friend."

We watched him go.

Sampson said, "Beer?"

"Definitely."

He went to a fridge in his garage, got two bottles, and handed me one. I took a long draw off it, loving the cold pouring down my throat.

Lowering the bottle, I said, "I was on my way here to see you when Pseudo-Craig splattered me."

"Is that right?"

"Yeah. I was upset and wanted to apologize again in person. I don't take our friendship or brotherhood for granted. It will never happen again."

Sampson's head bobbed before he looked me in the eyes. "We're good."

"Thank you," I said, holding out my beer. "I need everything about you in my life, John, now more than ever."

He clinked it, said, "Ditto, Alex."

CHAPTER 57

AROUND ONE THE NEXT AFTERNOON, I hurried into security at the visitors' entrance of the Alexandria detention center. Fairfax sheriff's deputy Estella Maines was on duty.

"Dirty Marty again?"

"Mr. Forbes, yes, please."

"Popular. You're the third visitor he's had today."

She buzzed open the steel door. Another deputy led me to a booth, where I waited a good ten minutes before the disgraced FBI agent shuffled in. He had two days' growth of beard and was shakier than I remembered, almost frail in the way he sat down opposite me.

Forbes stared at me for a long moment. "Thank

you for coming," he said finally in a strained, hoarse voice.

"I wish we could have done this on the phone."

"You wouldn't have believed me."

"Marty, I've got fifteen minutes."

He sat forward, hands clasped as if in prayer, his expression intense. "Guess who paid me a visit this morning."

"I heard you had two visitors this morning."

He nodded. "My lawyer, then an old friend of ours."

"Who was that?"

"Kyle Craig."

My stomach soured. "He's dead."

"Then he's risen. Like Lazarus. I'm telling you, Cross, the son of a bitch was sitting right there where you are not four hours ago."

My skin crawled, and I shivered. I said, "It's not Craig. He's dead."

Forbes got upset. "Cross, you've got to listen to—"

"Did he look exactly like he did the last time you saw him?"

He settled down. "No. He was older than I remembered, but we all are."

"He told you he was Kyle Craig?"

"He didn't have to. He just smiled at my reaction

to him being there, then he pulled out a handkerchief and used it to pick up the phone. And easy as can be in that drawl of his, he said, 'Been a long time, Marty.'" Forbes said he was dumbstruck because this was no ghost. The man was real, the appropriate age, and amused.

"Did you call him by that name? Craig?"

"I called him Kyle. I think I gasped and said it out loud."

"What did he do?"

"He just kept smiling at me, and then he laughed a bit like he was hearing a joke in his head. I don't understand how it could be him. After all these years."

"It is not Craig," I said. "What did this guy—let's call him Pseudo-Craig—want?"

"He wanted to give me and you a message."

"The two of us?"

"That's right. A message from M."

I sat up straighter. "What's the message?"

"'You'll never learn.'"

"That's it?"

"That's exactly what I said. But he smiled at me, hung up, and walked out."

I stared at him. "'You'll never learn'?"

"I don't know what he meant. You believe me, don't you, Cross?"

I thought of the blood balloon hitting my windshield right after that amplified voice had boomed out a similar message.

"Cross?"

I stood up. "I believe you, Marty. I just need to check on a few things."

CHAPTER 58

I FOUND MAHONEY AND SAMPSON eating cheeseburgers in a booth at Ned's favorite saloon on Capitol Hill. I slid a manila envelope to the center of the table.

"Pseudo-Craig paid a visit to Marty Forbes at the Alexandria detention center earlier. A deputy there helped me get some stills from the security footage."

"Really? Why Forbes?" Ned asked as he drew out the pictures. He put on his reading glasses and studied the stills, his eyebrows rising, then handed two of them to Sampson. "Jesus, you weren't kidding, Alex," Mahoney said, shaking his head.

"This guy looks exactly like an older Kyle Craig. Same sandy-blond hair, same haircut."

"Uncanny," John said.

"Check out the last page. There's a copy of his ID."

Mahoney flipped ahead and peered at the Pennsylvania driver's license.

"Gordon Harris, twenty-seven Flintlock Lane, Lancaster, Pennsylvania. Looks legit."

"Almost legit. There was a Gordon Harris who lived at twenty-seven Flintlock Lane in Lancaster until he was found strangled to death in his garage five months ago."

"With a tie?" Sampson asked.

"Piano wire. I haven't talked to the homicide investigators up there yet, but I'm assuming his driver's license was missing."

Mahoney thought about that. "Why did you visit Forbes?"

I explained the message from M, and Forbes's contention that someone with the same initial had set him up for the deaths of the sex traffickers off the coast of Florida.

"You never told me that," Mahoney said.

"Me either," Sampson said.

"I went to see Marty the first two times as his therapist. I couldn't share anything he told me in those sessions."

Ned didn't like that but let it slide and again studied the pictures of Pseudo-Craig.

I said, "See the second picture? The one where he has his hand on the counter in front of Deputy Maines? That was the only time we saw him touch anything inside the facility. Maines called in a tech to try to pull his prints, although it's a long shot because God knows how many people put their hands there in the course of a day."

"There have to be cameras in the streets outside that facility," Sampson said.

Mahoney said, "In multiple positions."

"Then we can follow him on tape as he leaves the jail."

"Maybe to his car," I said. "Black BMW."

Ned's phone dinged. He looked at the screen, thumbed it, and held the phone to his ear.

"You want something to eat?" Sampson asked me.

I checked my watch: two p.m. "I'll eat at home. I promised Nana I'd take her to her doctor at three."

Mahoney hung up, looking bewildered. "That was the lab with the results on the blood they took off your windshield last night, Alex."

"Human?" Sampson said.

"Definitely," he said. "But not just one. There was blood from eight different people in that balloon."

CHAPTER 59

EIGHT DISTINCT BLOOD SOURCES. All human.

Those facts gnawed at me on the way home. I put them aside when I found Jannie up and about and in better spirits.

"I'm feeling so good," she said, looking brighter than she had in weeks. "I could probably go for a jog."

"Not a chance," I said. "I read the instructions the doctor gave us. Part of what got you in this state was burning the candle at both ends. That has to stop."

"Dad—"

"I'm not kidding. Something's got to give so you can get the rest you need to compete."

To my surprise, Jannie didn't argue. "I definitely need to sleep more and eat better if I'm going to do everything I can to get Coach Wilson to offer me a scholarship."

I smiled. "I thought you might rise to her challenge."

"I'm going to at least try two field events at those meets this summer. I'll work at it, give it my best, and if it turns out I'm not a multi-discipline athlete, I'm okay with that. I'll just run at Oregon or wherever. Either way, I'll be fine."

I gave her a hug. "I think that's a good way to think about it."

"Nana says I can go to school Monday."

"No fever?"

"Not in five days."

"Let's see how you feel Sunday."

My grandmother came into the room.

"You don't look a day over eighty, Nana," Jannie said.

Nana Mama laughed. "I look every bit of my age, but thank you."

We left and drove over to her doctor's office, which was in the Cleveland Park neighborhood of the District of Columbia. We spent an hour with Dr. Patricia Long, a gerontologist who'd been treating my grandmother for more than ten years.

"Mrs. Hope, you continue to be a wonder," Dr. Long said, reviewing the lab work done the week before. "Your bad cholesterol is very low. Your good cholesterol is sky-high. You look like a healthy seventy-year-old!"

"So you're saying I'll be around for a while?"

"Barring some kind of accident, I'd put money on it."

That was comforting to know, and as I drove my grandmother home, I thanked God once again for putting her in my life and keeping her there for so long. She was both my anchor and my wind.

We had a nice, low-key evening. Bree called to say she'd be late. Ali had a good training ride with the Wild Wheels crew.

"There's a race in Pennsylvania in three weeks," Ali said. "Ten kilometers through the woods, like a time trial. Can I go?"

"How would you be getting there?"

"They have a van and chaperones. The coach said they'll have a handout about it on Thursday."

"Let's take a look at it Thursday."

"Captain Abrahamsen thinks it's a good idea," Ali said. "You know, for a first race."

Jannie shook her head. "What happened to your books?"

Ali frowned. "Nothing. Why?"

"You were supposed to be the family nerd."

"You're saying you can't be both smart and physical?" Ali said, annoyed.

"No, I...forget I even brought it up. Go mountain bike. Make the X Games."

Her brother grinned. "That would be awesome!"

After dinner, with Ali and Jannie studying and my grandmother watching a recording of *Antiques Roadshow,* I went up to my attic office, closed the door, locked it, and looked at the boxes containing the Kyle Craig files.

Part of me wanted to keep clear of the Craig files because they invariably made me upset. Craig had operated as an active serial killer right under my nose and under the noses of some of the best agents in the FBI. How many people might we have saved if we'd seen or understood evidence that could have identified him earlier?

It was those kinds of questions that usually kept me from opening his files.

And I had to go through two more boxes from the Edgerton investigation, which began in earnest a few months after Craig shot the tie-shop owner.

Just looking at the Edgerton boxes made me agitated. There might be something in those boxes that could lead me to M, but there were *definitely* things in them that would drag me down a mental black hole.

I chose what felt like the lesser of two evils and went to the boxes dedicated to Craig's crimes. I chose one at random and opened it to find a picture of Craig on the day he graduated from the FBI Academy.

Craig was twenty-six, already killing by then, but in that photograph, he had the face of an avenging angel. Or at least that's how it struck me. Even though he was young in the picture, his resemblance to Pseudo-Craig was unmistakable.

I spent the next hour studying files covering Craig's early life, paying special attention to members of his extended family. I made note of every male cousin who was roughly his age, plus or minus three years.

There were four who fell in that category. Two were the sons of Craig's mother's sister. One was his father's brother's son. And the fourth was his father's sister's boy.

I found a sheet dating back to when Craig was being considered for admission to the FBI Academy. There was a brief note saying that field agents vetting Craig had talked to his cousin Ted Shaw, the older of his maternal aunt's sons.

Shaw told the agents Craig had been cruel to

animals as a kid. *Stuck firecrackers in frogs' mouths,* the note read.

How had that gotten by the screeners? Cruelty to animals is a red-flag warning. Many of history's most heinous murderers started out being sadistic to defenseless—

A sharp knock came at the door, startling me.

"Alex?" Bree called.

"Hey, babe, I'm in the middle of something. Let me wrap up, and I'll be down."

"I'll be up the street, across from the Caseys'."

"You mean the house of the people with the barking dog?"

"Double homicide," she said. "It just got called in."

CHAPTER 60

UNIFORMED OFFICERS STOOD BY A cruiser parked in front of a bungalow across the street from the house of Nana Mama's friends Jill and Neal Casey. They stood outside their place, looking worried.

"We called it in," Jill said. She was in her eighties and still played tennis.

"I found them," said Neal, who was less spry than his wife but still sharp.

They explained that the house had been recently rented to the Richardsons, a young couple from Newark. Mary was a night nurse at GW Medical Center. Keith was a day trader who was "deaf as a post" without his hearing aids.

The Richardsons had a Jack Russell terrier named Otto.

"Barked all night," Jill said. "You could go over there and bang on the door, but if Keith had his hearing aids off, good luck."

"Which was going on this afternoon," her husband said. "I was trying to read, and the dog was barking, then finally stopped. I went over to talk to them about it and found their front door ajar. I looked inside and saw enough to call 911."

Bree and I thanked them, then crossed the street to the uniformed officers.

"You been inside?" Bree asked.

"We figured you'd want to go in clean, Chief."

"We do. Thank you, Officers," she said and led the way up onto the porch where we paused to put on blue booties, disposable gloves, and surgical masks.

Bree pushed the door open. We peered into an entry with a staircase to our right. On the bottom step, the barking terrier was dead, apparently of a broken neck.

In the living area beyond the stairs, Mary Richardson lay on the floor by a large table. She wore green hospital scrubs, surgical gloves, and a heavy-duty respirator and visor. A blue-and-red rep tie was cinched tight around her neck.

Slumped in one of the high-backed chairs around the table, Keith Richardson was similarly dressed. The tie that killed him was a loud yellow-and-red paisley.

The table between the victims was set up as a repackaging operation for crystal methamphetamine. There was a typed note on the table in front of a kilo of the drug.

> I'm usually as patient as a saint, Cross, but the damn dog would not stop barking, and these scum were selling to kids. Glad to be of service.
>
> —M

CHAPTER

61

IT WAS LONG PAST two a.m. when Bree and I returned home. We'd had to wait for a hazmat team to come deal with the chemicals in the kitchen before any more of the scene could be processed.

These scum were selling to kids. Glad to be of service.

Bree said, "How did he know the Richardsons were moving meth?"

"I don't know, but somewhere, I swear, he's made a mistake."

"Not so far," she said, yawning. "I have to sleep."

I did too, but sleep did not come easy. Every time I started to drift off, I'd flash on the stills of Pseudo-Craig, the blood of eight people bursting on my windshield, and the silk ties around the meth dealers' necks.

The dead dog was in my restless dreams as well, as were the remaining boxes of the Edgerton files, everything spilled along a path through the forest that I followed as I chased M, a dark figure, smaller than I'd expected.

Strangling someone is no easy feat. It takes strength and size. So does cutting off someone's head. And yet, my dream M was slight with narrow shoulders, and he could run and run and…

I woke with a start around five a.m. and heard birds chirping outside the window. Feeling dazed, I nevertheless remembered that slight, fast M who'd haunted my dreams and run past the Mikey Edgerton files in the forest.

The Edgerton files. I've heard it said that if fear is stopping you from doing something, you must take courage and do it anyway or be forever ruled by doubt and anxiety.

I got out of bed quietly and crept up to the attic.

After locking the door, I opened the final boxes of files concerning the serial rapist and killer I'd seen electrocuted a few weeks before. My tongue tasted sour when I began to read. Long-buried images of my past rose up, blurry at first, then gradually coming into focus, all of them deeply disturbing.

CHAPTER 62

Eleven years before

JOHN SAMPSON LOOKED OVER AT me and shook his head. My stomach lurched. My throat burned with reflux.

"There has to be something here besides the neckties," I said. "A guy like this? He has trophies somewhere."

We'd been searching a three-bedroom apartment in Arlington, Virginia, that had an expansive view of the Potomac River and the Jefferson Memorial. The apartment belonged to Michael "Mikey" Edgerton.

After Kyle Craig killed Gerald St. Michel, the necktie salesman with a history of predatory sexual behavior, most people believed that St. Michel was responsible for the murders of the other young women, including Kissy Raider. But I had my doubts.

Evidently, so did M, because I heard from him for the first time about three weeks after Kyle Craig killed St. Michel.

The two-sentence message came typed on plain white paper in a plain white envelope with no return address: *It's not St. Michel. Thank me later.—M*

I happened to agree with M, whoever he was, and set the message aside.

But then a man grabbed Gladys Craft, a young blond woman running late at night in Falls Church, Virginia. He used a necktie to bind her hands and then threw her in a van.

Craft managed to escape the van when he stopped at a light, and she was able to give police a rough description of her assailant and the last two digits of the van's Virginia license plate.

When we heard about the necktie, Sampson and I got involved again. We used computers to sift for possible matches between owners of cars with plates that had those last two digits and criminals who had histories of sexual assault.

We got a resounding match on Michael Edgerton, who lived in Arlington, ran an office of his family's import/export business, and had been a suspect in three assaults while he was in school at the Fashion Institute of Technology in New York.

Those cases had all been dropped at the request of the victims. Edgerton's parents had bought them off. When we contacted the women, all buxom young blondes, they were reluctant to talk until we described the women who'd died.

The second we mentioned that the women were strangled with ties, each of them started crying because Edgerton had used silk ties to control them all.

We became convinced that Edgerton, not the dead tie-shop owner, was responsible for the rapes and murders of Kissy Raider and the other dead women. We put him under surveillance and kept digging into his past.

When we were able to place him in the vicinity of six of the eight victims around the times of their deaths, a judge granted us a search warrant. Which had led us to Edgerton's apartment that day.

"I'm not seeing any trophies," Sampson said.

"I know," I said. "But he *is* our man. I know it in my gut."

"I think so too. But he's not keeping his trophies here."

"Probably not," I said and went into the bathroom.

The place was spotless for a man living alone. On the wall hung a photograph showing a younger Edgerton and his family on a sailboat, all of them beaming.

The whole family knew Mikey was a psycho even when he was that age, I thought. *Mom and Dad had already bought off three young women by the time this picture was taken.*

It made me angry to think that unless we found some evidence, and soon, this guy would get away with rape and murder again. At the very least, if we didn't find something, it would be more difficult to obtain search warrants for other places he might have used to store evidence of his cruelty.

Before I knew exactly what I was doing, I pulled out a small plastic bag. In it was a single strand of Kissy Raider's hair. I was drawing it out of the bag when Sampson came into the bathroom. He looked at the bag and the strand of hair.

"He's hidden the trophies somewhere else," I said, and I let the hair fall.

John didn't say anything for several long moments. Then he said, "I'll have forensics work in here next."

CHAPTER

63

Present day

IN MY ATTIC OFFICE THAT morning, I stared without emotion at an old copy of the lab report stating that the hair I'd dropped matched Kissy Raider's. I closed the file and opened another that contained a copy of that same lab report as supporting evidence for search warrants at all homes and businesses owned by Mikey Edgerton's family.

I found an evidence log noting various items discovered beneath the floorboards of Mikey's room in a vacation home the Edgerton family maintained at a lake in western Maryland. I scanned the list until I saw:

> Eight (8) locks of blond hair in specimen bags.
> Eight photographs, Polaroid, of eight women, all blond.

The actual photographs weren't in my files, but I remembered them as clearly as if I'd seen them yesterday. In every one, including the picture that showed Kissy Raider, each doomed woman was alive, bound, gagged, and terrified.

I shut the file and then the box, not needing to look further, not needing to see the DNA results that linked the eight locks of hair to Edgerton's eight victims.

And the strand of hair I dropped? I had not lost a wink of sleep over it. Ever.

Mikey Edgerton raped and killed those women. Of that there was no doubt.

You might ask if I believed the ends justified the means, and I'd answer that in this case, yes. The families of Kissy Raider and Edgerton's other victims got justice when he was convicted, and they got more justice when *he* opted for the electric chair. And the world, in my opinion, was made a safer place.

I'd picked up a burn phone the day before. A text came in over it from Sampson.

Wake the chief. She's not answering. Bring her and meet me at Seventeenth and R Southeast. She's going to want to see this.

CHAPTER 64

TWENTY MINUTES LATER, BREE AND I left her car and walked toward two patrol cars and barriers set up at Seventeenth and R in Southeast DC.

Sampson hurried over to us.

"How many victims?" Bree asked. The sidewalks were empty, but people, many still in their pajamas and robes, were looking out their windows at us.

"Six," Sampson said. "And we haven't brought in the dogs yet to look for more."

I saw Bree's shoulders adjust to the weight of that. Six victims.

Sampson led us to a brick building midway down the block, once a small job-printing facility but now abandoned and condemned, with a chain-link fence around it. The windows were all gone, replaced by plywood that had been spray-painted with graffiti.

Two-by-fours had been pried off the double front doors, which sagged open. We went inside and were hit by the smell of stale urine, feces, and body odor.

The place was trashed. John seemed uninterested in anything inside. He went straight through the building and out the back onto a parking lot of cracked pavement.

On the far side of the lot, three-foot concrete posts were anchored in the ground every fifteen feet or so; lengths of heavy chain were slung between them.

A decapitated head sat atop each of the six nearest posts, eyes open, blankly gaping at us. Blood seeped from the necks and dribbled down the posts, looking like the tentacles of red jellyfish.

Bree said, "We're going to need an army in here."

She tugged her radio from its holster and went back into the abandoned building. I could hear her barking orders, summoning crime scene personnel, as Sampson and I crossed the lot toward the severed heads.

"Equal-opportunity killer," Sampson said, and I understood.

The six victims were an African-American male, an Asian male, a Hispanic male, a Hispanic female, a Caucasian female, and a Caucasian male.

The Hispanic male and the Caucasian female appeared to be in their late thirties, early forties, and the rest looked to be in their twenties.

Noting the deep gray pallor of the Caucasian male, I put a gloved hand on his cheek and found the skin near ice-cold to the touch.

"The heads were frozen," I said. "That's why we're seeing the blood leaking."

"Pretty bold to move six frozen heads in the middle of the night. What kind of person does that?"

"The Meat Man would have," I said, feeling toyed with again. "Freezing heads was Tanner Oates's post-homicide fetish."

"Oates is dead. You saw him die."

"I saw Mikey Edgerton die too," I said. "And Kyle Craig."

Before Sampson could reply, I heard a dull thudding sound somewhere behind me, and then a huge explosion ripped through the abandoned print shop and blew out the plywood over the windows. The blast knocked me off balance and had my ears ringing, so it took me a moment to remember who had just gone into the building.

"Bree!" I roared and ran straight at the back door.

CHAPTER 65

OFTEN, WHEN I CLOSE my eyes, I can see myself sprinting toward the gray smoke and flame billowing from the blown-out windows, the rear door, and the loading dock.

My training screamed at me to stay out of the building, to wait for the firefighters. But I recalled the interior of the print shop—concrete floors. Steel posts. Trash. No wood. Little fuel. I leaped up the stairs, pulled my jacket over my head, and bulled my way into the chemical smoke and the heat.

"Bree!" I shouted. "Bree!"

My ears still rang from the blast. Fire blazed on mounds of trash to my right. The flames breathed slow and surreal.

"Bree!"

The heat got too intense, forcing me to my left; I was barely able to see. I stuffed the fabric of my jacket into my mouth and sucked cleaner air through it. Then I went down on my hands and knees to get beneath the heat and the rising smoke.

Visibility was better from that position. I could see the base of the steel posts like trees in fog as I crawled forward, pausing every few feet to scream, "Bree!"

No answer. I kept looking from side to side for a human shape.

And then I spotted one through the smoke, hard to my left, a woman lying on her side with her back to me. I crawled to her, fearing the worst.

When I reached her and turned her on her back, I saw it was one of the patrol officers. She'd been burned but was breathing.

I grabbed her by the collar, got to my feet, and started dragging her out.

The front entrance appeared, the sun shining through the smoke like a halo, and I stumbled toward it, coughing and hacking. When I got the patrolwoman outside, other officers ran to help me. My eyes felt singed. My vision was worse than blurry. I heard sirens coming.

"Chief Stone!" I shouted, feeling panic sweep toward hysteria. "Where is she?"

"Alex!"

I spun around, the despair of losing her disappearing at the sound of her voice as she came running across the street. It didn't matter that my throat and eyes burned when she grabbed me.

"Oh my God," she said as we hugged tight. "I was down the street and—"

"I thought you were inside," I said. "I thought I'd lost you."

"No, baby," Bree said fiercely. "You're never losing me. You hear?"

"I need to flush my eyes, get some oxygen. That smoke. It's chemical."

She was all business then. She turned to the people standing outside of their houses looking at us. "Who has a garden hose?"

A woman yelled that she did, and Bree was soon running cold water up into my eyes. Sampson had come around the long way from the back of the burning building and he got firefighters to bring me a mask and oxygen.

The female officer was rushed into an ambulance that vanished in flashing lights and the wail of a departing siren.

With every breath and every cough, I felt a

little better, less strangled inside by the taste of the smoke. And even though my eyes felt like I'd stared at the sun, my vision had improved by the time they brought the blaze under control.

"I still think you should go to the emergency room and have your eyes and lungs checked," Bree said. "Please?"

She said it with such concern and love, that I nodded.

"Just so you know?" I said.

"Yes?"

"I think those heads were bait. Someone wanted to get us here and then detonate that bomb."

Before Bree could reply, I felt my burn phone buzz. I pulled it out and looked at the screen, but my vision was still too blurry for me to read the words. I held it out to her. "What does it say?"

Bree took the phone from me, paused, and then replied, "It says, 'You and your family need to be more careful, Cross.' It's signed 'M.' "

CHAPTER

66

KEITH KARL RAWLINS CALLED THAT evening to tell me that my personal phone had indeed been hacked and compromised by an insidious piece of code that had most likely been written in China. The code evidently caused my phone to send a record of everything I did on it to an address on the dark web.

So M has been listening, watching, reading, I thought as I climbed into bed. For how long? And how had he learned of my burn phone number? I'd given it only to my family and close colleagues; were they bugged as well?

That last thought was the most upsetting. M had been listening to me through my phone, shadowing me electronically. And maybe he was doing the same thing to everyone else trying to catch him.

What else had he heard in the past week? Month? Year?

I barely slept. Despite an ophthalmic ointment given to me in the emergency room, my eyes still stung. And every hour or so, I had coughing fits.

But I was up before anyone else the next morning, padding around the house, checking windows and doors. I considered putting security cameras outside my home and wondered whether every electronic device we had should be checked.

My commitment to keeping my family safe and sound deepened after Ali and Jannie got up. I questioned them about their plans for the day.

Even though she felt even better than she had the day before, Jannie was staying home and working so she could get all caught up with her studies. Ali was going on a field trip to the Smithsonian and then on a Wild Wheels ride.

"I'll drive you to school today," I told him.

"I can take the Metro."

"I have to go in that direction anyway."

My son was remarkably perceptive for his age. Even though he didn't reply, I could tell he was suspicious. Bree came rushing down a few moments later, looking grim.

"You okay?" Ali asked.

"No," she said sadly. "Nancy Petit, one of our patrol officers, died last night from injuries sustained on the job."

My heart sank. Officer Petit was the woman I'd dragged out of the smoke. "I'm sorry," I said.

"The chief wants a task force, so I'm heading in now to organize."

"You want me there?"

"Yes," she said. "First meeting is at ten."

She had coffee and a piece of toast, and then I walked her out to her car.

"Stay alert. He was threatening all of us in that text."

"I know," she said. "Which is why I'm asking the chief to put officers here."

"Thanks. I'm hoping M made a mistake sending that text, that Rawlins can backtrack it."

"Let me know," Bree said. She kissed me, told me she loved me, and drove off. Twenty minutes later, Ali and I headed out too.

"So why are you really taking me to school?" he asked almost as soon as we got in the car.

I knew better than to skirt the question. Sometimes my youngest child is too smart for his own good. "A bad guy bugged my phone and threatened us," I said. "So I'm driving you to school to be prudent, and I want you to be prudent too. You know that word, right?"

"Like, level-headed?"

"More like cautiously smart."

"I can do that."

"I know you can, and that's the way I want you to be for the time being. If you're going somewhere, I want to know where, why, and with whom."

"I always do that."

"Good. Keep it up. If you see anything or anyone who strikes you as strange, you tell me immediately. Okay?"

"I can send you a Wickr message!"

I winced. "No more Wickr. I don't even have it on my new phone."

Ali seemed disappointed and was quiet the rest of the way to school.

But when I pulled up in front of the building, he looked at me with an expression that shouldn't be on the face of a ten-year-old.

"Are we going to be okay, Dad?"

CHAPTER 67

CHIEF OF DETECTIVES BREE STONE checked the black tape across her badge before striding to the lectern in the muster room in DC Metro's headquarters downtown.

The seats were filled with her hand-picked team of detectives, including Alex Cross and John Sampson. There were also liaison agents present from the Bureau of Alcohol, Tobacco, and Firearms and from the FBI, one of whom was Ned Mahoney.

Bree scanned the room a moment while she organized her thoughts, and she did not allow herself to dwell on the fact that her boss, Metro chief of police Bryan Michaels, was standing at the back of the room with his arms crossed. Ever since he'd given her the job, Chief Michaels had put pressure on her to perform.

Early on, she'd thought his expectations had been unrealistic, but she'd learned to accept his tight scrutiny as part of her job. If she was going to oversee the city's biggest cases, then Michaels was going to oversee her.

"Good morning," Bree said, quieting the room. "I appreciate you all coming here on such short notice."

She spotted an empty chair. "Does anyone know where Ron Dallas is?"

"I've called three times but he hasn't answered," his partner, Elaine Conrad, replied.

"We'll move on without him, then," she said, and she pressed a button on her laptop. A recent photograph of Officer Nancy Petit in uniform came up on a screen to her left.

"As you know, Nancy Petit was one of our finest patrol officers. You've read her file, you've read the multiple letters of commendation she received in a few short years, and you understand the loss. Not only to her family and to her fiancé, Bill, but to this department. We truly have lost one of our finest."

Bree paused, then she leaned into the microphone and, in her command voice, she said, "This will not stand. I want to be clear. *This will not stand.* We will do everything in our power to bring to justice whoever was responsible for those frozen heads and the bomb that took Nancy Petit's life."

She paused again, sensing the room shift from anger to resolve, which was what she wanted. Bree locked eyes with Chief Michaels and nodded before continuing.

"We have a target suspect," she said. "As you know, he calls himself M."

Bree brought the entire task force up to speed on the long history of M, from the first letter to Alex to the text that came in the wake of the bomb explosion that had taken Officer Petit's life.

Sampson said, "So we're operating on the assumption that M is responsible for the heads *and* the bomb?"

"Given the timing of the text, I think it's a reasonable place to start."

Alex said, "More than reasonable. It's him or people working for him."

Mahoney raised his hand. "Any IDs on the heads?"

"The ME's checking dental records and DNA on all of them," Bree said. "But figuring out who they are is going to take time."

A BATF agent named Fred Allen introduced himself and said his men had taken pieces of the bomb and samples of the chemical residue in the old printing plant to the lab and were forwarding samples to the FBI lab at Quantico.

Mahoney promised full cooperation but also gently reminded Bree that because M's crimes crossed many state lines and almost certainly involved kidnapping, the FBI would direct the hunt for him.

"Absolutely," Bree said. "But we are going to work this case hard, and we will share everything we find."

Chief Michaels took a few steps forward. A big, rawboned man, Michaels had been a U.S. Army Ranger in a previous life and carried it within him.

"We have no description of this M?" he asked. "No one's ever seen him?"

Bree said, "Not to my knowledge. Dr. Cross, is that correct?"

CHAPTER 68

I THOUGHT ABOUT THAT FOR a moment and then said, "I can't say positively that I've seen M, but I have absolutely seen someone who claims to be in contact with M. We call him Pseudo-Craig because he looks a heck of a lot like Kyle Craig, or what Kyle Craig might have looked like had he not had plastic surgery and had he lived."

Chief Michaels squinted at me. "You have a picture of Pseudo-Craig?"

"We do," Bree said and gave her laptop a command. The stills I'd gotten from the detention center appeared on the screen.

The chief said, "I can't remember what Craig looked like."

Bree typed and said, "I can show you the last known photo of him."

A third picture appeared, this one taken when Craig was first processed into the U.S. Federal Bureau of Prisons system. Despite the prison jumpsuit and the handcuffs, he sneered arrogantly at the camera.

"That *is* an incredibly close resemblance," Michaels said. "You're sure there's no way it could be Craig? What if he hadn't gotten his face changed?"

"He did."

"How do you know?"

"Craig told me. He mocked me with it right up until the time I saw him blown up."

"Still doesn't answer my question," Chief Michaels said. "Did you do DNA testing on whatever was left?"

Bree said, "I was there, Chief. He had a different face, but it *was* Kyle Craig. We didn't need to do any DNA testing."

Chief Michaels said, "Well, I think we need to do it now, don't you?"

I said, "I think we should. Just deal with it and get it done. But I'm telling you, there is zero doubt in my mind that the real Kyle Craig is dead."

Ned Mahoney said, "I'll submit the necessary

paperwork to exhume what's left of him, but it will take a few days."

Bree ordered detectives back to the neighborhood where the bomb went off, all of them armed with pictures of Pseudo-Craig. The BATF promised a preliminary assessment of the bomb by day's end, and the meeting broke up.

I was getting ready to leave with Sampson when a female FBI agent who'd been sitting behind Mahoney came up to me. She was in her early forties with short brunette hair and a no-nonsense style.

"Kim Tillis," she said, shaking my hand. "It's an honor to finally meet you, Dr. Cross. It turns out we have a mutual acquaintance."

"Oh? Who's that?"

"Marty Forbes," she said. "Once upon a time he was my partner."

"Okay?"

"I had a lot of problems with the guy, but—and this is not a popular position within the Bureau—I think Marty is innocent."

"As a matter of fact, I do too."

Tillis seemed both relieved and confused. "Chief Stone didn't mention Marty."

"Come again?"

"Marty said he's been contacted by M multiple times."

"It must have slipped Chief Stone's mind."

The veteran FBI agent raised her eyebrow and tilted her head toward her shoulder before saying, "And see? That's the key, I think."

"The key to what?"

Tillis twirled her finger around. "This whole thing. I tried to tell Mahoney, but he wouldn't listen when I told him to focus on Marty's case. Still, it's what my gut says will lead us to M, especially with all the headless bodies on that yacht and now these heads in play."

That took me aback for a moment, but then it made total shocking sense.

CHAPTER 69

SAMPSON, BREE, SPECIAL AGENT TILLIS, and I hustled into the DC Medical Examiner's office early that afternoon.

Every single one of us was a seasoned veteran of law enforcement. But none of us looked forward to what we were about to do. Dr. Stacy Abbott, a senior ME, buzzed us through and led us down a hallway past the three autopsy rooms.

In nearly every morgue I've been in, there's a distinct disinfectant odor in the air and an odd array of lights, some soft, others harsh, alternating in a way that throws me off a little and makes me slightly nauseated even before I confront a corpse.

I've learned to live with the feeling because, in

a murder investigation, a morgue is where the dead still speak. It takes a gifted pathologist like Dr. Abbott to hear them. But more often than not, their bodies will yield valuable information in homicide cases.

"How many have you examined so far?" Sampson asked Dr. Abbott before we pushed through the doors into the actual morgue.

"Several," she said.

"Similarities?" I asked.

"They were decapitated in the exact same way," said Abbott. She was in her late thirties, a little quirky, but very sharp upstairs.

The ME said the first cut was made from behind, a violent slice across the front of the neck, lateral left to right, and deep, going through the carotid, the larynx, and the esophagus to the spine. A second cut started on the right, went around the back, and joined the initial anterior wound.

The head was then twisted powerfully enough to rupture the spinal column below the sixth cervical vertebra. The exposed cord was severed to complete the process of detaching the head from the body.

"Any thoughts on the kind of knife?" Bree asked.

"A substantial one," Dr. Abbott said. "Three of the John Does in here were big men with muscular necks, and the initial cuts were still very deep. My best guess is you're looking for a stout knife handle with a razor-sharp ten- or twelve-inch scimitar blade attached. The kind of knife a butcher might use."

I closed my eyes a moment, thinking about Tanner Oates, the Meat Man. Every one of his victims had been killed by a butcher knife and then decapitated below the C6 vertebra.

"Ready?" Dr. Abbott said.

"As ready as you can be for this kind of thing," Special Agent Tillis said.

"You've never done anything like this before, have you?" Bree asked.

"A few times, but it's not on my regular diet."

"You'll do fine," Sampson said, and we followed the ME through the double doors.

The air was chilly inside the morgue, a tile-floored, rectangular space with cold lockers for bodies stacked three high the length of the room on both sides.

Abbott said, "Where do you want to start?"

"It doesn't matter," I said. "We want to look at them all."

Abbott consulted a chart, went to a locker on the right wall, and drew it open to reveal a thick, opaque plastic evidence bag with a head in it.

"Jane Doe number twenty-eight fourteen," Dr. Abbott said, lifting the head. "Female, Hispanic, roughly late twenties, brown-eyed, history of dental care."

Bree and Special Agent Tillis were looking at a laptop. They both shook their heads. "I'm not seeing her here."

After re-bagging the head and closing the locker, Abbott looked at her chart and went to another locker, this one on the lower level. She squatted down and opened it.

"John Doe number twenty-eight twenty-three," she said, removing the second head. "African-American, twenties, gold-cap incisors, two scars on the scalp."

Bree and Tillis studied the head and then the laptop. "Nope," Tillis said.

Abbott put the head back and pulled the third, an Asian male.

"Oh-for-four," Sampson said.

It got worse. None of the six heads matched any of the six headless bodies found aboard the sex traffickers' boat off Florida.

Tillis looked deflated. "I had hopes."

CHAPTER

70

BREE MOVED TOWARD THE MORGUE door as she said, "It was a good thought. But I've got places to be."

"Not yet," I said, then I looked at Dr. Abbott. "The FBI stores some of their caseload here, doesn't it?"

"They do, here and in Alexandria."

"Are there by any chance three other heads here? One female, Asian? And two males, one Caucasian, one Hispanic?"

"Yes, they're here," she said. "But technically, we should have written permission for you to examine them."

"I was there when all three of those heads were

discovered, working as a special consultant to the FBI."

Special Agent Tillis and Bree nodded in support.

Sampson said, "It's true."

"They're in a separate area. I'll have to go get them."

Dr. Abbott was back quicker than I'd expected, pushing a metal cart holding the three heads: the Asian female head put in our car during the Diane Jenkins kidnapping investigation, the male Caucasian head put in the locker in the subbasement of Dwight Rivers's anthill, and the Hispanic male head that rolled out of Rivers's Porsche before it blew up.

Abbott opened all three evidence bags, and we stared from the heads on the cart to pictures on Tillis's laptop.

"My God," Tillis said, putting her hand to her mouth. "Marty *was* framed."

"He was indeed," I said, walking to the heads, and gesturing to each one in turn. "Carlos Octavio, Ji Su Rhee, and Gor Bedrossian."

Dr. Abbott frowned. "I don't understand."

"Sex traffickers whose corpses were found beheaded on a yacht last year. An FBI agent named Martin Forbes is being held for their murders. But now it is clear these heads were all moved around and planted by the real killer while Forbes was behind bars."

"Unless Marty had an accomplice," Sampson said.

"Who?"

"M? Pseudo-Craig? How do we know Forbes is not—"

"He's not," Agent Tillis said sharply. "This kind of savagery? Taking people's heads? That *is not* Marty Forbes. He may be guilty of a lot of things, but this is not anywhere in his makeup."

"I agree," I said. "Forbes should get out of that cell."

Tillis smiled. "That would be a start."

"There was a finger with an engagement ring and a wedding band found with the Asian woman's head, Dr. Abbott," I said. "Did it belong to Diane Jenkins?"

Dr. Abbott pulled up a file on the computer. "The rings were Mrs. Jenkins's, but no, the DNA of the finger didn't match hers. We still don't know whose finger it was."

Bree's phone buzzed. She turned away and answered.

"So who are those others?" Sampson asked. "The six heads?"

I said, "I'm betting DNA from three of them

will match the three unidentified bodies found with the bodies of these three aboard that slave ship. The others? I don't know. But there have to be open cases of headless bodies out there."

Bree turned around, upset. "That was BATF. The bomb that killed Officer Petit was radio-controlled."

It took a moment for me to digest that and consider the implications. "He was watching us," I said. "M."

"I know," Bree said, puffing her lips. "Which means he could have targeted all of us when we went through that abandoned building. But he didn't. And he didn't when I went back through the structure alone. And he didn't wait for you to be in there, Alex. M chose to detonate the bomb when Nancy Petit was in that building. Why?"

Before any of us could reply, four different telephones started chirping, buzzing, and ringing, all of it echoing through the morgue.

CHAPTER

71

WHEN SAMPSON, DETECTIVE ELAINE CONRAD, Bree, and I reached the brick-faced home in Northwest DC where Ron Dallas lived, his partner was as shaken as I'd ever seen her.

"I'm sorry, Elaine," Bree said.

"Thanks, Chief," Conrad said, and then she broke down. "Jesus..."

Bree went and put her arms around her. "I know you were partners a long time."

"Five years," the detective said, wiping at tears.

"Tell us what happened," Sampson said.

Conrad said that after her partner missed the task-force meeting that morning, she kept calling him and kept getting no answer. She'd phoned

Ron Dallas's ex-wife, his daughter, and his sometime girlfriend, but they hadn't heard from him either.

"Ron and I have keys to each other's place," Conrad said, her voice quavering. "So if we ever had to...check in and...well, he's upstairs. The little room on the left."

We donned blue booties and gloves and entered a house not unlike my own, with a center hallway and a steep staircase. Bree led the way up the stairs onto a carpeted landing.

A bathroom door was ajar in front of us. To our right, I could see through an open door into Dallas's bedroom, which was military-neat. He had spent eight years as an army MP before joining DC Metro.

Bree stepped through the doorway on our left and stopped, stricken.

"Nobody goes in until forensics has a clean shot at it," she said, looking over her shoulder at us. "M has made a major mistake."

Bree moved aside to let us peer into the shambles of Detective Dallas's home office. The mementos of a lifetime lay shattered beneath overturned bookcases, filing cabinets, and boxes.

Sprawled diagonally across the debris of what had to have been an epic brawl was the body of

Dallas, who had been a burly, skilled fighter. His face was badly battered, and he'd been strangled by a silver-and-blue silk tie cinched up tight beneath his jaw.

A note was pinned to his torn work shirt. It read: *Detective Dallas is a disgrace, a cop on the take, cutting corners, playing fast and loose with evidence, Cross. You understand that, don't you?—M*

I stared at the note and felt slightly ill. Was he saying *You understand that* offhandedly, or was he playing with me?

What did M know? How did he know it?

"One hell of a man to take out Ron Dallas in his own home," Sampson said.

"Which is why Bree's right," I said, pushing aside my concerns and gesturing inside. "M *has* made a mistake. This kind of fight means there's blood or skin or hair in there that's not Ron's—"

"He wasn't on the take," Elaine Conrad said from the first floor.

We looked down the staircase.

"Ron was clean," the dead detective's partner said. "I promise you that."

"Because if he wasn't clean, then you aren't clean, Elaine?" Bree said.

"That's right, Chief," Conrad said. "And I won't have you or anyone think that of me or of my partner. We talked about that kind of thing first day I rode with him. Dallas believed in playing by the book. It's how we rolled. No cut corners. No planted evidence. None of that."

She'd said this last bit with a trembling lower lip.

"Detective," Bree began in a softer tone.

"I'm telling you," Conrad said. "The reason this madman gives for killing my partner? It's bullshit. Ronald Dallas had his faults, but he was a stand-up cop, one hundred percent blue through and through."

CHAPTER 72

WHEN BREE AND I GOT home that evening, we tried to put the brutal parts of the day behind us. But as much as I wanted to engage with my family at the dinner table, my mind kept drifting to what Detective Conrad had said.

Ron Dallas was a stand-up cop. No cut corners. No planted evidence. One hundred percent blue.

Was I a stand-up guy? I'd cut corners. I'd planted evidence. Was I one hundred percent blue? And what would it do to me if M somehow revealed my darkest secret?

It would end me, I decided. It would destroy my reputation, certainly. My life as a consulting investigator as well. And as a psychologist?

I could not help feeling as if M had me trapped no matter what he'd meant by *You understand that, don't you?* He'd gotten into my head, put me in a state of confusion and growing anxiety.

"Dad?" Ali asked, shaking me from my thoughts. "Is someone killing police officers here in DC?"

"Two were killed."

"Why?"

"We don't know," Bree said. "But we won't stop until we do."

"And that will be enough crime talk for tonight," Nana Mama said firmly. My grandmother asked Jannie about the book she was reading for her English class.

My daughter was not ordinarily an avid reader, but she sat up, looking awed.

"*Man's Search for Meaning,*" she said. "It's about this guy in a concentration camp and how he manages to somehow see life as, I don't know, a miracle. It's hard to explain, but it's really good."

Bree's phone buzzed. She looked and it, said, "I have to take this."

She got up and left the room. I watched her go, barely hearing Ali ask Jannie about the book, thinking that M might have found the chink in my armor.

"Alex!" Nana Mama said.

I started. "What?"

She said she'd like a word with me, which was never a good sign, but I nodded and followed her into the front room after she'd told Jannie and Ali to begin cleaning up.

My grandmother waited until she heard pots banging before crossing her arms, also never a good sign. "I won't always be here."

"Really? Folks on the street say you're immortal."

That only seemed to annoy her.

"I'm serious. I need you to remember what I told you when your children were young. Meals are no time to talk about work."

I held up my hands. "Ali asked."

"And I'm asking you to shut that talk down at my dinner table and at your dinner table when I'm gone."

Rather than argue, I went and hugged her and promised to do just that to the best of my ability. For the rest of the evening I was successful at keeping my children's chatter away from the two dead police officers and my mental chatter away from M.

But after Nana Mama and the kids had gone to their rooms and after I found Bree in bed, snoring, with a book on her chest, I realized I was still too wound up to sleep. I slipped the book from her hands, turned off the light, and went to my attic office.

The air was stale. I opened the window behind my chair, thinking about Ron Dallas. *How did M get into his house? How did he manage to kill a cop as formidable as Dallas? And why? He used a remote-control bomb to take out Petit.*

My thoughts drifted to Pseudo-Craig.

I got out the file I'd started on him and opened it, seeing the stills of him from the jail security feed and remembering how strikingly he'd looked like Kyle Craig when he'd driven past me and thrown the blood balloon.

For the first time since Martin Forbes raised the idea that Kyle Craig was alive, I felt a shadow of doubt about my convictions. I tried to shake it off, tried to remember Max Siegel, the FBI agent Craig had impersonated after having his face surgically transformed in Tampa.

The face I saw on the man who died wasn't Craig's face. But it was Craig.

It was...wasn't it?

I forced myself to confront a possibility I'd been denying. What if there wasn't any facial reconstruction? What if Max Siegel, or whoever that was who blew up and burned, was just another fiction crafted by Craig? Was Kyle Craig still alive? Was he M?

I stayed up long past midnight, my brain flashing back and forth between Pseudo-Craig and my memories of the real Kyle Craig, wondering if it could be true.

Ned Mahoney had said we were at least two, maybe three, days away from being able to exhume the body that had blown up and burned on my honeymoon.

I decided I couldn't wait, closed the file with the video stills of Pseudo-Craig, and started up my laptop.

Two minutes later, I was on the web, searching for cheap flights south.

CHAPTER 73

WHEN I EXITED A RENTAL car early the following afternoon in a parking lot in a slightly seedy neighborhood in North Miami Beach, the air was so hot and humid, it reminded me of Washington DC in mid-August, meaning that it was kind of like sticking your head in a panting dog's mouth.

Sweat burst out of every pore as I walked toward a two-story, faded green office building that had seen better days. The grass and shrubs were shabbily tended. The glass front door needed cleaning.

The directory on the wall inside said the two suites on the first floor were occupied by law offices that specialized in DUI defense. One of the suites upstairs was for lease, and the other was occupied by Cana Medical Arts.

I climbed the stairs to the suite of Cana Medical Arts to find a handwritten sign on the door that said *Clinic Hours 9:00 to 12:00 and 2:30 to 5:00, Monday through Friday.*

It was ten minutes to two, forty minutes until the clinic reopened, but I was there, so I tried the doorknob. It turned and I stepped into an empty, dimly lit reception area.

The front desk was unmanned, and the area behind it equally dim. I was about to call out when I heard snoring from down the hallway.

I followed the sound of the snoring and reached an office lit by a single lamp sitting on a large wooden desk. Behind the desk, a heavyset man in a rumpled blue shirt and jeans was sleeping in his chair, bare feet up on the desk.

His toes were positioned right under the lamp, as if he'd put them there for warmth. Unfortunately, the light revealed toenails that were long, abnormally thick, and yellowish with dark streaks, as if they were infected with something fungal.

I curled a lip at that distasteful sight but got out my ID, walked in, sat in the chair opposite him, and knocked on his desk. He didn't stir, so I knocked louder.

He woke mid-snort, flailed, and almost fell over backward, then he heaved his feet off the desk and lurched forward in his chair, looking befuddled. He had a jowly face, wrinkled, tobacco-colored skin, and bloodshot eyes and he appeared to be in his late sixties, though I knew for a fact he was only fifty-one.

The man's eyes widened and focused on me. He leaned back in alarm. "What is this?" he said. "Who are you?"

"I'm a detective, and I'd like to ask you a few questions."

Dr. Julius Bombay got angry and started sputtering. "Will this never end? I have paid my fines and endured the penalties and indignities. Enough already!"

"I'm not here about you losing your license to perform surgery, Dr. Bombay," I said. "I'm here about an old client of yours."

The disgraced plastic surgeon's entire demeanor changed. He quieted and studied me closely. "Who do you work for?" he asked. "I sense you're not real law enforcement."

"Try me. I'm here about Kyle Craig."

"I don't know who you're talking about," he said, taking his eyes off me and opening a desk drawer.

"He knew you. He told me you gave him a whole new face. This was back when you were operating at night and under the radar to fund your gambling addiction."

Dr. Bombay came up with a pistol and aimed it at my chest.

CHAPTER 74

I LOOKED AT THE PISTOL, a stout Remington 1911, probably .45 caliber. In the right hands, it was probably deadly.

But Dr. Bombay's gun trembled like his voice when he said, "Whoever you are, get out! This is persecution!"

I put up my hands and stood. "I'm not looking to pin another illegal cut job on you, Doctor. I'm just looking for corroboration that you did give Kyle Craig a new face."

He leaned across the desk and shook the gun at me. "Get out!"

"Calm down," I said, starting to pivot. "I'm going."

The instant I saw him begin to retract the

weapon, I spun back and smashed the inner wrist of his gun hand so hard, he howled in pain. The pistol went flying and disappeared behind him with a clatter.

"Asshole," he said. He looked miserably at his wrist, then up at me in alarm, and then he dropped behind the desk.

Knowing he was after the gun, I came around behind him, grabbed him by the shirt collar, and jerked him to his feet. I spun him around and drove my right fist into his solar plexus.

Dr. Bombay doubled over, his eyes bugging out, weird choking noises erupting from his throat. I guided him around into the chair I'd been sitting in, then went back behind the desk, found the gun, and unloaded it.

By the time I was done, he'd almost regained his breath.

"It's an easy question, so I want an easy answer," I said. "Did you give Kyle Craig a new face? The face of an FBI agent named Max Siegel?"

He shrugged. "I don't know. Maybe? Jesus, man, whoever you are, we didn't use names. I didn't want to know names. If I knew names, I could give them to people like you, so no names. Ever. Get it?"

I showed him the still shot from the jail-security footage. "You ever see him?"

Dr. Bombay leaned forward to look and then shook his head. “No. I mean, maybe, but I don’t remember much about their faces beforehand. It’s the after shot I always treasured.”

“What about an after shot? Is there one in your old files? I know the approximate date you would have operated on him.”

His eyebrows raised. “Well, that might have worked, actually. But all my old records were in a storage unit in Tampa until the last hurricane tore the place apart.”

“Dr. Bombay?”

A young woman with purple hair was standing in the doorway. She looked from me to the pistol and bullets on the desk to the doctor.

“Yes, Emma,” he said.

“Your patient is here.”

He shifted his gaze to me. “As you’ve heard, duty calls.”

The doctor said this with such an air of resignation that I nodded.

He sighed, getting to his swollen bare feet. “Emma, where are my sandals?”

Emma glanced at his feet. Her nostrils flared in revulsion, but then she pointed at a corner and moved aside to let me leave.

CHAPTER

75

I'M SURE I'VE BEEN TO worse airports than Miami International, but I can't remember when.

I didn't notice the problems as much when I flew in, but trying to depart, I waited for almost an hour to clear security, and I found most of the toilets broken and the floors filthy. There weren't enough benches or chairs, and the service people were deeply unhappy; some were downright rude. It put me in an even fouler mood than I'd been in when I left Dr. Bombay's office. I still had no answers to any of my questions, including whether Kyle Craig had indeed had his face surgically altered to match that of a missing FBI agent.

I'd hoped Dr. Bombay could prove that my idea that Craig might still be alive was wrong. But getting off my flight home, I felt no closer to doing that.

I grabbed a cab, gave an address a block from my house, and waited until I was on the Fourteenth Street Bridge before putting the battery back in my burn phone. When I turned it on, I found eight phone messages and eight texts waiting for me.

My phone rang before I could listen to or read any of them. John Sampson.

"Where the hell are you, Alex?" he asked after I'd said hello. "You haven't been answering your phone."

"I needed to disconnect for a few hours."

"Uh-huh," he said. "Okay, well, whatever. Can you receive text pics wherever you are?"

"I'm almost home, and yes."

"It'll take only a minute. I'll send them and call you back."

Stuck in traffic ten minutes later, I felt the phone buzz. I dug it out and glanced at the two pictures. I felt a blinding headache coming on.

Pseudo-Craig had been caught on-camera, in color, both in profile and straight on. He wore jeans, a tan leather jacket, no sunglasses, tooled cowboy boots, and a white baseball cap on backward.

My phone rang.

"You see him?"

"Couldn't miss him. Where was he?"

"Union Station. Four o'clock yesterday afternoon. Those are only two taken from the security footage, but I've looked at all of it, and...it's like he wants to be seen, Alex."

"Okay?"

"He deliberately walked in front of at least four cameras."

"Where'd he go after that?"

"We lost him when he dropped down the escalators to the Metro station. The cameras there were being repaired."

Of course they were. I groaned inwardly.

"What's he up to, Alex?"

"Let me think on it," I said. "I'll call you back."

The phone buzzed the moment I hung up. A text from Ned Mahoney:

We've got the federal court order to exhume Craig's remains tonight. I figure you'll want to be there.

CHAPTER 76

Quantico, Virginia

DRIZZLING RAIN AND FOG SWEPT over small black gravestones engraved with alphanumeric codes set flush in the forest floor.

Darkness had long fallen on that remote and piney part of the Marine Corps base, an area not specifically denoted on any map of the vast federal property, an anonymous graveyard in the trees created for criminals whose pasts were so evil, their families had declined to claim their bodies for proper burial.

Mahoney, two other FBI agents, three cemetery workers, and I were there, all of us dressed in rain slickers and rubber boots and waving flashlights, looking for B157, the code on the marker above the supposed remains of Kyle Craig.

"Why aren't they in order?" I asked.

One of the workers, an older man named Cecil who walked with a slight stoop, said, "The Marine commandant who authorized this burial ground after the Civil War wanted to make sure there would be no shrines to the dead here. Make them as difficult as possible to locate. Especially A-one."

I took my eyes off gravestone C42. "Who's under A-one?"

He hesitated, then said quietly, "John Wilkes Booth."

I frowned. "Lincoln's assassin? I thought he was buried in some cemetery in Baltimore under a blank gravestone that people cover with Lincoln pennies."

Cecil shook his head. "Family didn't want nothing of him. That headstone in Baltimore is over his sister's grave. Booth's here. He's the reason for this unholy place."

"Who else?"

"Can't say, but a bunch. People think they're

buried somewhere else, and there are headstones and all, but the truth is, most cemeteries don't want someone notorious or wicked defiling sacred ground. They send the real remains here. No one's the wiser."

I had never heard of this graveyard, not even during my days working on the base with the FBI's Behavioral Analysis Unit. I was fascinated. "C'mon," I said, glancing around. "Who else is in these woods?"

Cecil looked away.

"I promise it will be between us."

He hesitated but then said in a low voice, "You're within about thirty yards of all that remains of Oswald and of Ruby."

I gaped at him. "Lee Harvey Oswald? JFK's killer? Here? And Jack Ruby, Oswald's assassin?"

"John Wayne Gacy's not far either. Real hall of shame."

Before I could reply, Mahoney called out, "Here it is. I've got him."

Ned was three rows away, crouched down and shining the beam of his Maglite at the ground. "Bring the big lights and the digger over."

An FBI agent fired up a pickup truck carrying a bank of construction lights. Cecil crawled into a Bobcat earthmover with a backhoe arm.

I didn't watch Cecil drive. I was looking all around as the fog swirled off on a stiffening breeze and the true rain came on.

Booth. Oswald. Ruby. Gacy.

And only God and Cecil knew who else was in the ground there.

As I walked to Mahoney, I admit it was disturbing—okay, downright eerie—to know that I was stepping over the bones of psychopaths, assassins, and other cold-blooded murderers.

A worker used a pinch bar to pry up the headstone and then set it aside. Cecil was a master of the Bobcat and soon had the blade and teeth of the bucket digging down through last year's pine needles and into the wet red clay below.

It was pouring rain when the bucket hit metal, the heavy clank echoing up out of the hole. The other workers used a wooden ladder to climb down into the hole with a spade and two lengths of chain. In short order, they had the chains around a simple steel coffin and linked to the head of the bucket. Cecil toggled the controls. The box rose effortlessly, then swung and dangled above the hole.

"Small enough for a kid," Mahoney said, shaking his head.

I flashed back to the last time I'd seen the man I believed to be Kyle Craig alive, just before his miserable life exploded and burned.

"There wasn't much left of him," I said. "Two charred arms and a leg."

CHAPTER 77

I GOT HOME JUST BEFORE midnight, chilled and desperate for a hot shower and bed. Bree was up waiting in our room. She said nothing when I walked in, but her expression spoke volumes.

"I know I should have called," I said. "But I texted you that I had to go to Quantico."

Bree, stone-faced, didn't answer.

I went over and sat on the edge of the bed. "Look, I had to go somewhere today, talk to someone, and I had to do it in somewhat of a strong-arm manner. I did not want you involved in any way whatsoever, so I did not tell you where I was going, and I kept my phone off. I did not tell anyone where I was going. And when I got back, Ned called me to Quantico and took me to a place that isn't even supposed to exist."

She didn't reply for several moments, then said, "So there *is* a part of Alex Cross that his beloved wife is not allowed to know about."

I could see there was no good way out of this situation. I surrendered and told her about Dr. Bombay and then about the graveyard at Quantico.

"John Wilkes Booth?"

"I had the same reaction," I said.

Her hard expression was gone, replaced by genuine interest.

"What about Ted Bundy? Is *he* there?"

"We'd have to track down a groundskeeper named Cecil to know for sure, but I'd give it better than even odds that he is."

Bree shook her head. "That's incredible. And no one knows about this?"

"A select few."

"Do you think Craig's remains are in the box?"

"I'm so cold and tired, I don't know what to think."

"Poor baby," she said. "Take a hot shower and come to bed."

I kissed her and said, "Thanks for understanding."

Some of the soberness returned to her face as I stood.

"Don't think for a minute I agreed with your reasons for staying silent about Miami. We're supposed to be life partners, soul mates. Much more than a team."

"I apologize, and it won't happen again."

"Then consider it forgotten," she said, and she turned out her light.

The shower was wonderful. It not only warmed my bones but washed everything from repulsive toenails to coffins off my skin and down the drain.

I climbed into bed, the day far behind me, and drifted into dreamless sleep.

When Bree and I woke up, we decided we needed a family weekend.

We took Ali to the Tidal Basin, and he rode his bike while Bree and I went for our normal Saturday-morning run. You could tell almost immediately that the training rides he'd taken with the Wild Wheels group had improved his strength and technique.

I told him so when he circled back to us.

"So I can go to that race in Pennsylvania?" he asked.

"I read the flyer you brought home, and it looks good. I'll talk to the coach, but I think you can go."

He hooted with joy and rode off as Bree and I passed under the first of the Japanese cherry trees that line the basin.

"You seeing this?" Bree said, breathing hard and pointing up at the cherry trees. "The buds look ready to burst."

"You're right. Almost a week earlier than last year."

We puffed by the Jefferson Memorial and found Ali waiting for us at the traffic light on Maine Avenue. He held up his phone, upset.

"Captain Abrahamsen crashed his bike!" he said.

"What?"

"He hit gravel on a ride yesterday on the eastern shore and went over the handlebars with his shoes clipped in to his pedals. Says his shoulder got banged up. Plus he has to go to some army base in San Antonio to work for the week."

"How do you know all this?" Bree said.

Ali said that he'd texted the captain to tell him he was going to the race and wanted to know if they could ride before then. Abrahamsen said he was sorry, but he was flying to Texas in the morning after a doctor looked at his shoulder.

"He said it's going to be at least two weeks before he can think about a bike."

"That's too bad," I said. The light turned, and

Ali took off ahead of us as we jogged across Maine and then Independence. "But when's the race?"

Ali called over his shoulder, "Four weeks?"

"There you go," Bree said. "Plenty of time for him to heal up."

The rest of the weekend, it felt like we did have plenty of time. All of us. It rained on Sunday, and we stayed inside, watching the NCAA basketball tournament and eating Nana's food.

Bree was reading in our room after I put Ali to bed. I sighed, said, "I needed this weekend. Space to be us."

"I did too," she said, putting her book on the table, clicking off the light, and coming over to snuggle.

"Good night, baby," I said, kissing her.

"Who said the weekend has to be over?" she said and kissed me back.

CHAPTER 78

IT FELT LIKE THE SUN was coming in through the window and shining right on my eyelids.

I squinted and saw it was still dark in the room. But someone outside was shining a powerful, narrow spotlight beam on me.

I threw myself over and onto the floor, yelling, "Bree!"

No answer.

The light vanished.

"Bree!"

Our bedroom door opened, and in her bathrobe, she looked out at me crouched on the floor.

"Shhh!" she said. "It's only five thirty. Everyone's still sleeping."

I hissed, "There was someone outside just now, shining a light in on me."

That changed everything. We scrambled into clothes, got our service weapons, and went outside.

Judging from the angle, we figured the light had come from the roof of the Morses' house, next door, and well above the scaffolding that workers were erecting to sandblast the exterior walls.

We knew their lockbox combo, so we got the keys and went inside, guns drawn.

The house was empty. The interior windows, walls, and floors were covered with plastic sheeting coated with sawdust. There were small piles of construction debris here and there, swept up but not removed.

We found plenty of footprints of different sizes both downstairs and upstairs and definitely in the bedrooms that had dormers overlooking the roof. The plastic sheeting over one of the dormers had been cut away. From the window, we couldn't see anyone out on the roof or any dusty footprints.

Still, the only window in the house that wasn't covered with plastic was this one.

I climbed out on the roof and moved to where I

judged the flashlight had been held. I found traces of sawdust being blown away on the breeze.

"Someone was out there," I said when I climbed back into the house. "But the evidence is disappearing fast."

We went back to our own house, and Bree said, "It was him, M, wasn't it?"

"We have to assume so."

"I hate that he's watching us."

"When I think about it, I want to punch a wall."

"What about the cameras you were talking about?"

"Ordering them today. And for this place too. I'll bill the owners."

"Do we move Nana Mama and the kids? Send them to your dad's in Florida?"

It wasn't a bad idea, though I knew it would drive all three of them nuts for various reasons. "Let me think about that."

My phone rang. Keith Karl Rollins.

"You're up early," I said.

"I need only five hours a night," the FBI cybercrime consultant sniffed. "And I thought you should be the first to know."

He left me hanging. I said, "First to know what?"

"The Ethereum cryptocurrency used to pay the ransom on Diane Jenkins started to move late last night from all those accounts. I tracked the transfers through twenty-four different stops, most of them designed to strip metadata. A few of my bugs got through, though, and you won't believe where the funny money finally ended up."

CHAPTER

79

McLean, Virginia

THE NEXT MORNING, NED MAHONEY and I drove toward a gate in a six-foot wrought-iron fence that surrounded an estate in horse country. Set well back off the road, the sprawling Colonial home was white with green shutters and trim.

"I'm still not thinking it's a good idea for you to be here, Alex," Mahoney said when the pickup truck in front of us turned and rolled up to the gate. We came in behind it.

"I disagree," I said. "I'll be the rattler of cages."

"We have a search warrant."

"Who says we have to show our cards so soon?"

"What are you hoping for?" Mahoney asked as a hand came out of the window of the pickup and pressed a button on an intercom. "A confession? 'I'm M, and I organized all the mayhem because of you, Alex Cross'?"

"That's exactly what I'm hoping for," I said. We heard a loud buzzing noise and then the gate swung open. "And if we handle this right, we just might get it and save ourselves a whole lot of time and trouble."

Ned followed the pickup through the gate and up the drive. "Do me a favor, and let me do the talking?"

"I think my presence will provide more than enough leverage."

We parked on brick pavers in a circular area surrounded by azaleas, which were beginning to bloom. A row of dogwoods lined the walkway we took to the front door. We ignored the looks from the uniformed landscaping crew and knocked.

A Latina woman in her mid-forties answered the door. Somewhere inside, classical piano music played. "Yes?"

Mahoney showed his identification. "FBI, ma'am. We'd like to speak with the lady of the house."

The woman stared at the credentials. "FBI? She's not well. I'll call her son. He lives just down the street."

"We're going to see him next, but we need to talk to her now," Ned insisted. "What's your name, by the way?"

I suppose she thought Ned wanted this information so he could check her immigration status, because she crossed her arms, lifted her chin, and said, "I am Maria Joan, and I have a green card, six years now. I will be a U.S. citizen in seven months. I study for it. And I know the laws. Fourth Amendment. You cannot make me let you in without probable cause or a search warrant."

Mahoney smiled and reached for his inner breast pocket. "Well, Ms. Joan, you are right about that. But we do have a federal search warrant. So if you don't let us in to see your boss, you could be obstructing justice."

Mahoney held the warrant up for her to see. She scanned it, nodded, and grudgingly stood aside so we could enter.

The oval foyer was slate-floored. At the center, between us and a weeping wall fountain, stood a pedestal table with a vase holding a riot of a floral arrangement that scented the air with its perfume.

We followed Maria Joan down a hallway off the

foyer, past a library, and toward the sound of the piano music into a large open space that contained a kitchen out of a glossy magazine and a living area beyond with furniture of equally high finish and taste.

There were fresh roses in two vases and a nice tea service on the round table in front of a woman sitting in a wheelchair turned slightly away from us. She was watching Bloomberg Television on a large screen set into the wall.

The volume was on mute. Piano music played from speakers.

Maria Joan went around the front of the woman, shook her lightly, and said, "You have visitors, Mrs. M."

CHAPTER 80

I ALMOST LOST MY BALANCE when Maria Joan said those words.

You have visitors, Mrs. M.

Mahoney's face had gone slack, but it firmed before he came around in front of the wheelchair with me. I stopped short at her appearance.

The last time I'd seen Margaret Edgerton, she had had the poise and polish of a wealthy and accomplished businesswoman. But the polish had gone off her in the four weeks that had passed since that day at the Greensville Correctional Center when we'd both watched her son die the cruel and barbaric death he'd chosen.

She looked exhausted and wore tinted sunglasses, a plush blue robe, and thick socks. Her hands shook slightly, and there was an air of bewilderment about her when she turned her head and peered at me and Mahoney.

"Visitors?" she said in a sleepy, slightly slurred voice. "I thought the therapists had all gone for the day, and I'm tired, Maria."

"Mrs. Edgerton, I'm Special Agent Mahoney with the FBI," Mahoney said, stepping forward with his credentials and the warrant. "You can go now, Ms. Joan."

"She won't be able to read anything you show her," she said, walking into the kitchen.

Mrs. Edgerton looked puzzled. "What's this about?"

Mahoney said, "The kidnapping of a young mom named Diane Jenkins."

The old woman wrinkled her nose and then squirmed upright.

"Kidnapping?" she said, indignant. "Me? How dare you!"

She began to cough and hack. She waved her fingers in the air.

"Please," Maria Joan said, rushing back into the

room toward an oxygen canister set on a dolly in the corner. "You've upset her, and she can't breathe now."

I was beginning to feel bad about coming.

The aide got the oxygen line below Mrs. Edgerton's nose and then snarled at us, "Can't you come back? She had a stroke three weeks ago. It damaged her vision, and she gets anxious."

Now I felt really bad, but I said to Mahoney, "Tell her *exactly* why we came."

Mrs. Edgerton's head cocked and swiveled toward me. "Who else is here?"

Mahoney said, "A consultant, ma'am. But back to why we're here. The kidnapped woman's husband paid her ransom in what's called a cryptocurrency."

"I know what that is, blockchain nonsense," she snapped. "So what?"

Before Mahoney could answer, Mrs. Edgerton waved her shaky left hand in my direction. "You answer. Consultant."

"Mrs. Edgerton," Ned said. "I am in charge here."

"I don't care," she said, wheeling six or seven inches toward me. "I may be legally blind now, but I still have most of my hearing, my rights, and my wits about me. Mr. Consultant, tell me why you and the special agent are really here."

I cleared my throat and said, "The ransom money moved through hundreds of digital accounts all over the world and ended up in your personal cryptocurrency account. It landed there yesterday. All five million."

It was as if she hadn't heard. After I'd said about ten words, Mrs. Edgerton gripped the handles of her chair so hard, her knuckles turned pearly, and her face contorted into something bitter and vindictive.

"You're here to finish me off, aren't you, Cross?"

I hesitated, then said, "No, Mrs. Edgerton, I'm not."

She chortled at that. "Sure you are. You railroaded my son into that electric chair, and you'd like nothing better than to see me fry too."

"We're here about a completely different matter," Mahoney said. "Mrs. Edgerton, we have a federal warrant to seize any and all computers from your home and the Edgerton family office in Manhattan."

The old woman seemed not to hear. She strained forward in her wheelchair, looking as angry as she'd been when her son was executed.

In a harsh, cold whisper she said, "I told you

that you would burn in hell, Cross. Do you remember that?"

"I do. Are you M, Mrs. Edgerton?"

"Don't answer that!" a man behind us roared. "Mom, do not say another damned word, and you two are out of here. I don't care if you are FBI. You don't barge into my invalid mother's house and start asking her questions without counsel."

We'd both turned to see a bull of a man in his fifties coming at us across the kitchen. He was balding, fit, and wearing a hooded sweatshirt and workout gear. I remembered him from the execution.

"Peter Edgerton?" Mahoney said. "We have a warrant for your house too."

That stopped Mrs. Edgerton's older son in his tracks. "My house? For what? And what the hell do you think you're going to find in my mother's computers? She hasn't used one since the stroke!"

"Ransom money demanded by kidnappers ended up in your mother's crypto account," Mahoney said.

"Pete!" Mrs. Edgerton shouted. "I don't even have an account like that."

"Yes, you do, Mom," her son said sharply.

"What?"

"We'll talk about it later," he said. He studied us. "Are you bullshitting me? Did that crypto really go into *her* specific account?"

"It did."

"Then someone out there hacked it and sent it there, the real kidnappers."

"What would be the point of that?" I asked.

Peter Edgerton seemed to notice me for the first time, and his entire demeanor changed.

"No way," he said. He looked at Mahoney. "You get this son of a bitch out of my mother's house or I promise you, I'll spend every dime of my personal crypto fortune to sue you both into oblivion."

"Mr. Edgerton," Mahoney said.

"Get him out of my house, Pete!" his mother shouted.

Her son struggled to control himself as he glared at Mahoney. "If Cross goes, out of here completely, off the property, we'll cooperate, let you look at my house, my brother's place, the family office, whatever. I promise you we're not involved."

Mahoney looked at me and gestured with his head toward the door.

I left without argument. I heard Pete Edgerton

say in a soothing voice, "He's gone, Mom. He's never coming back."

I was heading toward the front door when his mother shouted, "You're still going to burn, Cross! No matter what you do, you're still going to burn for what you did to Mikey!"

CHAPTER 81

AS I WALKED DOWN THE driveway toward the gate, I decided there wasn't any point in my sticking around outside while Mahoney and his men conducted the search.

And I was having serious doubts that Mrs. Edgerton was physically capable of being M. Her brain seemed largely intact, but the stroke had left her all but blind, and she had serious respiratory issues.

Pete?

Now, that was a real possibility. Pete had the motivation to be M. He also had the money, and at least part of it was in largely untraceable cryptocurrency.

Or was there a conspiracy between mother and son? If it was a shared obsession, two hearts loathing as one, I could almost wrap my head around the Edgertons' putting revenge ahead of their personal fortunes, lives, and freedom.

Almost.

My doubts all stemmed from one question: Why would they be involved in a kidnapping in Ohio?

No answer I could come up with made sense. I walked through the gate and pulled out my phone to request an Uber to take me back into the city.

My phone buzzed in my hand. A text from FBI Special Agent Kim Tillis:

Going to Alexandria detention center at noon to tell Marty. See you there to deliver good news for a change?

It was ten past eleven, so I texted back: I will be there.

An innocent man freed. The thought made me smile in a way that putting the cuffs on someone guilty did not. This felt lighter, selfless, not like atoning for the dead at all.

That feeling was still building when I got out of the Uber at the appointed hour and spotted Agent Tillis beside a younger, chipper-looking woman in a navy-blue suit.

Sandra Wendover smiled and shook my hand after Tillis introduced her as an attorney with the federal public defenders' office.

"I'm so happy, Dr. Cross," Wendover said, still smiling. "We don't often get to make this kind of visit to an inmate."

I grinned back. "It does feel good."

Tillis teared up. "It's like we're bringing Marty the best present ever."

We went through the doors to the security checkpoint. I got out my identification and was ready to pass my shoes through the scanner when a woman called out, "Dr. Cross?"

I looked up to see Estella Maines, the sheriff's deputy.

"Did you get the message I sent over your way Friday?" she asked.

"My way?"

"To Metro PD."

"Oh, I'm only a consultant there these days."

"Well, the fingerprints you asked us to take of Dirty Marty's visitor? The guy in the stills from the security feed? We got a hit. He's an ex-con. We got him cold."

My heart raced. Finally, we were getting a break.

Before I could reply, Kim Tillis said, "Deputy, for the record, Martin Forbes is not dirty. He was unequivocally framed, and we've come to get him freed."

Deputy Maines didn't know what to make of that and she looked at me.

"It's true. The guy in the security stills was in on the scheme to put Forbes behind bars. Who is he? What's his name?"

CHAPTER 82

FORBES'S FORMER PARTNER AND HIS ATTORNEY went in to give him the good news. But after I'd learned the real name and most recent address of the man we called Pseudo-Craig, I'd decided not to go with them. I told them to give Marty my sincere best, and I left.

The first thing I did was call Keith Karl Rawlins to tell him to start digging. Then I called Ned Mahoney and told him to meet me in the lab beneath the FBI's cybercrimes unit at Quantico.

Mahoney was already there when I pulled open the lab's glass door and was met with the thudding techno dance music Rawlins listened to when he was working.

The cyber expert was sitting at his keyboard facing an array of six screens. Ned was standing behind him. I tapped Mahoney on the shoulder and he jumped.

"I didn't hear you come in," he said, almost shouting, and then he pointed to the silicon earplugs he'd stuffed into his ears.

Rawlins's head was bobbing to the beat, but at that point, he stopped and shut off the music. He looked over his shoulder at me as if he'd expected to see me there and then gestured with his chin toward my phone. "It's clean now. You can take it."

I picked the phone up off the bench, put it in my pocket, and said, "What about Nolan?"

"Oh, I've got a bunch of stuff on him already."

"Tell me," I said, coming closer. "And let's lose the techno soundtrack. I've already had a ridiculously long day."

Rawlins didn't like that, but he shrugged. "Your loss."

He gave his keyboard an order and up popped a digital rap sheet on one William Nolan, age forty-six, address in Encino, California.

"Look at him!" Mahoney said. "He is an absolute dead ringer for Kyle Craig."

"From all three angles," I said, shaking my head.

"But I ran Nolan's prints against Craig's old prints. Not even close to a match."

There it was, then, finally. Kyle Craig was still a dead man, and I wasn't crazy.

I let that make me feel better about things and listened intently as Rawlins gave us a summary of what he'd found. Nolan had been a stuntman and a B-movie actor in Hollywood until he'd developed a taste for cocaine, which got him involved in burglary and then grand theft auto.

The latter move had gifted him with a three-year swing in the California Institution for Men at Chino. Nolan had served his term and left prison four years ago.

There was a phone number for his parole officer, whom we caught at her desk. She called Nolan a model parolee. After his release, he'd worked in a car wash and then for a company that dealt with contamination on construction sites.

"Where would we find him?" Mahoney asked.

"The company's offices in Encino," she said.

But when we called, we learned that Nolan had quit his job six weeks before. He'd told coworkers he was getting back into the film business, that he'd gotten the role of a lifetime.

When we hung up the phone, Rawlins jumped

up from his console, flipped on the techno, and started pumping his fist overhead.

"You're killing me with this music," Mahoney said. "Nuke it."

The FBI contractor rolled his eyes and turned it off. "You know the problem with most Americans and definitely most FBI agents, Special Agent Mahoney?"

"Do tell," Ned said, crossing his arms.

"They're all stick and no carrot," he said. "They drive themselves day and night, but when they score, they don't celebrate. I believe in celebrating every victory, especially one as big as this."

"So let us in on the reason for the celebration," I said.

Rawlins smiled. "William Nolan has a bank account and two high-interest credit cards, the kind given to risky creditors like ex-cons."

"He use them?"

"Six weeks ago, he bought a ticket for a flight from LA to New York, then a train ticket to DC, and then twenty-two nights at a one-star in Gaithersburg called the Regal Motel. Snap! Eat the carrot, Cross! You've got him now!"

CHAPTER 83

Gaithersburg, Maryland

THE REGAL MOTEL WAS ANYTHING BUT.

For $22.00 an hour, $62.50 a night, and $213.00 a week, you could stay in a room that stank of stale cigarette butts and beer and featured threadbare rugs and bedcovers with suspicious-looking stains.

Hookers had used the place for tricks until the Montgomery County sheriff had cracked down a few years back. According to the desk clerk, the residents these days were homeless people, addicts, or women trying to hide from abusive spouses.

"We've got three or four of those, and their kids," the clerk, Souk, told me, Sampson, Bree, and Mahoney. She was a bright young woman who was taking night classes at American University. Souk nodded over her shoulder at photographs of men thumbtacked to the wall. "Any of them come in the drive, I call the sheriff," she told us. "They all have restraining orders against them, and I got copies."

"Good for you," I said. "Have you seen this man around?"

I pushed the still shot from the detention-center security feed across the counter to her.

"Sure," the clerk said. "Short, sandy-blond hair. Five ten, one seventy. Slips in and out of thirty-nine B. Pays weeks in advance."

"You sound like you studied him," Mahoney said.

"I study everyone who comes in while I'm working. I want to be able to testify if something bad happens here, which is bound to happen. Just the odds, you know?"

"Well, we're glad you're on duty, Souk," Bree said. "Is he here?"

She shrugged. "I just came on shift, and like I said, he kind of slips in and out. You catch glimpses of him."

"No car?"

"If he has one, it is not here. He says he's using the buses. Why? What's he done?"

"We just want to talk to him," Mahoney said. "Is there another way out of thirty-nine B?"

"A window in the bathroom to the back roof. But it's at least a thirty-foot drop."

"No fire escape?"

She shook her head. We moved outside, split up, and climbed to the motel's third floor. Bree and Sampson came at Nolan's room from the west. Ned and I slid toward 39B from the east. All four of us drew our weapons and stood on either side of the door. Mahoney knocked sharply. No response.

Mahoney knocked harder. "William Nolan, open up. This is the FBI."

For a moment, there was silence, and I thought Ned was going to use the key the desk clerk had given us. Then we heard the soft squeak of an old bed frame.

Mahoney shouted, "Mr. Nolan, we are—"

Inside, we heard running. A door slammed.

Ned spun the key and opened the door, which was latched with a security chain.

Sampson threw his whole weight at the door.

The chain snapped. The door fell. We swept

into the room and saw fast-food wrappers, empty booze bottles, and an open duffel stuffed with clothes on the unmade bed. A cigarette burned in the ashtray.

Sampson motioned to the shut bathroom door at the rear right of the room.

He slammed on the door with his fist. “Nolan, open this door.”

There was no answer, and Sampson broke down that door too.

The bathroom window was up, revealing a narrow roof.

I went to the window, stuck my head out, and saw Nolan, looking for all the world like Kyle Craig’s twin. He wore a camo knapsack and was crouched twenty feet to my left, six steps back from a thirty-foot drop into woods.

I shouted, “Nolan! Don’t do it!”

But he did.

CHAPTER 84

THE FORMER STUNTMAN SPRANG FROM his crouch, took four strides, and drove off his right foot. He exploded off the edge of the roof, legs and arms pumping as he fell.

I didn't want to see him die, so I averted my eyes and waited for the thud.

Instead, I heard a sound like a gunshot. I looked up, out, and down, and there he was—not on the ground but twenty feet above it, hanging on to a stout but cracked and cracking limb sticking out of a big pine in the woods behind the motel.

I spun around. "He's in a tree!"

Bree had been at the back, and now she led the way out of the motel room.

"How in God's name did he do that?" Mahoney said.

"Fear or lunacy," Sampson muttered.

"I'm calling the sheriff for backup," Bree called, scrambling down the stairs.

Mahoney took charge and shouted for me to go around the east side and for Sampson to go around the west. He and Bree would get the vehicles we came in.

Souk, the desk clerk, was by the office door. She looked worried as I raced past her and shouted, "What's in back of this place?"

"Trees and a swamp?"

"And after that?" I called over my shoulder.

"No idea."

Over the earbud I wore, I could hear Bree calling for backup as I ran along the side of the motel. The way was choked by weeds and vines. Thorns tore at my skin and clothes. There was trash everywhere.

I got to the rear corner of the building, gun up, and peeked around it fast. The trashy thicket went the entire length of the motel. Dead center of that space, a good twenty feet from the Regal's rear wall and eight feet up the pine tree, Nolan was looking over his shoulder right at me.

For a split second, I saw sheer terror in his eyes,

as if he saw clearly who was pursuing him. Then he launched backward out into space and managed a quarter turn before hitting the ground in something like a parachutist's roll. He grunted in pain, but rolled over onto his hands and knees and then scrambled over the bank out of my sight.

"He's heading north into the swamp," I barked into my radio as I fought forward through the thorny vines and trash.

At the other end of the building, Sampson was doing the same. But there were old mattresses, abandoned refrigerators, and other no-tell-motel relics piled up and blocking his way.

Bree's voice crackled over my earbud. "Sampson, go east. You'll hit a north/south road."

"Copy."

"I'll stay on him," I said into the mike at my collar.

When I reached the spot where Nolan had disappeared, I could tell where he'd gone into the mud from the busted skunk-cabbage leaves and bent little saplings.

I slid on my butt down the steep bank. My athletic shoes sank in the mud when I hit the bottom. They almost came off when I lurched up and tried to gain ground on Nolan. The going was tricky, solid earth one step and then six inches of oozing mud the next, a veil of vegetation ahead of me.

In the distance, I thought I heard thunder, and I noticed the sky clouding fast.

"How wide is this swamp?" I said, breathing hard.

"Maybe three-quarters of a mile?" Bree said.

"Then what?"

"State route. Major artery."

"Close it off."

"Already asked."

"I'm heading there right now," Mahoney said.

Sirens began to wail far away. The wind was picking up, the clouds gathering.

I reached an opening where the swamp became more of a slough marsh for sixty yards. And there Nolan was, flailing and crawling out the other side of the wetland, caked in mud and swamp grass.

The marsh grass grew in dense, tightly clustered clumps with spiky flowered heads above the water. I jumped to one clump, wobbled for a moment, and then hopped to another.

Luck and stability were with me almost all the way across the slough. But right at the end, with maybe six feet to go, I lost my footing and sprawled on my face in the goop.

I crawled and flailed up the far bank just as Nolan had. I wiped the mud from my eyes and kept on, seeing that he was leaving mud tracks that I could follow.

Suddenly I was aware of engines revving somewhere ahead, gears shifting, and then the clank and scrape of metal on rock.

"Is there a big machine working out there?" I called. "Am I near that highway?"

No answer. When I'd gone into the slough water, my mike must have died.

The machines grew louder. But where was the sound of traffic? I should have been hearing tires whine and the sigh of air brakes.

Two minutes later, the thicket thinned before a large, clear-cut area. Hundreds of pine-tree trunks were stacked to my left beside a flatbed trailer. Two white Chevy pickups were parked to my right about seventy yards. Beyond the trucks, three men in hard hats stood with their backs to me watching a bulldozer and grader at work.

None of the men seemed to see or hear William Nolan running behind them toward a black BMW SUV parked on the far side of the clearing near a red dirt road that snaked north.

CHAPTER

85

I BOLTED FROM THE THICKET and went down the steep grade, one eye on Nolan, who was closing fast on the SUV, and the other on the three men still watching the machines working. They seemed oblivious to what was happening behind them.

As I sprinted to the men, I happened to glance through the open passenger window of one of their pickups and saw keys on the dash.

Nolan was already inside his car. I felt like I had no choice.

Less than fifteen seconds later, I threw the Chevy in gear, hit the gas, and spun the wheel, throwing dirt and gravel toward the three men, who had finally turned and were running at me.

I didn't care. Nolan had already left the construction site.

I accelerated across the clearing, bumping over ruts, just as lightning flashed overhead. The skies opened and it began to pour buckets.

If you've never driven in a mid-Atlantic spring deluge of three or even four inches an hour, I can tell you it's a disorienting event. So much rain falls so fast that your wipers can't possibly keep pace with it, and you're forced to slow to a crawl.

It was a good thing I slowed because when John Sampson suddenly jumped out in front of me from behind a debris pile, I was able to slam on the brakes and skid to a stop.

He jumped in. "Go!"

I smashed the gas pedal and we slid in the greasy mud but then found gravel and I was able to keep the truck fishtailing toward that dirt road leading out.

"How the hell did you get in front of me?" I asked, peering through the downpour.

"Road goes around the swamp." He gasped, chest heaving for air. "Saw the clearing from it and came in from the side just in time to see Nolan getting into that SUV and you running for the truck, looking like the swamp thing."

I had no time to reply or laugh because we'd

made the road, which narrowed and offered little improvement over the raw ground behind us. We bounced and slid and almost went off it twice.

"He can't outrun a truck in this muck," I said. "My mike's dead. Call Bree. Tell her what's happening."

"Chief Stone," Sampson called.

"Right here," Bree called back.

"Suspect is in a black BMW SUV, leaving a construction site on a new—"

"There he is!" I shouted.

We'd come around a curve in the road, and the BMW was sliding all over the place. I was barely keeping us on the road but I sped up. Or tried to.

Neither of us was wearing a seat belt, and we hit one rut so hard our heads smacked into the ceiling of the cab. I let up on the gas, trying to orient myself, and I realized that Nolan had slowed, not stopped, just before we were hit by a spray of mud and gravel slurry thrown by his spinning back wheels. Even with the rain pouring down, it coated our windshield in reddish brown.

I couldn't see a thing and slammed on the brakes.

"He's high-centered!" Sampson bellowed. He threw open his door and shot out, only to slip and sprawl sideways in the mucky road.

I was already exiting the other side of the truck, arm up to shield my face and head from the hail of mud and gravel, which suddenly stopped. The SUV's door flew open, and Nolan jumped out.

I started to go for my weapon, but even through the driving rain, I could see he was unarmed as he took off toward the paved road. I tried to sprint after him, but almost immediately my right foot submerged in the mud up to my calf and I went to my hands and knees.

I fought my way back to my feet, losing my right shoe when I pulled my leg free, but I was buoyed by the fact that Nolan had fallen into a low spot in the road filled with mud that looked like pudding. He'd gone in face-first and was wallowing around, trying to find his footing, while I took a wider stance and made short chopping strides toward him.

I came around the front of the vehicle. Nolan was up and staggering. Sampson was abreast of me and also charging Nolan.

It felt like old times. John and I had played high-school football together, both defensive ends. Each of us knew what the other was going to do without either of us saying it.

My feet found the far edge of the bog, and I drove off it, hurling my head and shoulders low toward the back of Nolan's legs. Sampson aimed high.

We hit the Kyle Craig lookalike at the same time and slammed the dirtbag down so hard he made something of a man-shaped crater on impact. And his flimsy knapsack tore open, revealing stacks of hundred-dollar bills inside.

CHAPTER 86

NOLAN CLAIMED WE'D BROKEN HIS knee, separated his shoulder, and cracked his ribs when we tackled him. He demanded a doctor and an attorney and then clammed up, as was his right. Mahoney took him into federal custody, and we parted with plans to meet again in the morning.

Bree drove us home. The storm had passed by the time we'd dropped Sampson at his house and parked in front of our own. I peeled myself off the passenger seat. My clothes were torn and caked in that thick copper-colored slurry.

"You look like an extra in a zombie movie," Bree said, and she chuckled.

"Feel like one," I said, rubbing my sore ribs. "I hit something hard."

We started up the porch stairs, and I barely gave the scaffolding between our house and the Morses' a second thought.

"You think Nana Mama's going to let you walk on her clean floors with you looking like that?" Bree said. "Go on around to the basement shower."

I sighed. "All right. And I'll hose off my pants before I go inside."

"Even better," she said.

I leaned to kiss her. She jumped back and laughed. "Not on your life."

"Kiss of the zombie!" I said. I threw my hands up Frankenstein-style and chased her a few feet.

Bree shrieked with laughter and then scrambled up the stairs and across the porch. She opened the front door, looked over her shoulder, grinned, stuck her tongue out at me, then went inside.

I loved seeing Bree light up like that, more girl than woman, more regular person than cop, and all because I acted like a little boy. It made me feel pretty darn good at the end of a long and complicated day that had gone sideways more than once.

But all in all, we'd made serious progress. If we didn't have M in custody, we had someone who knew him. Nolan had said as much. To me and to Marty Forbes.

The shower was long, hot, and wonderful. Dinner—roast chicken in a citrus-mustard sauce, a recipe Nana Mama had gotten from the *Rachael Ray Show*—was on the table when I entered the kitchen, feeling like a new man.

"You clean up nice," Bree said.

"Every once in a while."

"Bree said you were covered in mud," Ali said.

"Head to toe."

"I wanted a picture."

"That wasn't happening."

"Dad?" Jannie said. "Aren't you going to ask me how my first day back went?"

I'd completely forgotten. "School. Yes. How are you feeling?"

She sat up straighter and smiled. "Pretty good, actually. Those vitamins really do work after a while."

"No tiredness during the day?"

"Just once, in study hall. I put my head down and took a ten-minute nap. When do you think I can start training again?"

My grandmother said, "I know you're champing at the bit, but the last thing you need is a relapse."

Jannie looked glum.

I said, "Nana's right, and you know it. So, let's say the rest of this week, you stay on that vitamin regimen and stretch all you want while we see how you do at school. Things go well, you can start to run next week."

My daughter chewed the inside of her cheek before saying, "So, right now, I'm, what, twelve weeks from the first of those meets?"

"Sounds right, but you have to take it easy, no pushing hard out of the gate."

"But I like to push hard out of the gate," Jannie said with a playful moan.

"And you will," Bree said. "In twelve weeks."

Jannie held up both palms. "I officially surrender."

"Sometimes you have to surrender in order to fight another day," Nana Mama said.

"Who said that?" Ali asked.

"I did," my grandmother said. "Just now."

"You should write that down, Nana," he said.

"No, *you* should write that down," she said.

Ali stared off into space for a second and was about to say something when his phone dinged. He pulled it out and looked at the screen, and a smile bloomed softly on his face.

"See?" my grandmother said. "They can't keep their attention off their screens and on real life.

I say write that down, but then—ping!—off he goes."

Ali stuffed his phone back in his pocket, got up, and grabbed a notebook and a pen. "No, Nana, I'm going to write down all the stuff you say, and we'll put it up on Twitter once a day. You know, like, hashtag-crazy-good-stuff-my-great-grandma-says."

There was dead silence for a moment and then Jannie started laughing. "That could work!"

"Right!" Ali said, holding up his fist in triumph. "Nana Mama goes viral!"

My grandmother stared at both of them as if they'd lost their minds, which caused Bree and me to start laughing. It took only a few moments before Nana started to chuckle with us. "Honestly, I have no idea what's so funny," she said, "but it doesn't matter. A good laugh will keep you from going toes up and six feet under."

"Write that down!" Jannie cried, and we started laughing all over again.

CHAPTER 87

THE FOLLOWING AFTERNOON, WILLIAM NOLAN'S attorney notified us that her client was willing to talk. Bree, John, and I were cleared through FBI security at the Bureau's downtown headquarters soon afterward.

As we rode the elevator and walked the length of several hallways, I was still hearing the mental echoes of how hard we'd laughed the night before. We'd stop and then Nana Mama would say something else, and we'd yell, "Write that one down!"

I couldn't remember having that much fun at dinner in a long time. It was all Ali had talked about that morning at breakfast before school.

He was going to write down at least thirty good Nana-isms before he "launched the hashtag."

"You get the feeling the mountain-biking bug might be over?" Bree asked now.

"I was thinking the same thing. Especially after he said he was skipping tonight's Wild Wheels ride to work on Nana Mama's social media presence."

Sampson laughed. "The kid does jump from one thing to the next."

"He's exploring," I said. "It's what kids do."

Ned Mahoney stepped out of a doorway near the end of the hall. He gestured at me, said, "Alex, you were his target, so you are observing today. If you have something you want asked, we'll hear you over the earbuds. Chief Stone?"

Bree straightened her shoulders, glanced at me with mock pity, then followed Mahoney inside. John and I went into the observation booth with Special Agent Kim Tillis, who had just arrived.

On the other side of the one-way mirror, William Nolan had his left wrist cuffed to his chair and his right arm in a sling. He was hunched over and looked miserable. I was surprised to see Sandra Wendover, the same federal public defender who'd worked on Martin Forbes's case, sitting beside him.

"Hey, c'mon," Nolan said as Bree and Ned took chairs. "I'm dying here."

"You're not dying, Mr. Nolan," Mahoney said.

"I'm in serious pain," he insisted in a hoarse whine.

Wendover said, "My client has three broken ribs, a blown ACL in his right knee, and a separated shoulder. That could be construed as brutality."

Mahoney snorted. "Except your client jumped off a roof into a tree and then took off trying to elude federal officers who were forced to subdue him."

"Who cares?" Nolan said, irritated. "Because I know for a fact I've done nothing wrong. A misdemeanor, maybe. But not something you go away for."

Mahoney said, "Well, Mr. Jailhouse Lawyer, here's a news flash for you: We are holding you as the prime suspect in a federal kidnapping-and-mass-murder investigation."

That got Nolan's attention in a big way. He rocked back in his chair, eyes big as sand dollars, then he winced and said, "Whoa! Whoa! What are you talking about?"

Wendover said, "Wait—he's involved in Martin Forbes's case?"

"He is."

"Then I must recuse, and I advise my client to stay silent until federal defenders can send over another lawyer to represent him."

"What? No," Nolan said. "No, just sit here, I'm not admitting to nothing because I didn't do anything."

Bree said, "How about cutting off people's heads? You did that, didn't you, M?"

Wendover said, "Mr. Nolan, I advise you not to answer."

Nolan shook his head violently. "I do not know what they're talking about."

"Are you M?" Mahoney asked. "Simple question."

Nolan's brow knitted. "That a name or something?"

"You know it is."

"What, like some rapper?"

"You're saying you are not M?" Bree said.

"I can say without a doubt that I am not Em or Eminem or whoever this dude is, and I have never, ever killed anyone, much less chopped off a bunch of people's heads."

On the other side of the mirror, behind Mahoney and Bree, I keyed my mike, said, "The blood he splattered on my windshield."

Bree nodded, said, "You're sure, William? Because Dr. Cross says you threw a blood balloon at his windshield out on the Beltway."

"Blood balloon?" Wendover said. "Do not answer that question, Mr. Nolan."

He ignored her. "That was fake blood, and so what? It's like a kid's prank."

"Except that wasn't fake blood," Mahoney said. "That was a blood cocktail taken from several different human beings. We haven't done the entire DNA workup yet, Mr. Nolan, but the smart money is on the blood matching the heads and, therefore, you."

Nolan lost all color and looked dazed by what he'd just been told.

"Okay," Wendover said, gathering her things and standing. "I am out of here."

"Stop!" Nolan said. "Why?"

She glared at him. "Because, Mr. Nolan, I represent an innocent man who's in jail, accused of the heinous crimes you've been involved in."

"Heinous?" he said, looking after her as she left the room. "I've never done anything heinous in my entire life!"

Wendover shut the door behind her. I was about to go out into the hallway to talk to her when Nolan said, "I admit I've done things I'm not proud of, and I did time for them, but nothing heinous. Nothing remotely heinous."

"But you can see where this is going, William," Bree said. "Your blood balloon. The heads. The bodies. You must already be fearing the day they execute you."

"Wait, now. I…" He struggled and then apparently came to a decision. "I was given the balloon. I was told the blood was fake, you know, movie-prop stuff."

In the observation booth, we all leaned forward as one.

"Who told you that, Mr. Nolan?" Bree asked. "Who gave you the balloon? And who told you to visit Marty Forbes in jail and act like Kyle Craig?"

Nolan closed his eyes, said, "He calls himself M."

CHAPTER 88

SHORTLY AFTER SEVEN THAT EVENING, in the Homeland Security offices at Union Station, Mahoney, Sampson, Bree, and I crowded around Lieutenant Edith Prince, a TSA officer with access to the archival feeds from cameras mounted in and around the transportation hub.

We asked her to bring up the footage from several days before, when Nolan had been caught on-camera. The time stamp said 4:01 p.m. when the Kyle Craig lookalike appeared in the feed, walked through the main hall of the rail station, and disappeared into the Metro.

"He told us he went to a locker before going to the Metro," Bree said.

It took a few tries before Prince picked him up on another camera feed, this one overlooking a bank of lockers open for use between six a.m. and midnight.

On the TSA lieutenant's screen, Nolan appeared at 3:54 p.m. He went to locker C-2, one of the larger storage bins. It was open.

Nolan reached inside and up. He groped around, then pulled his hand out in a loose fist and put it in the pocket of his jacket. The door swung shut. Nolan left.

Exactly the way he had described his actions to Bree in the interrogation room.

"What happened just there?" Prince asked.

"Nolan says he retrieved a claim check for a piece of carry-on luggage in storage at the Willard Hotel," Bree said.

"Now we just need to figure out who put the claim check in the locker, and the luggage at the hotel," Mahoney said.

"Can't help you with the hotel," Prince said, and she gave her computer an order. "But just maybe..."

The viewer played backward at six times normal speed. I had trouble keeping my eyes on the screen. My mind kept leaping back to the Kyle Craig lookalike's claim that he was contacted two years before through an anonymous Panamanian server and an e-mail account belonging to someone named M.

The sender was aware of Nolan's circumstances, that he was an ex-con trying to stay clean years after his release from prison, that he was working too many hours for too little pay.

M also knew Nolan had been an actor and a stuntman and thought he'd be perfect for several roles he had coming up. The first role would involve five days of work, and the pay was one hundred thousand dollars, twenty-five up front, seventy-five on completion.

"For doing what?" Bree had asked.

Nolan had shifted and winced. "I don't think I should answer that, actually."

Mahoney leaned across the table. "Headless bodies, William. Blood from those bodies in your possession. Start talking or start thinking about what you want for your last meal."

The stuntman wasn't happy, but he spilled everything. He'd been the one who chloroformed Marty Forbes in that Fort Lauderdale motel room. He'd been the one who'd put an IV in Forbes's arm and run drugs into him. He'd been the one who'd kept the maids away the entire four days Marty had lain in a chemical haze.

"I waited until Forbes was starting to come around, and then I left," Nolan said. "Five days later, I get a UPS box filled with seventy-five grand in cash. I'm still not sure what I did to earn it."

"You were part of a frame job that put Forbes behind bars for murders he did not commit," Bree said.

"I didn't commit them either!" Nolan said. "And I didn't know about Forbes being in jail until ten days ago, when I was told to go see him but say nothing."

Nolan claimed M had contacted him again back in February and offered him a month of work that would pay two hundred grand. For that he was supposed to stay at the Regal Motel and wait until he was told what to do.

"Still via this Panamanian e-mail account?"

"No," Nolan said. "He made me switch to this phone application called Wickr."

That's when I believed everything Nolan said. I'd already been inclined to believe him when he said M had made contact with him through a Panamanian e-mail account, just like he had with Marty Forbes. But Wickr, the anonymous, disappearing digital-telegram system, was how M had contacted me, goaded me to—

"Stop!" Bree said, startling me from my thoughts.

The feed froze on the screen inside the Homeland Security offices. It showed a young Caucasian woman wearing a peasant dress and a woolen cap over blond dreadlocks. She was standing in front of locker C-2.

CHAPTER

89

LIEUTENANT PRINCE STARTED THE FEED in slow motion. At 2:29 p.m. on the same day that Nolan retrieved the claim check, a young woman went to the locker, pulled out a backpack and a woven purse. She put the purse over her shoulder and across her chest, bandolier-style, took the backpack, and left.

We could see the young woman from all angles, and she never seemed to reach up toward the top of the locker. Prince rewound the footage and found the same young woman earlier, at 12:40 p.m., when she first deposited her gear in C-2 and locked it.

Sampson said, "She could have put the claim

check in there when she loaded the locker. You can't see her hands for a good eight seconds there."

"Maybe," I said. "Keep going backward and speed it up."

Prince gave her computer an order. The footage went in reverse again, this time at sixteen times normal speed. We had to concentrate, had to stare right at locker C-2 and nothing else. My iPhone buzzed, alerting me to a text. I ignored it.

"There," Bree said, pointing at the screen.

"Got it," Prince said and slowed the pace to normal speed.

At 10:22 a.m., a man in a long, dark raincoat wearing a black cowboy hat with a clear plastic rain cover over it unlocked C-2. He retrieved a valise and left. The hat brim made it impossible for us to see his face. When he turned, I noticed the hat had some kind of band around the crown, but it was obscured by the rain cover.

I couldn't see it earlier, at 9:54 a.m., when the cowboy entered the locker area the first time. He put the valise inside C-2, locked the door, and departed, never giving us a single view of his face.

"I don't see when he could have planted the claim," Bree said. "It's all business. He puts the valise in and takes it out."

"I think you're right," I said. "But mark that place, Lieutenant Prince, and then keep going back in time."

At 8:12 a.m. on the day Nolan got the claim check, a big man, African-American, wearing a blue sweatshirt, hood up, entered the locker area and looked around. He wore dark sunglasses and seemed agitated before going to C-2, unlocking it, and reaching inside it up to his elbow.

The big man's shoulder moved as if he were groping for something, and then he pulled out a laptop computer in a sleeve. He tucked it under his arm and left.

"He definitely could have done it, right there," Mahoney said. "Why else put something so small in a locker that big?"

"I agree, but let's look when he puts the computer in there," I said.

Prince ran the feed backward until finding the same guy at 6:48 a.m. He carried a large, heavy messenger-style bag then, and he put it in C-2.

Before locking it, however, he apparently reconsidered and then reached back inside the locker for the bag. From it, he took the computer in the sleeve and put it deeper into the box. Then he locked it and left with the messenger bag under one arm.

"Both times he could have done it," Sampson said.

"He's our guy," Bree agreed.

"I think so too," Mahoney said.

My phone buzzed a second time, then a third and a fourth.

Exasperated, I dug it out, and looked at the screen, seeing two texts from Jannie and three from Nana Mama. All of them said the same thing: Call! Now! It's important!

I said, "I have to take this."

I crossed the room and called home. My grandmother answered on the first ring.

"I just want you to tell me things will be fine," she said in a tense, trembling voice.

"What's going on, Nana?"

"It's probably nothing, but Ali's an hour late for dinner, and he told me this morning he was coming home to study for a geography test. We've tried his cell phone, and he won't answer or he doesn't have it with him or he forgot to charge it again."

My stomach felt slightly hollow, but I said, "Did you check the shed, see if his mountain bike's there?"

"Jannie already did. It's there."

I started to feel sick.

My phone buzzed in my hand, and my heart soared. "He just texted me."

"Oh, thank God," Nana cried.

I thumbed the icon to read the text, and felt my knees threaten to buckle.

The past is now present, Cross. Come find your son.—M

CHAPTER 90

THREE HOURS AFTER RECEIVING THAT text, Bree and I were back at home with Sampson, Mahoney, and Rawlins. Though a team of FBI agents was already working on Ali's kidnapping from the Bureau's headquarters downtown, we'd decided to contain knowledge of his abduction, fearing what M might do to Ali if the media's spotlight swung his way.

Jannie's eyes were puffy from crying. Nana Mama was shaken but trying to stay busy; she was brewing coffee for the agents. Outwardly, I was doing my best to remain stoic, professional, detached, and focused on the safe recovery of a kidnap victim.

But inside, as a father, I was deathly afraid for my little boy, afraid because, as a detective, I knew what killers like M could do. They were divorced from their souls.

In my experience, there was no other explanation for truly depraved acts. It took someone divorced from his soul, someone turned absolutely amoral, to kill with no conscience, to hack the heads off people, guilty of crimes or not. Or to kidnap an innocent mother and threaten to cut off her finger. Or to frame an FBI agent in order to toy with me in a depraved, ruthless game played out over a dozen years.

And now Ali, my baby boy, was a pawn.

As Mahoney, Bree, and Sampson attempted to put together a timeline of Ali's day, I tried to put myself in M's shoes, tried to anticipate what he might be thinking, how he could use my son against me.

M could torture Ali to torture me.

M could kill Ali to torture me.

M could kill Ali to destroy my family.

M could—

"Dad?" Jannie said, startling me.

"Yes?"

"They've got a rough timeline," she said. "You should take a look."

I went into the dining room and saw that a whiteboard had been set up on Nana Mama's china hutch. Sampson, Bree, and Mahoney were studying it.

John said, "Ali is at school until three twenty p.m., when classes let out."

Bree said, "His friends the Kent twins said the last time they saw him, he was on foot, heading for Fort Totten Metro station to go home to work on Nana Mama's Twitter account. They said it was all he talked about all day."

"Cell phone?" I said.

Rawlins turned from his computer and said, "His cell phone was on after school. We picked up his location a block from Fort Totten Metro at three thirty-seven p.m. and then nothing until it surfaced again briefly south of Harrisburg, Pennsylvania, at seven twenty p.m."

"Which is about the time M texted me," I said.

"Correct," Sampson said. "Signal dies completely after that."

"And nothing since," Bree said. "Just over three hours since last contact."

Mahoney said, "I think he's going to let you hang on the hook a bit, Alex."

I nodded. I'd anticipated that at a bare minimum.

"How are you holding up?" Bree said.

"You're all here," I said. "This isn't all riding on my shoulders. Have we gotten access to his texts?"

Rawlins said, "Working on it. And that hat."

"What hat?"

"The one the cowboy was wearing at Union Station."

"Dad!" Jannie screamed in the kitchen.

I spun and bolted around the table, past the two agents setting up computer equipment, and into the kitchen. Jannie was on the floor, cradling Nana Mama's head in her lap and crying.

"She had trouble breathing, Dad," she said, sobbing. "And then she just kind of sagged into me!"

CHAPTER

91

I GOT DOWN ON THE floor next to my grandmother. Her eyes were shut, her breathing rapid and shallow.

"Nana?" I said, checking her pulse. It was elevated but not racing.

"I'm here," she said weakly, and her eyelids fluttered open. "I…I just got dizzy there all of a sudden."

Bree said, "Should I call an ambulance?"

"No," my grandmother moaned. "I am not spending another night in a hospital. I just got anxious thinking about Ali and how scared my sweet boy has to be. Someone bring me my inhaler from my bed stand. I'll be okay."

"I'll get it!" Sampson said, and he rushed off.

"And you take slower breaths, Nana," I said.

She tried, and once John returned with her inhaler, she got a couple of puffs into her lungs. Ten minutes after she'd sagged into Jannie's arms, she felt better. Five minutes after that, she sat up on her own.

My grandmother looked around at us all and said, "Note to self: If you want to keep living, you need to keep breathing."

We all smiled and laughed.

"Write that down," Jannie said, tears welling as she hugged my grandmother.

Nana Mama got to her feet, and, with me trailing, she climbed the stairs under her own power. At her door, I said, "Do you want Bree or Jannie to come and help you get ready for bed?"

"No," she said. "I can take care of myself from here."

But she held my hand for a long moment and gazed sadly into my eyes. "I'll pray for him before I sleep, and I'll pray for him when I wake up."

"I know you will."

She squeezed my hand. "I've seen my share of senseless tragedies, and God knows you have too. But I have faith."

I kissed her forehead and hugged her, trying

not to break down. "I know you do. We both do. Thank you for reminding me."

She went into her room and shut her door.

I met Jannie on the stairs. She said she was suddenly exhausted and was going to bed.

"I'm going to try to sleep too," Bree said.

"I'm not there yet," I said, and I headed to the dining room.

Rawlins looked up from his computer. "We'll have text access in five minutes. Meantime, this is the clearest image I can get of that cowboy at Union Station."

He swiveled his laptop so we could all see that he'd come in tight on the front of the crown of the hat, right where it met the brim. Even through the rain-splattered plastic cover, you could see two crossed sabers in scabbards and knotted gold cord below it.

"What's that insignia?" I asked.

"U.S. Army Cavalry," Mahoney said. "Like Custer wore."

That confused me a moment. Rawlins turned his computer around, started typing, said, "Okay, I'm inside Verizon and your account, Dr. Cross, and your data."

That sickening feeling came back as I walked around the table to stand behind the cybercrime expert, and I didn't know exactly why. He had the screen split, half of it showing the cowboy hat and insignia, the other a long string of data.

"Tell me what I'm looking for," Rawlins said.

"Everything Ali texted for the last three days. Calls. Data usage. Browser history. All of it."

"You got it," he said, typing.

I was about to turn away but I looked at the insignia again.

"Cavalry," I said. "That's tanks now, right?"

"Tanks and heavy armor," Mahoney said. "Why?"

"Here are Ali's texts," Rawlins said. "Last one to this number. It's a San Diego area code. Recognize it?"

I shook my head. "What's it say?"

He highlighted the phone number, clicked it, and the text came up: I'm here. Can't wait.

"That's at three thirty-two, five minutes before Ali's phone goes off," Sampson said.

"Go backward," I said. "Open them all up."

There were twenty-two texts to and from that number. But I didn't have to read them all to understand who had my son.

The back-and-forth was all about mountain biking and what route should be taken on a ride after school got out. The first text of the day, from the California number, read Captain Where.

Change of plans and phone. Got mine drowned and it died. I'm going to take a chance and ride this afternoon. You up for it?

And the day before, Ali had gotten a text from Abrahamsen's regular number at dinnertime, when Nana Mama was spouting one-liners. I remembered how he had smiled as he read the text.

Yes, I am back from Texas, that text read. Shoulder's still a little too sore to be riding. Hope you are well, my young friend.

"He's M?" I said, shaking my head in disbelief. "Former tank commander, now with defense intelligence, U.S. Army captain Arthur Abrahamsen?"

CHAPTER 92

AT FIVE THE NEXT MORNING, the two-story Colonial on the east side of Eaglebrook Court in Fort Hunt, Virginia, was just as dark as it had been when Sampson and I parked a surveillance van down the street shortly after midnight.

There was a large dumpster in the front yard. According to records Rawlins pulled, Abrahamsen had a permit to remodel the house. Beyond the dumpster was that van with the decal wraps of the U.S. Armed Forces bicycle team.

In my mind, I could see Abrahamsen pulling up in front of Ali in that van and my son jumping in.

Mahoney trotted up to the surveillance van, climbed in, shut the door quietly.

"People are going to start waking up and wondering what this van is," I said.

"Just waiting for a judge to give us the okay," he said. "I brought an infrared sensor. Should pick up anyone inside."

The sensor looked like a large, fat gun with a screen attached to the rear. I opened the window, aimed the gun at Abrahamsen's house, and turned it on.

The screen showed the house radiating massive amounts of heat.

"He must have the furnace turned up to ninety," Mahoney said. "Can't make out any heat differentiations in there."

"Maybe why he's got the heat cranked up," Sampson said from the driver's seat.

Ned's phone rang. He answered, listened, and said, "ETA?" Then he listened again and hung up.

"Judge is reading our support material," he said, pulling out an iPad and calling up the Google Earth view of the house. "If we get his signature, they'll bring the warrant to us. I'm going to have HRT start to filter into position."

The FBI's Hostage Rescue Team. The best in the business. I should have been elated that HRT was coming to rescue my son, but the father in me wanted to be the one to lead the charge, knock Abrahamsen silly, and bring Ali home safe and sound.

"What was that?" Sampson said, pointing at Abrahamsen's house. "I saw something move on the side of the house there."

I threw up my binoculars and saw nothing in the shadows. Then I pointed the infrared sensor at the house again.

The house was still pulsing heat, especially through the windows and around the doors, which were depicted in red. But the walls were hot too, a deep, undulating orange.

I was about to flip the sensor off when out of the orange on the side of the house, a blob appeared and became the yellow silhouette of a man.

"Unidentified man outside," I said. "Right there. He's—"

The silhouette straddled something, then got into a sitting position and rolled out of the sensor's range.

"He's on a bike!" I said. "He's going out the back."

"Mount Vernon Trail," Mahoney said, then he snatched up a handheld radio and triggered the mike. "We've got a runner."

CHAPTER 93

SAMPSON STARTED THE ENGINE, threw the van in gear. Part of me wanted to jump out, go straight into Abrahamsen's house, and find Ali.

But we had no cause yet, at least no warrant with a judge's signature. And Abrahamsen or M or whoever he was—he was getting away.

The first gray light of morning showed when Sampson took a hard right onto Waynewood Road and accelerated toward the Mount Vernon Trail and the George Washington Parkway. He pulled up where the bike trail crossed the road.

He looked north and I looked south. We saw nothing, but you could not see far.

"He can't have gotten by us this way so fast," Mahoney said. "He has to be heading south."

Sampson swung hard onto the GW Parkway and accelerated. I rolled the window down and peered out into the dawn light, finding the snippets of the ribbon of the bike trail through the still-leafless trees.

"Slow down," I said. "We could miss him in there."

"He's right," Mahoney said, looking at his iPad. "Satellite shows the path veers away from the parkway and goes through a big block of woods up ahead."

"What's the next crossing south?" Sampson asked.

Mahoney said, "Fort Hunt Road."

"Call in a helicopter," I said as Sampson hit the gas again.

Mahoney picked up his radio just as his phone rang.

I was still hanging out the window, looking for anything that suggested a bicyclist back there in the woods.

Where are you, M? Where are you going? And where's my son?

"Fort Hunt Road coming up fast," Sampson said, hitting his blinker.

You could clearly see the bike path where it ran through open ground north of the intersection. He wasn't there yet.

"Stop alongside the path up ahead," I said. "We'll wait for him."

Sampson pulled over on Fort Hunt beyond the bike path. I looked north, saw nothing, and then west, where I spotted a bike farther down the trail and crossing the street.

"There he is!" I cried.

Sampson threw the van in gear again and sped toward the crossing where the trail cut back to the east toward the parkway and the river.

"We've got the warrant!" Mahoney said. "They're faxing it to HRT."

"What's ahead?" I said.

Mahoney looked at his iPad, said, "Take a hard left. He's going to come out of the woods and go under the parkway. If he gets much beyond there, we won't be able to stop him for a good four miles."

"That's not happening," Sampson said. He downshifted, skidded into the hard left turn, and then accelerated again.

"There he is!" I said again, seeing Abrahamsen biking out of the woods and heading toward the parkway and the Potomac River. "Get under the overpass and ahead of him!"

Sampson sped by Abrahamsen, who didn't give us a second glance. His head was down and he was pedaling furiously.

Mahoney's radio crackled. "HRT is a go."

"Go," Mahoney said.

We went beneath the overpass and turned hard right toward an on-ramp to the parkway. Sampson pulled over and I jumped out, crossed the street, and ran across forty yards of grass.

Abrahamsen was coming so fast I barely had time to step in his way, crouch down, and aim my pistol at him.

"Stop or I will shoot you, Captain!"

CHAPTER 94

ABRAHAMSEN HIT HIS BRAKES SO HARD, he skidded; he hit gravel, the bike went out from under him, and he crashed into the grass. On the ground, he grabbed his shoulder and yelled out in pain.

"Oh God! That broke ribs, and there goes the shoulder again. Oh God."

"Keep praying, and keep your hands where I can see them," I said, grabbing him by the back of his bike shirt and wrenching his upper body my way. "You're going to need all the help you can get."

Abrahamsen screamed. "Don't move me! What the hell are you doing?"

"Placing you under arrest," Mahoney said, running up with his FBI badge out.

"What?" he said, panting. "What are you talking about?"

"Murder and kidnapping," I said. "Where's my son?"

"Arthur Abrahamsen, you have the right to remain silent," Mahoney began.

"Ali?" he cried. "I have no idea where he is. I haven't seen him since before I—"

"We know you have him," I said, pushing hard on his right shoulder, ramming his busted left side into the ground.

The captain screamed again. "My God, Dr. Cross. Believe me!"

"We have the texts," I said. "Now where is he?"

"Texts?" he said. "I don't know what you're talking about. I texted him once, the day before yesterday, to tell him I was back."

"Before you drowned your phone and texted him repeatedly with a burner," I said. "Invited him for a bike ride. Where is he, M?"

Abrahamsen groaned. "Who's M? I did no such thing. You've got the wrong man."

"I don't think so," I said as Mahoney unclipped Abrahamsen's shoes from the bike pedals. "We're searching your house."

"Good," he said. "You won't find him there. You won't find much of anything in there. You've got it all wrong."

Ned's radio crackled with the voice of the HRT commander. "SAC Mahoney."

Mahoney raised the handheld to his lips. "Come back."

"No one here. Place is virtually empty. Looks like they just applied some kind of textured plaster to the walls and the heat's jacked up like a sauna."

"To dry the plaster," Abrahamsen said, grimacing as he looked at me. "Dr. Cross, I adore your son. I think he's one of the more remarkable boys I've ever met. I will swear on a stack of Bibles, I don't have Ali. I haven't seen him in more than ten days."

My cell phone dinged in my pocket, and I reached for it with my gut sinking again. I looked at the Wickr message, then back at Abrahamsen, wanting to sit down and cry.

"I believe you, Captain," I said. "I apologize. I should have suspected M would try to use you to get to me."

CHAPTER 95

SOMEONE SHOOK MY SHOULDER, and I came groggily awake into a splitting headache. I opened my eyes, and saw I was in my attic office chair, head down on the Edgerton files, an empty pint bottle of Jack Daniel's beside me.

Bree was crouched next to me, looking concerned.

"Why didn't you use the bed?"

I gazed at her stupidly and then remembered. "I thought I'd find something up here, and then I realized I couldn't control this. M. Any of it. So I put my forehead on my fists, and I prayed for him. I must have fallen asleep."

"I imagine you did, with that much whiskey in you."

"For the first time in my life, I felt so afraid, I needed to black out."

"Oh, baby," she said, throwing her arms around me.

We hugged in silence for many minutes, and in the love I felt from her and gave to her, I began to come more alert.

When we broke apart, Bree kissed me and then gave me a disgusted look. "Your breath could stop a train, and you look even worse."

"Thanks."

"Anytime. Sampson said he sent you a Wickr message?"

I nodded and gestured to a piece of paper on the desk where I'd written it down because I'd forgotten to take a screenshot of it. But the words were indelible in my mind:

Have you noticed I'm always three steps ahead of you? Your son now suffers the sins of his father. Soon the rest of the family will be like him and Granny, gasping and clawing for air.

Bree read it.

As she did, my hungover mind keyed on the words *now suffers,* unable to control the things my imagination threw at me. Then *the sins of his father.*

What were my supposed sins? What had I done to M to make him come after me like this for so many years? I couldn't…

"I think we need to get Nana Mama and Jannie out of here," Bree said.

I looked at her dumbly.

"He said that the rest of the family would be gasping and clawing for air, Alex," she said. "We have to get them somewhere safe."

I didn't reply, just read the last sentence again. *Soon the rest of the family will be like him and Granny, gasping and clawing for air.*

Something there bothered me, but I couldn't quite put my finger on it.

"Alex," Bree said again.

And then I got what was bothering me, and held up my hand, seeing all the implications of that last sentence. I cleared my throat. "I agree. I'll call Ned, ask him if you, Jannie, and Nana Mama can use his beach house. It'll be safe. You can work from there."

"What about you?"

"I want to stay close to home."

Bree gazed at me, puzzled, but said, "Okay, I'll get them packing."

CHAPTER 96

ON THE SEVENTH EVENING AFTER Ali's kidnapping, I trudged up the stairs to my front porch, feeling lost, heartbroken, and dreading the loneliness inside.

My head was splitting again. At the front door, I was shaking so bad I had to put down the heavy brown paper bag I was carrying and use both hands to get the key in the lock. The door opened and swung inward.

I picked up the bag, but then I stood there, unable to take the first step inside.

The past few nights I'd been unable to detach from the case. I'd gotten so worked up and was so sleep-deprived, I'd had terrible visions of what M might be doing to Ali.

The nightmares had been so real, I'd screamed out several times and then cried myself back to sleep. I didn't know if I could face another night in my empty home and considered taking the car right then and driving to the Delaware shore to join my family.

But Ali needed me, even if it was the wreckage of me. I stepped inside and closed the door. I felt my way into the kitchen. After setting the bag on the counter, I finally turned on a light and looked around dully before pulling out my phone.

Nothing. No texts. No Wickr messages.

I was about to set the phone down when it rang. Bree. I put her on speaker.

"Anything?" she asked.

"Report came in. DNA seals it. That was Kyle Craig in the box."

"Kind of makes it worse, you know?"

"I do."

"Nothing else?"

"Not a word from M in six days," I said, my stomach in knots. "He's getting his torture in."

"Do you have to stay there all by yourself?"

"I ate dinner with Ned, John, and the others."

"I'm worried about you, Alex," she said. "You haven't seemed like yourself at all."

"I can't imagine why."

"Ali's counting on you to be strong."

"And here I am feeling weaker than I've ever felt."

After a beat, she said, "Have you been drinking again?"

"Today? No, and I have no plans to."

"Do you want me to come home, baby? Keep you company?"

"I'll come tomorrow, spend the day."

Bree's voice came back lighter. "That would be good. For you and for us."

"Family therapy."

"I think you need a good dose of it."

"I do."

"I love you, baby. Call me before you go to sleep, no matter what time it is. Promise?"

"Promise. And I love you too. Kiss them good night for me."

"I will," she said, and she hung up.

After I put the phone down, I stood there at the kitchen counter for a good two minutes, staring at that brown paper bag. Then I got the television remote and turned on the small screen we had mounted for Nana Mama above the refrigerator.

I thumbed through the channels, pausing on the two stations broadcasting local news. There'd been a fire overnight that took the lives of four children.

I shut the television off, muttering bitterly, "Media bastards. How long until the cameras start feeding on us?"

I put my hands on the counter and hung my head, despondent.

And no wonder. We'd made no significant progress in days. Security cameras at the Fort Totten Metro station hadn't picked up Ali after his friends the Kent twins had seen him walking in that direction.

FBI agents had discreetly canvassed the seven blocks between the school and the subway stop, but no one seemed to remember seeing Ali or anything out of the ordinary the afternoon he vanished.

Other investigative threads had led nowhere. The Willard Hotel, for example, did not keep a security camera in its storage area, and the bellmen had no clear memory of the carry-on bag M had supposedly left for William Nolan two weeks before.

And no word whether my boy was alive or…

We were stuck, and I was left alone in my house to wait M out. As it had every night that week, my anxiety level rose with each passing minute. And as I had every night that week, I pulled a bottle of Jack Daniel's from the bag and opened it.

I poured twice what I'd consider healthy into a tumbler and downed it. I shuddered at the fireball that went down my throat and boiled in my belly. I poured another in anticipation of a third.

In twenty minutes, I knew, I'd be feeling less pain. In an hour, I'd find moments of pleasure where I wouldn't think of Ali at all and stretches of suffering where all I could see were memories of him.

And sometime after that, I thought, picking up the bottle and tipping it to my lips, my world would go blank and dark again.

CHAPTER 97

I WAS WELL INTO THE whiskey bottle but not yet into the darkness when I began to feel claustrophobic, and then I was simply unable to stay inside. Weaving slightly, I went to Nana Mama's pantry and found a go-cup.

I poured the cup full, put on the lid, slurped a little, and then a lot. I set the cup down, my mouth open to soothe the caramel burn in my throat, my hand on my belly to calm the nausea and cool the fire.

I left the kitchen but had to grab at the wall with my free hand before going out onto the porch. April coming on, and the night air was warm, thick, and breezy; somewhere upwind, azaleas were blooming.

A good night for walking drunk, I decided.

I did not want lights. I wanted shadows. So I headed not toward Capitol Hill but deeper into Southeast DC, toward the Navy Yard and eventually Anacostia.

In general, Southeast wasn't as dangerous as it was back when crack cocaine was king and violence erupted at all hours on every corner. But parts of Southeast remained mean streets by anyone's definition.

I should have been swiveling my head, on the lookout for potential threats. Instead, I drank the whiskey and wandered aimlessly.

Shortly before eleven that night, I went into a liquor store and bought a pint to refresh my go-cup. That's when things started to go hazy for me.

I walked through one dark, nameless alley, stumbled into another, and then went down a third. At one point in one of those alleys, I tripped and fell. I almost stayed down, but then I heard voices, people arguing.

I got up, drank more, and moved toward the voices, but they soon stopped. I finally came to a halt by a dumpster, and I held on to it, barely able to stand. I hallucinated Ali ahead of me in the shadows, and M menacing behind him, faceless, soulless.

"C'mon," I slurred. "C'mon, M. I'm not armed, and I'm the one you really want. I'm right here. You don't have to hurt Ali. He's just a little boy, like you once were. Take me instead. Get it over with. Right here. Right now. Take me instead."

But nothing moved in the shadows. And no one spoke.

Enraged, I lumbered toward the spot and swung wild haymakers at the night.

"C'mon," I shouted. "Be a man."

But there was nothing, and I felt more lost and hopeless than I had when I'd gotten home earlier in the evening. I wasn't helping Ali. Unable to cope with the threat of losing my youngest child, I was numbing myself. I was a fraction of what I'd once been.

"That's it," I said. "I'm done."

I pressed my back against a chain-link fence, slid down, and sat in trash, uncaring.

"You win, M," I mumbled as my mind fell into a dark void. "I am a broken man."

CHAPTER

98

I HAVE NO IDEA HOW LONG I was passed out in that alley, lost in the darkness. Then air brakes squeaked and sighed close to me. Lights played over my face.

My head was burning. I squinted my eyes and saw in double vision a garbage truck coming for the dumpster, its headlights on.

My brain felt so boiled that at first, I didn't know where I was or how I'd gotten there. And then some reptilian part of my brain said, *Go home, Alex. Sleep it off.*

I lurched to my feet, dizzy, still drunk, although I somehow knew the direction of home. I staggered past the garbage truck.

"Get some help, brother," the driver called out his open window. "I been there, and you can find help if you want it."

I waved at him, said nothing, and kept on toward the mouth of the alley. Dawn glowed. The city was just waking when I turned north.

Passing shops not yet open for the day, I couldn't help seeing myself in the windows: shuffling, unsteady, filthy, a drunken bum, a shattered man who hung his head and wouldn't look at passing strangers.

"Gotta stop," I said at one point when the pounding in my head became too much. "Go to detox."

I knew where to go for that, but the GPS in my brain kept sending me toward Fifth Street and home. I was almost there when I heard a boy laughing through an open window, and I sobered into the waking nightmare of Ali all over again.

From there it was one step after another until I was in front of my house. I climbed the porch steps, hearing thunder rumble in the distance. The wind was picking up, bringing the smell of spring rain.

As I fumbled for my keys, I was blearily aware of a fluttering piece of pink surveyor's tape tied to the lower bars of the scaffolding between our house and the neighbor's place. The lower outer wall had been sandblasted to reveal the natural brick beneath, and the scaffolding had been raised to the roofline.

My stomach soured as I opened the front door. I went inside, felt sicker, and rushed to the bathroom beyond the kitchen.

The whiskey came up, which helped my stomach but made my head ache all the more. I guzzled two full glasses of water in the kitchen before I noticed my phone, forgotten on the counter.

I looked for messages, saw none, and put it down again. I needed to clean myself up and sleep before driving to the shore.

But when I got to the top of the stairs outside my bedroom, I felt a stiff breeze coming from my attic office. I must have left one of the windows open, I thought, and there was a storm coming.

I climbed the stairs like a zombie and ducked under the low doorway into my office. But then I stopped short, jolted stone-cold sober by a surge of adrenaline.

A man divorced from his soul sat behind my desk.

He was aiming a silenced pistol at my chest from point-blank range.

"Good morning, Dr. Cross," he said. "I see you've been having a tough time of it. A real pity. For years, I've thought of this moment, and I was honestly hoping for so much more from you when your boy's life was on the line."

CHAPTER 99

HE WAS IN HIS MID-FORTIES, athletically built, with pale skin and facial bruises. He wore an olive workman's shirt flecked with sawdust. A white hard hat rested on the desk near his right elbow. There was a carpenter's tool belt beside it.

His neck was thick. His pale head was completely bald, his lashes were fine and blond, and his steady eyes were ice blue. I had never seen the man before in my life, but I knew who he was just the same.

"M," I said. "Where's my son?"

M took me in with those eyes, which spoke of violent desire and something profoundly evil. "He's buried deep. The bugs are probably already on him."

My worst fear hit me like a blow to the solar plexus. My knees jellied. *Ali? Gone?* "No," I mumbled. "Why?"

M said nothing, just tilted his head slowly left and then right, studying me. It was as if he were mentally recording every twitch and ripple of grief passing through my body. The longer he gazed at me, the more his eyes brightened. The barest smile came to his lips.

I understood. The man was enjoying himself. He was a sadist, and in my experience, sadists liked to play with their prey. It was part of the power trip.

Feeling stronger for that understanding, I straightened up, said, "You're lying."

"Am I?"

"Yes."

He shrugged. "When I left Ali, he *was* doomed. It really doesn't matter when he goes for good, not him or your grandmother or your wife or your daughter out there at Ned's beach house in Delaware. In my mind, Cross, you and yours are already bittersweet memories."

He's equivocating, I thought, feeling another surge of hope. Ali had been alive when M left him. I just had to keep him talking to find out where and how long ago. "What's your real name?"

"It's whatever I'm calling myself at any given moment. I have found that a name really doesn't matter in the long run."

I glanced beyond him at the thin curtains billowing as the wind and rain came in the open window. He must have come out of the Morses' house and across the scaffolding.

M reached back and shut the window. The thin curtains settled.

"You're here to kill me?" I said.

"Hate to say it again, but you are a big disappointment. Time to move on to new and bigger challenges."

"Who are you really? Why are you doing this? I think the doomed man has a right to know before he dies."

He smiled outright. "Who am I really? Why am I doing this? I am a multitude of names and purposes, Cross. But all the world really needs to know is that I bested the greatest detective on the planet, the Sherlock Holmes of his time, at his own game and on his own turf. And too many times to count."

My mind raced back years and years, and I remembered a *Washington Post Magazine* profile of me and the writer saying something ridiculous like that.

"You read that damn article years ago?" I said.

"And in my spare time, I've been playing you ever since. Plotting, executing, outfoxing. All while you bumbled and choked at every turn. World's greatest detective." He snorted. "I don't think so."

Despite the put-down, I realized M, or whatever his name was, had just told me quite a bit about himself, intrinsic things. He'd shown me the cracks in the facade and perhaps given me tools to widen those cracks.

"You won," I said. "It's true. You beat me. Whatever your name is, whatever your reason, I suppose you are now the greatest criminal on earth."

He made a low humming noise in his throat but said nothing, just watched me.

"It follows, doesn't it?" I said. "You defeat the best detective, you're number one."

After a moment's pause, he said, "I suppose it does follow, yes."

"They'll be talking about you for years."

M hummed again.

"Right there with the immortals," I said. "John Wilkes Booth. Ted Bundy. Lee Harvey Oswald. John Wayne Gacy. Kyle Craig."

M made a clucking sound, said, "I am more than all of them combined."

"You're not too far off. They'll write books about your life. Maybe make a movie. But that will be long after you're dead."

M said nothing, and he never took his eyes off me.

I said, "Do you know they have a place where they bury people like you?"

"You don't understand, Cross. There's no one like me."

"But there are. Sadists. Serial killers. Assassins. Predators so vicious, whose crimes are so heinous, that their own relatives refuse to retrieve their bodies for proper burial. Cemeteries refuse the bodies too, something about not wanting them to defile a sacred place. So you and all your buddies are taken to this remote corner of Marine Base Quantico and buried under nameless headstones. I thought you'd want to know where you're going to end up eventually."

As I spoke, I watched his eyes shift from impassive to soulless.

"Many other men have made the mistake of trying to get inside my head," M said, raising the pistol. "They had no idea what I was capable of, and neither do you."

Starting in the pit of my stomach, terror swept through me.

I held up both palms, said, “Please, don’t shoot, M—”

“Shut up,” he said, losing all affect, turning asocial, amoral, and moving his gun to aim at my face. “Alex Cross, welcome to the dead.”

CHAPTER 100

I HAVE HEARD OTHERS DESCRIBE the surreal moment when they faced certain death. They say that time seemed to slow.

Neuropsychologists know that time doesn't slow in these moments.

Instead, the brain, faced with the possibility of extinction, secretes chemicals that ignite parts of the mind rarely used. The brain lights up, electrically brilliant, and runs so fast that it is able to receive and process information at hundreds of times its normal speed.

And so, for a person confronted with death, events seem to slow.

In the split second between M's last words to

me and his finger tugging the trigger, I saw every nuance in that man's face, smelled the foul odor coming off him, and heard glass tinkle and bones crack before blood burst from his chest.

M arched and twisted as he shot.

His bullet almost took off the tip of my right ear and embedded in the wall behind me.

His lower body sagged. His left hand slammed on the desk, and he tried to get the pistol back on me.

I'd already taken two strides and launched over the top of my desk. My left hand knocked his gun arm aside. My right forearm and all my weight hit him square in the chest.

We crashed against a bookcase and fell to the floor. My fist was instantly back, elbow high.

But M wasn't moving.

For one heart-wrenching moment, I thought I'd gone too far and killed him before he could tell me where my son was.

Then I saw his chest moving as he labored for breath, and blood still spurted from his wound.

"Great shot, John," I said, gasping. "He's down, but alive. We need an ambulance."

I threw his pistol aside, tore off my sweatshirt, and pressed it against the exit wound. M's eyes came half open, and he coughed and choked, trying to get air.

"Don't move," I said. "There are EMTs coming. You have the right to remain silent. You have the right to an attorney."

I continued through the Miranda warning, and M's eyes opened wider. I thought I saw fear in them.

"Can't move my legs," he whispered when I was finished. "Can't feel a thing."

Sirens wailed toward the house.

"Where's my son?"

He closed his eyes.

"It's over, M. Where's my son?"

He didn't reply.

I felt like smashing him in the face, but boots were pounding up my stairs.

I got up, shaky, nauseated. Ned Mahoney was first through the door, with Bree right behind him.

"You good?" Mahoney asked.

"Better than him," I said, going to hug Bree.

She had tears in her eyes but pushed me back. "I love you, baby, but you're covered in blood."

"His blood," I said as the EMTs came into the little office, which was now packed. "Let's get out of their way."

We climbed down the stairs and stood there looking at each other.

"I am never watching you act as bait ever again," Bree said.

"And for the rest of my life, I will never drink another drop of whiskey."

CHAPTER 101

Soon the rest of the family will be like him and Granny, gasping and clawing for air.

That text had been M's undoing.

The week before, in the moments after I got that text, I'd had a strange reaction that I couldn't explain at first.

Granny, gasping and clawing for air.

Then I realized that M had to have known about Nana Mama's attack.

Except that was impossible. Only six people had known: Me, Bree, Nana, Jannie, Sampson, and Mahoney. That was it.

We hadn't called for an ambulance. We hadn't called anyone.

There was only one explanation: M had bugged our house.

Two hours after Bree left with Nana and Jannie for Ned's beach house, there was a knock at my front door. Keith Karl Rawlins, the FBI cyber-crimes contractor, was there, posing as a fumigation specialist. He said the construction next door had turned up signs of termites, and he offered me a free check.

Soon after, we knew that M had not only been listening to us via bugs in four different rooms but also watching us on two separate fiber-optic cameras, one in the kitchen and one in my attic office.

How and when he'd placed them was a complete mystery to us, but there was no doubt the cameras and bugs were feeding wirelessly to a small transponder mounted high on a telephone pole across the street; the transponder sent it to the internet by satellite.

When Rawlins and I met with Mahoney away from my house later that day, Rawlins wanted to take down the transponder and analyze it, but I overruled him.

"He doesn't know we know he's watching," I said. "We can use that, draw him out."

"How?" Mahoney said.

"By setting me up as bait," I said. "Ultimately, he wants me in some kind of showdown, I think, lured by the promise of rescuing Ali."

We decided I had to start acting as if Ali's abduction had been a crushing blow that left me a weak, despondent, self-destructive loser, incapable of playing any game, much less a life-or-death one. M would fear that he'd never get that final conflict.

With plainclothes agents watching my house from every angle and a pin mike inside my collar, I'd started drinking that night.

Every evening afterward, I escalated, some of it acting drunk, but most of it real as I tapped into every fear I had about the situation and threw it out there in long drunken monologues.

It had taken six nights of personal humiliation and liver damage before one of Mahoney's men picked up the infrared image of an individual entering the Morses' house at three a.m. and crawling across the scaffolding into my attic office an hour later.

That same agent put up the pink surveyor's tape as a signal that I had a visitor waiting.

When I entered my office, Rawlins tapped into the wireless feed. He, Mahoney, and Bree were watching in a surveillance van around the block.

With M's focus on me, Sampson was able to slide out on the porch roof and get a clear shot.

He came onto the front porch as the EMTs were taking M out.

"Where's my son?" I demanded as he went by on a stretcher.

"Deep," he said.

I could tell that, even shot and paralyzed, he was enjoying my misery.

CHAPTER

102

FOR ALMOST FOURTEEN MADDENING HOURS, we could not talk to M, much less ask him where he'd taken my son. He underwent immediate surgery for the chest wound and spent a long time in recovery after having an adverse reaction to the anesthesia.

CT scans of his spine found that the bullet had glanced off the right side of his fourth thoracic vertebra, then passed through three inches of his right lung before exiting the rib cage. The energy of the bullet's passing had broken ribs, cracked vertebrae, and severely bruised the spinal cord.

"He told me he couldn't feel a thing," I told the surgeon.

"With that kind of swelling, he probably won't feel from mid-sternum down for a long time, if ever," the doctor said.

"When can I see him?"

We got the go-ahead to interview him around ten that night, shortly after M was brought into the ICU and shortly after an evidence tech reported that the suspect had no fingerprints. It looked like they'd been burned off with chemicals decades ago.

"I want to go in alone," I told Bree, Mahoney, and Sampson in the hallway outside his guarded room. "I think he'll try to play us if there's more than one of us there."

"I had a camera put in before he was transferred," Mahoney said. "We'll watch from down the hall."

Sampson said, "Good luck."

"Thanks, brother."

The two of them walked away.

I took a deep breath and gazed at Bree. "This feels daunting."

Her eyes were glassy as she squeezed my hand and smiled. "You were born for this, Alex Cross. Go get your boy."

She kissed me and then followed Ned and John. Nodding at the officer standing guard, I prayed for the right words to come and then went through the door.

M, or whatever his real name was, lay semi-upright in his hospital bed, a bank of monitors and medical devices cheeping and whirring around him.

He opened red, watery eyes. He tracked me as I came to the foot of his bed.

"Can you tell me where you took my son now?"

"Told you," he said, his voice thick and his words slurred due to the pain meds. "I buried him deep underground."

"Then tell me where I can dig him up and give him a proper burial."

"You're bright. You'll find him eventually."

"Look—you win. I concede. You outplayed me. You're still outplaying me." I said that last with as much sincerity as I could muster.

"And yet I'm the one who might never walk again and will spend my life behind bars."

Maybe the drugs had loosened his tongue, because that felt like an honest comment, and an open one, and I decided to radically change tactics.

"So when did you stop listening to your heart?" I asked.

"Don't know what you're talking about."

"Yes, you do. There had to be a time in your

long-ago past when you knew right from wrong instinctively. Do you remember that time?"

He swallowed, shrugged. "One set of foster parents brought me to church when I was a kid. Read scripture and other such nonsense."

"But apart from that, there *was* a time when you felt in your heart what was right and wrong. Do you remember that time?"

M's eyes narrowed. "What does this have to do with your son?"

"Do you remember?"

He closed his eyes. "Yeah, sure, I guess."

"Of course you remember. Of course you do. It was there when you were born. It was there before you were born. Did you know that the heart has its own nervous system? It's true. The heart is alive and alert long before the brain develops. It's a deeper organ of thinking, another way of knowing."

M's eyes opened. "So?"

"When did you stop listening to your heart?"

He shook his head. "I don't know what you're—"

"Yes, you do," I said. "You stopped listening to your heart because you thought it was broken. And that's when you started listening to the angry voices in your head. Were you thirteen? Fourteen?"

CHAPTER 103

I HAD NOT ASKED THESE questions idly.

A remarkable number of suicidal or homicidal adults endured some traumatic event in their late tweens to early teens, when their hormones were surging and going haywire and their emotions were swinging wildly.

In essence, the experience of that trauma is magnified by the hormones and amplified by the mood swings. I believe such a brutal event in those years wounds the brain, causes short circuits, and etches in hatred, self-loathing, and neuroses.

When I asked M about his early teen years, a shadow came over his face, and he shut his eyes.

For almost five minutes, I waited for an answer. The only sounds were our breathing and the monitors.

"I was fourteen," M said at last, opening his eyes. "My sister was raped and murdered. I found the man who did it and beat him to death with a chain."

"That's when you stopped listening to your heart? Before you killed him?"

"Afterward," he said. "When I realized I'd liked beating that son of a bitch to death, and I wanted to do it over and over and over again."

I nodded. "That would do it."

"Do what?"

"Silence your heart. Divorce you from your soul."

I stayed in eye contact with him, saw the twitching of his cheek muscles.

"I don't have a soul or a heart."

"Of course you do," I said. "The bullet missed it completely, and it's still there. You can listen to it if you dare. You might find hope."

"Of what?"

"Redemption."

He laughed softly. "There is no redemption for a man like me."

"Yes, there is. Close your eyes."

I had a moment of doubt when I thought he might shut me down. But then his eyelids closed.

"Listen to your heart," I said quietly. "It's still there. It *will* tell you what to do."

He breathed, swallowed, shifted uncomfortably, and then opened his eyes. "I've done too much."

"You can still listen. Just like you did when you were a young boy, like my son."

M's jaw stiffened. His lower lip curled against his teeth.

I gazed at him steadily, trying not to show how desperate I was. Every minute that passed was worse for Ali.

"I'm sorry, Cross," he said. "I went deaf to this kind of crap a long time ago."

"No, you didn't. You just unplugged the receiver."

"Does it matter now? It won't change things."

"Maybe not, but it will change you."

I could tell that caught him off guard, and I wanted to keep him that way. "You must have liked Ali. You can't meet my son and not be swept up in his enthusiasm."

"Kid talks a lot."

I smiled. "Nonstop."

"Smart."

"Brilliant."

M glanced at the ceiling, then back at me. "Life is full of injustice."

"You watched my family," I said. "You've seen Ali smile. Heard Ali laugh." I paused, trying to channel my love for my son but not wanting my emotions to overwhelm me. "That boy has a lifetime ahead of him," I went on. "Who knows what Ali will be able to do if you'll just take a chance and listen to your heart."

M stayed silent and would not look at me.

I waited a full ten minutes, sighed, then turned and headed for the door.

I'd opened it and was leaving when M said, "Cross."

I wanted to melt but stood tall and pivoted to look at him.

"The anthill," he said.

CHAPTER 104

THE FBI HELICOPTER FLEW IN over Dwight Rivers's property in the Shenandoah Valley and landed in the meadow between the solar panels and the house. It was past midnight. A full moon lit the place in a strange blue light.

We'd called Rivers, who'd gone home to heal after being released from the hospital. He said he had not been in the anthill since returning. The FBI had sealed the bunker because of the head found in there.

"Exceptional hiding place if you think about it," Mahoney said.

"Who would look in a sealed crime scene?" Bree said before the pilot gave us the all-clear.

We jumped out and started running toward Rivers's bunker. There were lights on in his house, but we found him on crutches next to an ATV waiting by the main entrance to the anthill.

"Padlock's still in place," he said. "So is the seal."

We all shone flashlights on the seal, which showed no signs of having been tampered with. Mahoney took two pictures of the seal, then broke it.

Rivers gave us the padlock combination, and we were quickly inside. The doomsday prepper hobbled in behind us, flipping switches, starting generators, lighting the anthill up from top to bottom.

"If your son is in here, you'll find him, Dr. Cross," Rivers said.

My thoughts were on Ali, but I couldn't help noting the irony that I'd suspected the man enough to break into his bunker, and yet here he was, helping me to find my boy.

"Thank you, sir," I said, then I led the way down the short hallway to the staircase.

Mahoney and Sampson climbed. Bree and I descended.

"Ali!" we shouted. "Ali Cross, can you hear us?"

We opened doors and went into every level of the maze, calling and looking in the kitchen, the armory, the security hub, the battery operation, and the water-filtration room. The workshop, where the head was found, was still sealed tight off the main staircase. I broke the seal and we went inside.

The first thing I noticed was that the heavy steel door at the opposite end of the space was on the floor in the hallway beyond. That door had been locked and sealed. The rest of the workshop looked much as I remembered it except there weren't any bloody tools or equipment; the FBI had seized those as evidence.

Then I noticed an empty plastic water jug by one of the lockers and empty tins of food strewn in the corners.

"Smell that?" Bree said.

I did, faintly. "Human waste."

It didn't take long to locate the smells. The floor drain stank of stale urine, and in a closed locker, we found zip-lock bags filled with feces and used toilet paper.

Mahoney and Sampson came in. "Anything?"

"He played me again," I said, shaking my head in helpless anger.

"Someone *was* confined in here," Bree said.

"I have a forensics team on its way from Quantico," Mahoney said. "Let's back out, let them do their jobs, figure out for sure if it was Ali being held here."

"I know he was," I said, and I gestured at dust by one of the lockers, where a single finger had doodled a design. "Ali draws those in his notebooks all the time."

Bree nodded, said, "And there are small footprints over by that door."

I went over and saw multiple shoe prints on top of each other, including several that looked Ali's size. I shone a light into the hall and spotted an acetylene blowtorch and tank by the ladder and a discarded hacksaw blade.

Bree said, "M must have come down this interior ladder and blowtorched and cut his way in. With the seal and lock still on the main staircase door, he'd know no one was coming in here. Perfect place to keep a kidnap victim."

That made me furious.

"Ali!" I shouted up the ladder. "Ali, can you hear me?"

"Alex?" Mahoney said. "He's not here anymore. We need to back out. Be sure."

"I'm staying," I said.

"No, you're not," Bree said. "You're coming home with me. I need you. So do Nana and Jannie. We'll go back to talk to M in the morning."

I stared at her, feeling overwhelmed at the idea that Ali had been right here sometime in the past few days, and now he was gone again.

But I nodded and left the workshop, unable to fight off the thought that I might never see my little boy again. My eyes welled up with emotion when I thanked Dwight Rivers for his help.

"You'll find him," Rivers said. "And I figured out how they were getting in and out. Someone's been using the roof winch. The cable line's hanging on the side."

"We left that," Sampson said.

"What?"

"It's a long story, sir, and it's late," I said, and I set off toward the helicopter.

Bree came alongside me and took my hand. My mind kept up a flashing slideshow of Ali moments: His birth. The first time he walked. The first time he talked.

Riding a bike. Playing in the ocean out in front of Ned's place on the shore.

The memories kept coming for me as we buckled ourselves into the helicopter seats: Ali obsessed with zombies. Obsessed with darts. Obsessed with mountain bikes. Obsessed with everything and, more often than not, grinning from ear to ear.

As the helicopter lifted off, Bree broke down

sobbing and fell against me. I wrapped my arms around her, feeling her shudder as tears poured down my face in the darkened cabin. I imagined Ali alive so vividly, I could have sworn I heard his voice on the wind.

CHAPTER 105

BOTH OUR PHONES STARTED BUZZING and ringing at four thirty a.m.

I took a look at the text from Mahoney and cursed. "That's impossible!"

"Goddamn it!" Bree yelled.

We dressed in seconds and pounded down the stairs.

"What's happening?" Nana Mama cried after us.

"Go back to bed."

"You've barely been to bed!"

We didn't answer, just ran out to the car. I threw a bubble on the roof and we took off, me driving, Bree on her radio, barking orders. Sirens wailed all around us as we sped through the deserted city.

Six minutes later, we pulled up in front of George Washington University Hospital.

"Go out ten blocks with the perimeter," Bree said into her radio. "No one in or out. All vehicles searched."

Sampson was already in the hall outside the ICU. "He's armed and dressed as a uniformed Metro police officer."

"What?" I said as Bree broadcast the news. "How?"

"Take a look."

We walked to the open door of the room where M had been.

Ivan Marky, the same young officer who'd been on guard when we left the evening before, was in the bed. He was naked. His throat had been cut.

Sampson said, "M put his clothes on, went to the nurses' station, put the officer's gun in the faces of the two on duty, and ordered them to give him all the narcotics and antibiotics they had. Then he took their cell phones, locked them in a closet, and left."

"How long ago?"

"Forty minutes."

"Forty minutes," Bree cried. "Are you kidding me?"

I closed my eyes, seeing M in the moments after

Sampson shot him, remembering how he'd shown fear and said he couldn't feel a thing. And the surgeon had said his spine was cracked and bruised, hadn't he?

"I don't understand how he's standing, much less walking," I said. "And if he had help, he's way beyond that ten-block perimeter. He could be long gone out of the city."

Bree said, "He can't last in his condition."

"He got up in that condition, yanked his IVs out in that condition, and killed a cop in that condition!"

"We'll catch him, Alex."

"What if he gets to Ali before we do?"

"Alex, we can't think that—"

"What other way is there to think, Bree? He obviously moved Ali out of the anthill before he came to our home. He's obviously heading to wherever he has our son stashed now. God only knows what he'll do," I said. I paused and then shook my head in disgust. "'Listen to your heart, Mr. Psycho Killer.' Could I have been more of an idiot?"

"You tried to reach him the only way you thought possible. It was brilliant."

"And he brilliantly used it against us."

"Go home. Get some rest. You'll think straighter."

"You've had less sleep than me."

"But for some reason I'm more clearheaded. I feel in my heart that he's coming home. So sleep a few hours, then call me. You're no help to me or Ali like this."

I didn't reply, didn't say a thing to Sampson, just turned and left. On the elevator, on the cab ride home, and going back into the house, my emotions swayed from enraged to demoralized to defeated.

I had tried to stir some reconnection to humanity in M. That failed miserably.

I tried to think about the other things he'd said to me in his hospital room. Had he really been in foster care? Did he really beat a man to death with a chain for raping and murdering his sister? Or was that all made up on the fly?

Our kitchen clock said five minutes past six when I went in and flipped on the light. I hadn't slept enough in weeks, and yet I felt wired, unable to even contemplate going to bed. If I went up there now, I knew I wouldn't be able to get Ali out of my mind.

What was he going through? Was he suffering? I closed my eyes, terrified by the thought that, with M on the loose, I might end up finding my son strangled with a silk tie or missing his head.

I looked at the coffeemaker and then past it to the cabinet where we keep the liquor. I couldn't stomach the thought of whiskey, but I knew booze could take me where I wanted to go, to the darkness, to no past, no future, no now, no—

The front doorbell rang.

At ten after six in the morning?

The bell rang again, and I hustled into the hall, not wanting to wake Nana or Jannie if I could help it and feeling dizzy and disoriented, as if I were about to be hit with a migraine on top of exhaustion.

I opened the door. Dwight Rivers stood there, leaning on his crutches and breathing hard.

"Mr. Rivers?" I said.

"I drove straight here, Dr. Cross," he said. "I thought you should be the first to see this."

"What is it?" I asked as he started down the stairs.

Rivers didn't answer. He reached the sidewalk and crutched his way to a pickup with a camper on the back. He opened the camper's rear door and motioned with his chin for me to look inside.

The sun was up and strong enough now to throw a glare that made me squint at the shadows inside. For a moment, I couldn't make out what Rivers had brought me.

But then I saw movement in the lower bunk at the back.

"Who's that?" a woman's soft, shaky, frightened voice asked. "Who's there?"

In the top bunk, a weaker voice said, "That's my dad, Mrs. J."

CHAPTER

106

MY HEART SPOKE ITS OWN language and nearly exploded with joy as I leaped inside the camper and went to the bunk. Rivers flipped on a light, and there my little boy was, looking like he'd been through a war and trying to smile through tears of pain and hope fulfilled.

"Ali," I whispered, gazing at his sheer presence in wonder and at his condition with much deeper concern.

He was barefoot and bare-chested, covered with scratches, cuts, and welts. The shirt he'd worn to school the day of his disappearance was wrapped around his head and soaked in blood. His eyes seemed a little unfocused before they shut.

"Call 911!" I shouted to Rivers.

"I don't have a cell phone!"

"What?"

"I don't like to conform, man."

"We both fell last night," said the woman in the bottom bunk, who was also filthy and banged up. "After everything, he hits his head, and I break my arm and probably my leg."

I had my phone out and was punching in 911. I said, "Hold that thought, ma'am."

The dispatcher answered, and I described the situation.

"Keep your son awake," she told me after I said there was a possible head injury.

I shook Ali lightly, and he opened his eyes a little.

"Stay with me, pal."

He smiled lazily. "Dad?"

"Right here," I said, and I held his hand.

"Ambulance ETA two minutes, Dr. Cross," the dispatcher said.

"Is this a dream, Dad?"

Though I knew I had to be calm and collected for his sake, that question broke me in a way I'd never expected, and I choked out, "No. No, Ali. This is no dream. You're here, and I'm here."

Tears rolled down his cheeks as his grin broadened.

"I knew we'd make it," he said. "Right, Mrs. J.?"

"You never doubted it," the woman said. "Even when I did."

Sirens wailed down our street.

"I'm sorry, ma'am," I said. "Who are you?"

"Diane Jenkins," she said. "I live in Ohio."

My jaw sagged a moment before I smiled in disbelief and said, "Of course. We've been looking for you."

"Can I call my husband?"

"Right after we get you some medical help."

"Dad?" Ali said as two ambulances wailed and sped down our street toward us.

"Right here," I said, squeezing his hand.

"Mrs. J. is really good with a blowtorch."

"It was his idea," she said.

Ali's eyes started to wobble closed.

"C'mon, stay awake, pal," I said, shaking him again.

"I really wanna sleep, Dad. I'm tired. We've been up all night."

"I know you do," I said, stroking his cheek. "But I need you to stay awake a little longer."

"Do I get to ride in an ambulance?" he said as the sirens whooped up beside the camper and stopped.

"You do," I said, feeling more love for him than I'd thought possible.

"You should see your face, Dad," he said, smiling and licking his lips as the EMTs came to the door behind me.

"I know," I said, tearing up again. "The happiest father alive."

"We're coming in," the medic said.

I let go of my son's hand.

His eyes widened. "Don't leave."

"Don't worry, pal," I said. "Dad will be with you every step of the way."

CHAPTER

107

TWO DAYS LATER, on the third floor of the neurology unit at Georgetown University Medical Center, an orderly wheeled Diane Jenkins on a gurney toward me. Her right arm was in a cast; her leg was heavily bandaged.

Her husband, Melvin, walked at her side. He came straight to me and shook my hand. "I'm sorry for the things I said to you, Dr. Cross."

"Water under the bridge," I said, then I looked at his wife. "You gave us quite a scare with that leg."

She shook her head. "I'd never heard of compartment syndrome, but the surgeon said I'm lucky I didn't lose it below the knee. How is Ali?"

I smiled. "Concussion, but no skull fracture.

The gash is what caused all the blood and made it look so bad. And he was exhausted. Do you want to see him?"

"How could I not?"

I looked over at Bree, Ned Mahoney, and John Sampson, who were waiting down the hall outside a hospital room. The orderly pushed Mrs. Jenkins toward them.

Melvin Jenkins gazed at me, apparently uncomfortable. "Look, Dr. Cross, I'm deeply, deeply grateful Diane's alive. And, well, I'm wondering if we have any idea where he put the five million dollars I borrowed?"

I put my hand on his arm. "We do. And I'm sure the person who has it will return it to you once she understands that the money went to her to throw us off M's trail and implicate her in his crimes."

Jenkins's shoulders relaxed, and he hugged me. "Thank you. Shall we go in?"

I patted him on the back. "Melvin, I'd appreciate it if you'd watch on the feed. I need to do this alone."

You could tell he didn't want to leave his wife, but he nodded. "Right next door?"

"Right next door."

He went to join the others inside an adjoining

room set up with monitors so they didn't miss a thing. The orderly pushed Mrs. Jenkins through the next door down. Before I entered Ali's room, I paused outside, bowed my head, and for the thousandth time thanked God for the miracle of his survival.

They'd been giving my son fewer and fewer drugs the past day, bringing him slowly up out of a tranquilized state the doctors wanted him in while they assessed the extent of his injuries. He was semi-upright in his bed, and as alert as I'd seen him.

"Mrs. J.!" he said when he saw Diane Jenkins. "Why's your leg like that?"

"I bashed it good enough to pinch the blood supply, and it got all swollen, so they cut it open to fix it and drain it," she said. "It's still draining."

He gave her a slightly disgusted look that made her laugh.

"We're alive," she said. "Thanks to you, young man."

Ali looked at me. "Mrs. J. did as much as I did."

I held up both hands. "That's why you're both here. I want to hear everything. From the beginning."

CHAPTER 108

DIANE JENKINS SAID THAT ON the day she disappeared, there had been a man hidden in the back of her car. He clamped a gloved hand across her mouth, and the last thing she remembered clearly was being terrified and getting jabbed in the neck with a needle.

She remembered being in multiple places before the anthill but had trouble recalling much about any of them or saying how much time had passed, though she did have recollections of a vehicle he used to transport her from one place to the next.

Mrs. Jenkins woke up for good in the workroom in Rivers's bunker, her hands zip-tied in front of her, and the doors locked from the outside. There was water, food, and no way out. Her wedding and engagement rings were missing.

She said she'd screamed for a while, but no one came. Sometime later, a day, maybe two, but well after the effects of whatever she'd been knocked out with had finally worn off, she awoke to find M bringing in Ali, who was drugged, bound, and unconscious. She'd begged M to let them go, but he'd ignored her and locked them both inside.

"I didn't know what to do," she said. "But Ali did."

Ali said that he thought he was meeting Captain Abrahamsen after school, but M had pulled up in a Suburban. He was wearing U.S. Armed Forces biking gear and said he rode for the team with Abrahamsen and that the captain had had an emergency meeting and sent him.

"I know it was stupid, but he was wearing the same uniform as Captain Abrahamsen, so I got in. I was looking out the window for my friends, and he stuck a needle in my leg. That's the last thing I remember until that room he kept us in."

Ali said he was initially frightened and then confused and angry when he realized he'd been duped by the texts. "But after that, I was only thinking of a way to escape."

"It's true," Mrs. Jenkins said. "He became... obsessed."

"Sounds familiar," I said, and I winked at Ali, who went on.

Even with his wrists bound, Ali had managed to go through every cabinet and drawer in the workshop, and he found all sorts of things, including a hammer, a chisel, a portable drill with bits, three headlamps and two extra batteries, a hacksaw with two replacement blades, an old watch that was still running, and a new acetylene torch still in its box, along with a small tank of the gas.

Ali had wanted to use the torch immediately to cut their way out. The instructions were in the box. How hard could it be? But Mrs. Jenkins had pointed out how small the gas tank was and wondered whether it would be enough to take down the steel door.

They decided instead to first weaken the hinges and the handle mechanism with the other tools and then finish the job with the torch. Using the watch, Ali kept track of M's comings and goings and found their captor was checking on them roughly every twenty-four hours or so, consistently between two and three thirty a.m.

With the tools hidden, Ali had asked M if they could have their wrist restraints cut because their skin was getting rubbed raw. M had done it without comment, then he gave them antibiotic ointments to dress their wounds and left, locking the door to the hallway and interior ladder behind him.

Before Ali and Diane Jenkins could start on the door, they became woozy, which made them believe that M had put drugs in their water. They decided to limit their liquid intake, but nonetheless, their ability to work was slowed.

They began with the middle hinge and the hacksaw, trying to keep the cut as inconspicuous as possible.

"We made sure everything was cleaned up way before M was supposed to come back," Ali said. "But every time he came, we were scared he was going to see where we'd been weakening the door."

But M did not discover what they were doing, and two days later, with the middle hinge down to two inches of quarter-inch steel, they turned to the lower bracket.

That took another two days. Cutting the upper hinge to three inches took them a day and a half. They waited for M to arrive at the usual time on the sixth morning, but he did not return until the seventh day around one a.m.

M seemed agitated, distracted; he tossed cans of food and bottles of water to them and left some two hours before he crawled out of my neighbor's house and across the scaffolding into my attic office.

Ali and Mrs. Jenkins said that in retrospect, they probably could have escaped in that twenty-two extra hours they'd spent waiting for M to return. But they'd wanted to start the final cutting process when they knew they'd have at least a full day to drop the door and get as far away as possible from wherever they were being held.

CHAPTER

109

AT ROUGHLY THE SAME TIME I was face to face with M in my attic office, Ali and Mrs. Jenkins began drilling into the door around the handle and locking mechanism.

Dwight Rivers had built the doors by cutting them out of the sides of railroad container cars and installing reinforced locking mechanisms so, as Ali put it, "Zombies could not break through them during the Apocalypse."

The practical result was that they were trying to drill through three-quarters of an inch of steel plate with a household portable drill that required changing batteries and recharging constantly. Progress on the lock slowed to a crawl.

While we were waiting for doctors to give us the okay to interrogate M, Ali had picked up the blowtorch and the striker and told Diane Jenkins to turn on the gas.

Diane Jenkins, thank God, told him that a ten-year-old running a blowtorch was not happening, and over his protests she took it from him. When she'd been kidnapped, she'd had her prescription sunglasses around her neck. While not a welding mask, they'd been enough to let her work without going blind.

"You should have seen her, Dad," Ali said. "She was scared, but once she got it lit, she started cutting like she'd done it all her life. Bottom hinge to top."

When the top hinge broke free, she turned the torch on the gaps between the holes they'd drilled around the handle and lock. Just as the gas tank was starting to lose pressure, she completed the circle, and Ali hit the area with the hammer.

After fifteen blows, it fell out the other side, and the door dropped after it with a booming clang. In the hall beyond, they spotted the ladder coming out of the ceiling, went to it, and felt the downdraft.

Using the headlamps, they climbed and stumbled around inside Rivers's doomsday bunker before reaching the roof and finding the same winch cable and rope Sampson and I had used to escape the anthill nearly two weeks before.

Mrs. Jenkins had balked at the idea of rappelling and told Ali she would wait for him to come back with help. He convinced her that M had to be using the rope to get in and out of the bunker and that they should get away from it as fast as possible.

"It was the most frightening thing I've ever done in my life, but he just kept talking me through it," Mrs. Jenkins said.

When they were both at the bottom, they heard a vehicle and turned off their headlamps. Then they saw headlights up near a house and thought it was M returning for them.

They took off running west, crossing the meadow toward the woods. Having no idea where they were, they kept going once they reached the trees and could turn on their headlamps. They walked for an hour and a half and never crossed a road.

The forest got thicker, and the ground started to climb. Though they did not know it at the time, they were well inside Shenandoah National Park when they decided to stop and wait for daylight.

But then they heard our helicopter fly overhead

and land in the meadow back toward the anthill. They heard sirens coming a few minutes later.

"We figured that was good, sirens," Ali said. "So we started back in that direction, except once the sirens died, we couldn't tell exactly where they'd come from."

"That's when the headlamps started to dim and we walked off the side of a cliff," Mrs. Jenkins said.

I pulled back. "What?"

"Or tumbled down it," she said. "I guess it was more like a ravine."

"It was steep," Ali said. "I sort of remember that."

Mrs. Jenkins said she hit rocks and boulders in the bottom of the ravine. She felt her arm break and her lower calf smash.

Ali didn't remember hitting the rock but he'd blacked out for a time.

"I got a new battery into my headlamp and found him," she said. "There was a lot of blood, but he came around."

Then it started to rain and our helicopter flew back over them.

"It went almost over our heads," she said. "We were both yelling, but no one could hear anything."

I wanted to say that I'd thought I'd heard Ali's

voice, which was impossible. I decided to keep that for later, between me and Ali.

Mrs. Jenkins said they had to keep moving or they'd die of hypothermia.

"Between us we had three legs," she said.

"And one and a half heads," Ali said, and he sniggered.

She laughed. "No, you were three-quarters of a head at least."

They hobbled through the woods, relying on the headlamp until the rain stopped and dawn arrived.

"It got light," she said. "And there was this rock wall, and on the other side of it, there was a path through the woods, and then the dirt road was just there."

They hadn't walked three hundred yards down that road when Dwight Rivers came driving by in his camper truck, heading to the hardware store to get new locks for his anthill.

"He stop right away?" I asked.

"He drove way past us, even when we were waving at him," Mrs. Jenkins said. "But then he hit the brakes hard and came fast in reverse."

My son spoke up. "He said, 'Are you Ali Cross?' I said I was. And Mrs. Jenkins told him who she was and asked could we use his phone. He said he gave up cell phones in protest of something, I don't know. Then he told us to get in the back of the camper, warm up, and sleep a little, and he'd drive us all the way home."

"End of story," Mrs. Jenkins said. "Your son is my hero, Dr. Cross."

"Mine too, Mrs. J.," I said.

Ali beamed. "When can the hero go home and have ice cream?"

"The doctor will decide about home, but I have a feeling Nana Mama might bring you two or three different kinds when she visits you later on."

My son looked at Diane Jenkins in a way that spoke of the deep bond they'd formed in captivity. "Do you want to meet the real hashtag-crazy-good-stuff-my-great-grandma-says and eat ice cream?"

She laughed, glanced at me, then said, "I would, Ali. Very much."

CHAPTER 110

Eleven weeks later

JANNIE LOOKED LIKE HER OLD SELF when she came bouncing out of the players' tunnel and onto the track at the University of North Carolina, Chapel Hill.

We were all there, even my older son, Damon, who was out on summer break from college. We all jumped to our feet and clapped and whistled for her.

Ali still had a long, livid scar on his scalp, but other than a problem staying asleep and a few harsh mood swings, he seemed back to himself.

The stands in the shade were crowded, but we didn't care. We were all together and giving our girl love on the second day of a USATF invitational meet for high-schoolers.

Ted McDonald, the independent coach who'd first taken an interest in Jannie, described the series of four meets as similar to football combines, where scouts are looking for pros. In this case, the scouts were NCAA Division I coaches, at least fifteen of them, by my count.

Several of the coaches had visited our home already, and we'd heard from most of the rest by telephone or letter sometime in the past year. Though the coaches were there to watch all of the nearly two hundred athletes attending the meet, it was no secret there were lots of eyes on Jannie.

So far, she'd handled the pressure with relative ease. It helped that Coach McDonald had flown out from Texas for the event.

McDonald was there when she qualified for the finals in the four-hundred, her best event, and just missed a slot in the eight-hundred. She'd also competed in javelin for the first time and took eighteenth of twenty-five in the field, which was not bad, considering.

Jannie ignored the college coaches as she jogged

past them, then blew kisses at us and grinned like she was having the most fun ever.

"It's good to see her so relaxed again," Nana Mama said. "And strong."

"Thanks to sleep, vitamins, your good food, and the weight training."

"And Coach McDonald," I said, seeing him out on the infield, sandy hair, long and lean, talking with one of the officials. "I don't know how we would have handled all this without him."

"I like him too," Bree said, standing. "A lot. He keeps her grounded."

She went to get us drinks. Damon and Ali walked down by the fence to talk with Jannie before the long jump.

My grandmother started reading her paperback, and I was left with my thoughts.

Despite a massive regional manhunt and a nationwide alert with multiple photographs and video clips of him, the man we knew as M had not surfaced.

But we knew a whole lot more about him now. When we ran his DNA samples through the FBI's and Europol's vast databases, we were stunned to get twenty-six different matches to DNA gathered at homicide scenes around the world.

M had definitely been in that broken-down

cabin at the fishing camp. His skin cells were on the dead preschool director. They were on Katrina Nixon as well.

His DNA was also found aboard the sex traffickers' yacht and in the apartment of Detective Ron Dallas.

But with no fingerprints and no other solid information about him, it was as if the man did not exist.

Ali could have easily let the experience traumatize him. But other than enduring confusion as to why M had targeted him, he'd gone right on to new obsessions, the Galápagos Islands and computer coding. And he continued to mountain bike and carry on his friendship with Captain Abrahamsen, who was thrilled Ali was okay.

Another positive was I got to see Martin Forbes walk out of court a free man, determined to spend the rest of his days wisely.

"You saved my life, Cross," he'd said before hugging me. "I'll never forget it."

And Bree and I could not forget that M remained a threat to our family. We installed our own cameras inside and outside the house and insisted that Jannie, Nana Mama, and Ali never travel alone.

Bree and I were constantly swiveling our heads

at large public gatherings, like the track meet. So far, we'd seen no one who resembled M anywhere in the stands.

The long-jump event started. Jannie's early attempts were middle of the pack but enough to qualify for the finals, where she finished seventh of eight and twenty inches off the winner. She came out of her last jump shaking her head, shoulders slumped.

"I can do better," she said to me afterward.

"I know you can."

"I just wanted to show Coach Mac something."

"So show him in the four-hundred."

That brought back the bounce in her step. It didn't leave her the rest of the day.

In the four-hundred finals, Jannie broke clean in the fifth lane, ran easy off the outside shoulders of the three leaders through the backstretch and into the final turn.

With a hundred and twenty yards to go, and despite all the injuries and illnesses she'd fought in the past two years, my daughter seemed to find a gear we'd thought she'd lost and began bounding more than running.

We went crazy when she chewed up the gap, caught the leaders with fifty meters to go, and won the race by three-quarters of a second.

"She's back!" Ali shouted, jumping up and down. "Jannie's back!"

"Did you see that?" Damon crowed. "It was like those other girls were standing still at the end!"

"We all saw it," Nana Mama cried. "So did all those coaches."

She was right. Most of the coaches were on their feet and looking at their stopwatches, some grinning, some shaking their heads in wonder. Coach McDonald was looking at us from the infield, smiling and pumping his fists.

Down on the track, Jannie had slowed to a stop, her head thrown back, a delirious smile on her face, and her palms raised to the sky.

CHAPTER 111

JANNIE AND I HAD COACHES coming up to us the rest of the day with offers of campus visits and mentions of scholarships. We were grateful to listen to each and every one of them, including the coach at the University of Oregon, who reminded us that he had been the first to show an interest in her when she was a freshman.

As he walked away, she said, "I don't know what to do."

Coach McDonald, who was also there, smiled. "Luckily, you don't have to make any decisions today or anytime soon."

"Thank you for flying out, Coach Mac," she said, hugging him. "It helped."

"Thank you for giving me the gift of watching you soar today. And we'll talk Tuesday?"

Jannie's eyes watered as she nodded. "Tuesday."

He walked off.

"Can we get something to eat?" she said. "I'm starving."

"Dr. Cross? Jannie?"

We turned to find Coach Wilson of the University of Texas walking toward us in the tunnel that led to the locker rooms. She was the only coach who had not yet approached us that day.

"The unicorn is back," she said. She smiled and shook Jannie's hand and mine.

Then Coach Wilson looked at me. "Jannie *is* a unicorn. In more ways than one. That was a very impressive win in the four-hundred today."

"Better than the other three events," Jannie said.

"No, that's where you're wrong. You didn't win or even place in those individual field events, but you were competitive in all of them. That's the mark of a great all-around athlete, which is what I am looking for."

Wilson paused. "But I can't tell you to give up the four-hundred, where you are clearly exceptional Division One talent, to chase the idea of the heptathlon, an unknown but one in which I believe you have the potential to be a world-class talent."

Jannie puffed up her cheeks and blew out air. "I don't know, Coach."

"And you don't have to," Coach Wilson said. "But whatever path you decide to take, know that you have a full scholarship offer at the University of Texas. And may I remind you that Coach McDonald lives in town?"

Jannie smiled. "I know."

"You're lucky to have him on your side."

"Yes, ma'am. I am."

Wilson said she'd be in touch and left. Jannie wiped at her eyes with her sleeve.

"You okay?"

Jannie smiled through tears. "Of course I'm okay. It's just, how many seventeen-year-olds get to live their dreams like this?"

"Every seventeen-year-old girl who lives in my house," I said, and I hugged her. "I can't tell you how much—"

"Dad!" Ali yelled, running at us from the stands.

I held up a hand and looked at Jannie. "I can't tell you how proud I am of—"

"Dad!" Ali said.

"Ali," I said sharply. "I am trying to tell your sister how—"

I stopped in midsentence, seeing the phone he held out in front of him and the petrified look on his face.

"It's him, Dad," he said. "Wickr, but I took a screenshot of it."

I took the phone, read it, and knew the M game was not over.

You are quite the little escape artist, Ali. And Jannie, the stellar track champion! Say hi to your father for me. Tell him that from where I sat, his daughter clearly ran with heart.

ABOUT THE AUTHOR

JAMES PATTERSON is the world's bestselling author and most trusted storyteller. He has created many enduring fictional characters and series, including Alex Cross, the Women's Murder Club, Michael Bennett, Maximum Ride, Middle School, and I Funny. Among his notable literary collaborations are *The President Is Missing,* with President Bill Clinton, and the Max Einstein series, produced in partnership with the Albert Einstein Estate. Patterson's writing career is characterized by a single mission: to prove that there is no such thing as a person who "doesn't like to read," only people who haven't found the right book. He's given over three million books to schoolkids and the military, donated more than seventy million dollars to support education, and endowed over five thousand college scholarships for teachers. The National Book Foundation recently presented Patterson with the Literarian Award for Outstanding Service to the American Literary Community, and he is also the recipient of an Edgar Award and six Emmy Awards. He lives in Florida with his family.

For a complete list of books by

JAMES PATTERSON

VISIT
JamesPatterson.com

Follow James Patterson on Facebook
@JamesPatterson

Follow James Patterson on Twitter
@JP_Books

Follow James Patterson on Instagram
@jamespattersonbooks